DUBIOUS PERSUASIONS

JOHNS HOPKINS: POETRY AND FICTION

John T. Irwin, general editor

Guy Davenport, *Da Vinci's Bicycle: Ten Stories*
John Hollander, *"Blue Wine" and Other Poems*
Robert Pack, *Waking to My Name: New and Selected Poems*
Stephen Dixon, *Fourteen Stories*
Philip Dacey, *The Boy under the Bed*
Jack Matthews, *Dubious Persuasions: Short Stories*

DUBIOUS PERSUASIONS,

Short Stories by Jack Matthews

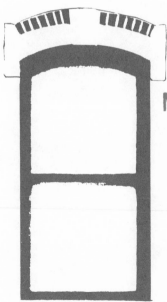

The Johns Hopkins University Press
Baltimore and London

This book has been brought to publication with the generous assistance of the Andrew W. Mellon Foundation, the G. Harry Pouder Fund, and the Albert Dowling Trust.

The Johns Hopkins University Press, Baltimore, Maryland 21218
The Johns Hopkins Press Ltd., London

Library of Congress Cataloging in Publication Data
Matthews, Jack.
  Dubious persuasions.
  (Johns Hopkins, poetry and fiction)
  I. Title. II. Series.   ?
PS3563.A85D8   813'.54   81-47581
ISBN 0-8018-2692-6   AACR2

All of these stories have appeared previously in journals, and grateful acknowledgment is made to their editors for permission to reprint. "Another Story" was first published in the *Sewanee Review* 77, no. 3 (Summer 1969). Copyright 1969 by the University of the South; "The Terrible Mrs. Bird" in *Western Humanities Review;* "First the Legs and Last the Heart" in *Carleton Miscellany;* "The Project" in the *Southern Review;* "The Girl at the Window" in *Jeopardy;* "Elma" in *Today;* "Gluck, the Silent Oracle" in *Ante;* "Love Song for Doris Ballinger" in the *Carleton Miscellany;* "The Descent" in the *English Record;* "Polly Sue and the St. Louis Dodgers" in *Focus Midwest;* "The Eternal Mortgage" in *Southwest Review;* "Irma, the Good Sport" in *Montrealer;* "The Kitten" in the *Kansas Quarterly;* "The Pilgrimage" in *Prism International;* "Who Is Who, and When Will We Be Real?" in the *Yale Review;* "No More Babies" in *Quixote;* "The Last Abandonment" in the *Georgia Review.*

To the memories of my father, mother, and sister

CONTENTS

DUBIOUS PERSUASIONS

THE TERRIBLE MRS. BIRD

Nan stood by the wheelbarrow, one hand resting on the handle as she spoke. "It doesn't happen every night," she said. "Only sometimes."

"Nan-SEEE!" Mother called from Grandmother's screened-in back porch.

"Yes, Mother," Nan sang, looking at me. She knew what Mother was going to ask.

"Are you keeping your eye on him?" Mother said. "Is he there with you?"

"He's right here, Mother," Nan said.

"Well, keep your eye on him," she said. "It'll soon be dark. Is he warm enough?"

"Are you warm enough?" Nan asked, wrinkling her nose at me.

"Yes," I said.

"He's warm enough," Nan cried, sitting down on one handle of the wheelbarrow, so that the opposite side eased off the ground. But she still sat there, poised delicately with one bare foot in the grass. She turned her left arm around, making it bend the wrong way, and gently scratched at an old scab on her elbow. Mother always said that Nan had rubber joints.

"Will she come out after it's dark?" I asked again.

"Will you stop asking that?" Nan said. "I just now told you that sometimes she does, and sometimes she doesn't."

"How did she die?" I asked.

"A mean old man cut her throat one night. *Isn't* that how it happened, Patty?"

I was surprised to see Patty right behind me. She had come up without making a noise.

"Isn't *what* how it happened?" Patty said. "You mean, Mrs. Bird?"

Nan said, "He was asking me again."

"I'm not scared," I said.

"You haven't seen Mrs. *Bird*," Patty said, biting into an apple. Patty was our first cousin, older by two years than Nan, and Nan was always asking her questions and telling other people what she said.

"There'll be a mist tonight," Patty said, looking down into the orchard. "A *lot* of mist."

"That's the kind of night Mrs. Bird likes, all right," Nan said, nudging me with her bare toe. Then she sighed and fell loosely back into the wheelbarrow, saying, "I wish the apples were ripe."

"They are in that tree in front," Patty said.

Up on the back porch, there was a loud laugh, and Patty smiled and said, "Honestly, that Uncle Ned and his laugh."

"That was Daddy," I said.

"Crazy!" Nan said to me. "Patty calls him 'Uncle Ned.'"

"He's my uncle," Patty said. "Why don't you go get some apples. They're just right for eating. Those down in the orchard are late, Daddy says."

Nan got out of the wheelbarrow and said, "I think I *will* have an apple."

"No, stay here and I'll get you one," Patty said. "Do you want one too?" she said, asking me.

I nodded my head and said, "But not if it's green. Green apples give me a bellyache."

"Shush," Nan said. "Mother says not to use that word."

"Bellyache, bellyache," I said.

"Will you please be quiet?" Nan whispered rapidly, hitting me in the stomach.

"That didn't hurt," I said.

"Well it will the next time."

"Bellyache," I said in a low voice.

"If you don't behave, you won't see Mrs. Bird. She doesn't like nasty boys."

"How old was she when she died?" I asked.

"Oh, about thirty-five," Nan said, closing her eyes and pulling a strand of hair from her forehead, the way she'd seen Patty do.

"Why did he cut her throat?"

"You mean that old man? Because he didn't like her. He used naughty words all the time, and she didn't like him, so he didn't like *her*."

"Bellyache," I said.

"Oh, shut up. Mother says that's vulgar, and you know it very well! She says it's coarse."

"What's coarse?" Patty said, coming up behind me again.

"What he's saying," Nan said.

"Here are the apples," Patty said, handing one to Nan and then one to me. She had another one herself, and wiped if off on her shorts. Back and forth, across the Scotch plaid of her shorts. Her legs were tanned and smooth, and she kept rubbing the apple back and forth across the Scotch plaid, looking down. When she lifted the apple, she shook her hair out of her face and stared at me. Then she bit into the apple and chewed, looking out at the orchard.

"I'll bet it's dark in there at night," I said. "Why did they bury her in the orchard?"

"Because she loved apples," Patty said, and Nan giggled.

"They give me a bellyache," I said.

Up on the screened-in porch, Daddy laughed again with his big laugh, and Nan said, "He'll hear you."

"Where's Greta?" I said, chewing on my apple.

"I don't know," Nan said, collapsing back into the wheelbarrow.

"You'll get dirty sitting in that thing," Patty said to her.

"No I won't," she said. "I don't care, anyway."

"Where's Greta?" I asked.

"She's sick," Patty said. She sat down on one of the wheelbarrow's handles, exactly the way Nan had been sitting a little while ago. Every time before she'd bite into the apple, she would toss her head, making her long hair fly out of her eyes. She was pretty, and I liked her. Some people said Nan was pretty, too, but she was my sister and I didn't like her. Most of the time, anyway.

"What's wrong with her?" I asked.

"Nosey," Nan said.

"Why is Greta sick? She's *always* sick."

"She eats too many apples," Patty said, and then they both giggled. I laughed too.

"Is she my cousin?" I said.

"Don't ask silly questions," Nan said.

"That's not a silly question."

"It is too," Nan said.

"She's Grandma's helping girl," Patty said.

"Kind of like a *maid*," Nan said.

"She's fat," I said.

"She is not," Nan said. "At least, boys don't think so." Then she and Patty both giggled so hard, they got all tangled up together, like dirty clothes. They ended up with Nan's bare foot sticking up in the air, the bottom of it about three inches from my face.

"Your foot's dirty," I said, even though I couldn't see it very well.

"Well, what do you expect when I'm going around in the grass barefooted," she said. Her voice was muffled. It was coming from around in back of Patty, who was still eating her apple. They were both kind of sitting inside the wheelbarrow, only Nan was more in it than Patty was.

"Why does she talk funny?" I said.

"You ask too many questions," Nan said.

4

"Why does Greta talk funny?" I repeated.

"She's Swedish," Patty said. "Grandma took her in from the Children's Home, because she was too old to stay there any more, but too young to go out on her own. Or maybe it's German."

"How old *is* she?" Nan asked.

"Sixteen," Patty said, getting up out of the wheelbarrow and bending her arm back and throwing the apple core over the fence and into the orchard.

"I can throw farther than that," I said.

"Sure," Nan said. "Sure."

"Well, I can," I said.

"Sure."

"Will Mrs. Bird come out tonight?"

"If she does, she'll scare you to death," Patty said. "She hates men. Even little boys."

"Why did he cut her throat?" I asked.

"I've explained that to you," Nan cried.

"Nan-SEEEE!" It was Mother's voice from the back porch.

"We want to stay out, Mother," Nan called back. Then she pinched me and said, "Don't we."

"Sure," I said. "I want to see Mrs. Bird."

"Well, not too late," Mother called.

"If you once saw her, you wouldn't want to see her again," Patty said. "But if you really *want* to see her."

Nan whispered something to Patty, and Patty whispered back. I heard her say, "She'll be ready."

"Who'll be ready?" I asked.

"Oh, shut up," Nan said. "Patty and I were talking."

"Mrs. *Bird* will be ready," Patty said. "She'll be ready to climb up out of her grave and walk through the orchard as soon as she finds out it's a misty night."

"I want to see her," I said, shivering. It was dark already and the mist lay among the apple trees like smoke from a grass fire.

"Well, you'll have to promise to do as we say," Patty said.

Nan hit me on the shoulder and said, "Well?"

"Well what?" I said.

"Do you *promise*?"

"Yes," I said.

I sat down in the grass and took off my shoes. Nan and Patty were talking. Patty was standing by the wheelbarrow, tying a rose in her hair. She had plucked the rose from the climber on the fence, saying, "Grandma doesn't mind it if you take a rose now and then." Nan said that Patty lived nearer to Grandma than we did, and visited her at least once a week.

Nan watched her as she wound the rose in her hair, but they were talking about something else. I took off my socks. The grass felt cool to my bare feet.

"What do you think you're doing?" Nan said.

"I'm going barefooted."

"Put those shoes back on," she said.

"*You're* going barefooted."

"But I'm older than you are. Put them back on or I'll call Mother, and she'll make you go inside."

"I don't want to," I said.

"I'll call Mother."

"If you put them back on," Patty said, "you'll be able to run faster when you see Mrs. Bird."

I sat down on the ground and started to put my socks back on. Nan and Patty were whispering.

Far up in the woods, there was a strange sound, repeated again and again. I heard it and said, "Listen! What's that?"

"That's a whippoorwill," Patty said. Then she started whispering again to Nan.

"That's a bird," Nan said, interrupting Patty to tell me.

"Mrs. Bird," I said.

"No, not *Mrs.* Bird," Nan said, and they both started giggling.

"Maybe it is," Patty said after a few seconds, and then they were both silent.

I heard a high moaning sound from the orchard.

"What's that?" I said.

"*That's* no whippoorwill," Patty said, doubling up her fists. Her voice sounded scared.

"Let's go down by the gate," Nan said. She lurched out of the wheelbarrow, turning it over on one handle, and both of them started walking to the gate. They were several steps ahead of me before I could catch up. I was making a humming noise because I was scared.

"Now you just be quiet!" Nan said, shaking my arm.

"Listen!" Patty hissed. "Listen!"

I listened, but I couldn't hear anything. It was dark out, and there was a big yellow moon in the sky. It was uneven, like the yolk of an egg just ready to drop out of the broken shell. The mist was thick and white in the orchard, like the white of an egg when Mother poached it. Some of the little trees planted near the road were almost buried in the mist. All you could see were the black scratchy tops sticking up out of the mist.

Up on the porch, Daddy laughed again, but he sounded farther away, as if the porch were floating down a river. I grabbed Nan's leg and squeezed it as hard as I could.

"Now you stop that," Nan whispered. "You're hurting me! Stop it!"

So I let up a little, and she put her hand on my head, letting me keep on hugging her leg.

Then I heard the moaning, and Patty whispered, "It's Mrs. Bird! It's Mrs. Bird!"

"Oh my God!" Nan whispered. "It really is!"

I started dancing around in circles then, because I couldn't see anything. One shoelace was untied and the shoe wobbled on my foot.

"Don't let her get behind us, whatever you do," Patty said. "She's awful quick."

"I just *knew* she'd come out on a night like this," Nan said.

"So did I," Patty said.

"Look. There she is!" Nan threw her arm out straight, and I saw something white deep down the path that led along the apple trees. It moved slowly up and down.

"Oh God, I saw her face," Nan said, turning me around and burying my face in her stomach. I strained and strained until I burst away from her, and said, "Where? Where?"

"She's gone now," Patty said.

"But where is she?" Nan said.

"I don't know. I only hope she isn't behind us."

"One of us should look," Nan said.

"But I'm afraid," Patty said.

"I'll look," I said.

"You better not," Nan said. "You're a boy. It'd better be one of us who looks."

"Why?" I asked.

"Because Mrs. Bird *hates* boys! How many times do we have to tell you?"

"She's awful quick," Patty said. "She can move faster than a dog can run, and you can't hear a thing."

"That's because she's *dead*," Nan said.

"I'll look," Patty said.

There wasn't any noise at all for a second, and I swallowed, my heart going a hundred miles an hour.

Then Patty hissed, "She's there. She's back there *behind* us!"

Both of them took off through the gate, then, and I lost my shoe, but ran after them anyway. They ran as fast as they could up the orchard path, and then I couldn't see them any more. The weeds and bushes were higher than my head, and the mist was thick. The moon bobbled back and forth overhead as I ran, and then I could hear a noise coming from somewhere, and it was myself, crying.

Suddenly a great white shape jumped in front of me, and I tripped and fell right into it, scrambling with all my might. The screaming was louder, now, and my face went into something soft and round and warm ... something like a hot-water bottle, and I couldn't get my breath, and I bit down on it as hard as I could, and then the screaming changed, and I was dropped to the side, twitching all over, and there suddenly was Greta, holding her hands up to her chest and shrieking, with her chin raised to the moon.

Beside me were Nan and Patty, standing absolutely still. Greta could not stop screaming. I lay there in the grass, my heart pounding, my legs and arms still twitching, as if they wanted to run off by themselves, and escape.

Greta could not stop screaming. All that night she screamed. I could hear it in my sleep. It was like scalding-hot water spilling over into my dreams, and it wouldn't stop. Nobody talked to me or paid any attention to me at all, except that Mother hugged me once, and said, "He doesn't understand. He doesn't understand."

"Are you *sure* you girls weren't teasing him?" Mother said.

"Cross my heart and hope to die," Nan said.

"Of *course* he had no idea!" Aunt Polly said.

Nan and Patty would not look at me. Other people stared at me without saying anything. They seemed to be thinking of something else.

All the while, Greta was screaming. Somebody said that she was just an ignorant girl, and hysterical, that it wasn't all that bad. I didn't know who said this, or if anybody answered.

Greta kept on. Nobody could stop her.

Once during the night I thought I could hear Mrs. Bird down in her grave, laughing. Patty had said that Mrs. Bird liked to laugh a lot, but it was the kind of laughing that would scare anybody.

When we returned to our home in the city, Nan would not play with me unless she had to. She told me this. She said, "Mother says I must never tease you again, and that's all right with me."

Sometimes I would ask her about Mrs. Bird, but she wouldn't answer my questions.

It was a long time later, and it was snowing out. It was Christmas.

Daddy and Mother and my baby sister Paula and I were all in the car, bundled up like Eskimos, Daddy said. The car's heater wasn't working. Nan had forgotten her new glasses, and we were all waiting for her. I was in the back seat, holding a big airplane Daddy had bought for me. Mother was holding Paula in her lap.

"What's taking that girl so long?" Daddy said.

"She can't find her new glasses," Mother said. "She sent Patty her school picture, and Patty said she looked attractive in her glasses. That's why she wants to wear them." Mother laughed gently and reached over and spread some hairs on the top of Paula's head with two fingers.

"Will Patty be there?" I asked.

"Yes, she'll be there," Mother said.

"And Greta?" I said.

There was a slight pause, and Mother said, "Yes, she'll be there too."

I had heard them talking about Greta just that morning. They were standing in the kitchen, and they thought I was in the front room with my new airplane, but I heard them anyway. They said they were worried about Greta. They called her "poor Greta."

"They say she's just eaten up with it," Mother said. "All inside."

"That's certainly too bad," Daddy said. "But that doesn't have anything to do with what *he* did."

"Oh, of course not."

"Although that must have been a terrible bite he gave her."

"It *was*," Mother said. "But he didn't *know*, poor thing. It's just one of those things."

When Nan came out to the car, she got in without looking at me. She was wearing her glasses. She started reading a book and read it all the way to Grandma's house. When we pulled our car into Grandma's driveway, she closed the book with a bang and looked up. It was a big book.

Patty did not look at me either.

When we were eating dinner, I asked where Greta was, and Grandma said, "She's upstairs, Dear. She isn't feeling well. Greta is sick."

"Like the night Mrs. Bird came out?" I asked.

The minute I asked, I was sorry I had said anything. I remembered that Nan had made me promise on that night I had bitten Greta that I must not tell anyone about Mrs. Bird.

Everyone was silent. They were looking at me. Patty and Nan were sitting together on the far side of the big table, and they were both looking down, eating.

"Who is Mrs. Bird?" Mother asked.

"Oh, nobody," I said.

"Well, it has to be *somebody* if she has a *name*," Mother said.

"Nan told me about her," I said.

"Nancy," Mother said. "Who is Mrs. Bird?"

"Oh, just somebody we made up," Nan said.

"Anybody for more turkey?" Grandma said.

"I'll go for some," Daddy said.

Nobody mentioned Mrs. Bird again.

But after dinner, I followed Nan into Grandma's big hallway, and I asked her where Greta was, and she said, "Didn't you hear Grandma say she was upstairs in her room, sick?"

I didn't say anything, and Nan said, "You never give up, do you?"

"I just asked where she was," I said.

"If you only *knew*!" Nan cried in a soft voice.

Patty came up, and she and Nan whispered together, and I said, "Why doesn't she come downstairs."

"Because she just happens to be *dying!*" Nan hissed.

"What is it?" Mother asked. She had come into the hallway.

"He was asking about Greta again," Nan said. "Honestly!"

"I think he should be allowed to go up and see Greta," Mother said.

"Oh no," Nan cried. "You can't be *serious!*" Patty walked out of the hallway into the front room.

"I certainly am serious," Mother said. "You don't expect that little boy to *understand,* do you?"

"I don't expect him to. . . ." She didn't finish, because Mother gave her a look.

"Go upstairs and ask Greta if she feels like seeing him," Mother said. "And see if she's decent."

Nan didn't answer, but she went upstairs as Mother had told her. Then Aunt Polly came through the hallway and mussed up my hair.

Nan came back to the top of the stairway and motioned to me with her wrist limp. She looked tired enough to die, as Great-Uncle Wallace was always saying.

"If you say anything about her dying," she said, when I had climbed the stairs, "I'll kill you. Do you understand?"

I said I did, and Nan led me to the second stairway that went up to the third story, where Greta's room was. When we went in, Greta watched me from the bed. She was sitting up in bed, and her skin was white. Her eyes looked wet and heavy. She didn't smile or anything, and I didn't either, but when I just stood there, Nan pushed me a little bit and said, "Say something, Dummy."

I still didn't say anything, and neither did Greta. She just stared at me as if she had never seen me before.

Nan pushed me forward another step, and Greta said hello to me with her lips moving, but she didn't make any sound at all.

"Hello," I said. Then I noticed something: Greta was pretty, because she had lost so much weight. Her eyes looked very dark, and there was a sad expression on her face.

"Can't you ask how she's *feeling?*" Nan said, pushing my shoulder again.

But I didn't say anything. Instead, Greta took my hand in hers and held it. Her fingers were cold. She squeezed my fingers, and then she closed her eyes tightly and tears began running down her cheeks.

Nan took me out of her bedroom, and I said, "Why was she crying? Is she *that* sick?"

"Yes," Nan said. "Now please don't speak about it anymore."

We went downstairs and opened the Christmas presents. Outside, it was snowing again. "A real old-fashioned Christmas," Great-Uncle Wallace said.

I went out and played in the snow and got all wet. When I came back in, Mother changed my clothes. Everybody seemed happy, but a little bit quiet.

"Don't you ever mention Mrs. Bird again," Nan whispered to me later, "or she'll come back and cut your throat."

"Is she still out in the orchard?" I asked.

"I won't tell you where she is," Nan said, closing her eyes.

When spring came, Daddy brought me a new tricycle. He said it would hold me until I could ride a two-wheeler in a couple of years.

Then one night we got a long-distance telephone call from Grandma, and she said that Greta was dead.

"Well," Mother said in a soft voice, "we expected it. It was meant to happen."

Later she said that Grandma had been crying.

"She wasn't any relation, was she?" I said.

"You know she wasn't," Nan said.

"Nancy, don't be so *cross* with him," Mother said. "You know he doesn't understand."

"That's so *obvious,*" Nan said, and Mother said, "Now, Nancy, you heard what I said."

Then Nan started crying and ran upstairs to her bedroom.

"Why is she crying?" I said to Mother.

"Girls that age," Daddy said, "are often weepy."

"Also, she's sad about Greta," Mother said.

The next evening I was riding my tricycle down in the park. I was circling the pond on the old cement sidewalk, following the cracks with my front wheel.

Nan came up to me and said, "Where have you been?"

"I've been right here," I said.

"Well, Mother's been calling you for hours. Don't you know it's past dinner time?"

"I've been right here all the time," I said.

"Listen," Nan said, "we're going to Greta's funeral tomorrow."

"Are we going to Grandma's?" I asked.

"Of course, where do you think we would go?"

"Why did Greta die?" I asked.

"Because she was terribly, terribly sick."

"Why was she sick?"

"I promised Mother I would never say anything about it, as long as I live."

"About what?"

"Never mind. But I will tell you this: don't ever, ever, ever, as long as you live, and cross your heart and hope to die, ever, *ever,* bite a girl or woman there."

"Where?"

"You know where. You know very well where."

I thought a minute, but I didn't say anything. I was thinking of one day long, long before, when I had walked into Mother's bedroom and she was letting Paula chew on her body. Her body was pale and soft, and it moved back and forth, because Paula was chewing so hard. But Mother didn't mind, and she just smiled at me. She seemed to be sleepy, and didn't want to talk.

"Will you promise me?" Nan said.

"Yes."

"You and your promises! You promised you would never mention Mrs. Bird, but you did."

"Will they bury Greta with Mrs. Bird?"

"I don't know," Nan said. "Now come along. Mother's furious with you."

"Will Greta come back on misty nights?" I asked.

"I don't know," Nan said. Then she looked at me with her lips twisted up in a kind of grin so that she looked mad.

Then, after I had climbed on my new tricycle and started to pedal back home with her following behind, I heard her whisper, "Maybe."

ANOTHER STORY

He remembered thinking for a moment that the boy couldn't be serious. He was tall and slender and seemed candid; he was impressively American. But there he stood in his heavy cloth bathing trunks, holding a flashlight and speaking nothing but a rapid, slangy German. Peters could see the goose flesh on his forearm, the blond hairs of his wrist bristling out in angry toothbrush spikes. Even the goose flesh looked familiar, recognizable, "American." But everything else was hopelessly muddled. He supposed he had been too anxious for this boy to be an American. God knows why he had thought this way. Maybe he looked like a long-forgotten boyhood chum.

Reluctantly, Peters dragged his mind away from this possibility. Obviously, the boy was about nineteen, and couldn't (or wouldn't) speak a word of English.

"Mädchen," Peters said, setting his hands about a foot apart and vibrating them tensely up and down. He recognized it as a Harry Truman gesture. Frances would have said that. And she would have whooped with laughter; and all the German bathers would have turned and stared at her.

"Wo ist die Mädchen?" Peters said, vibrating his hands and frowning to show this fellow he meant business. "Sie war mit mich," he concluded lamely. "Ich kan ihre finder nicht. Verstehen Sie?"

The boy slapped his palm against his leg, and the sound, although loud, was strangely similar to the lapping of the lake waves. He grinned and nodded once, curtly, and spoke so swiftly and so colloquially that Peters was once more exasperated.

Then the boy said something else and turned back to the group sitting in a glum circle on the beach. Peters had noticed them before. Irrationally, he had even then had the impression that they were all German but this boy (who might have had German blood; his name might have been Clarence Schultz, for instance, or Victor Fischer, and he might have come from Wisconsin . . . but it just didn't seem that he was German). The others had been saturnine, drinking from dark, long-necked bottles of beer so gravidly that Peters had heard their mouths plopping when they took the bottles away. The boy had been mercurial, however. . . .

He was now returning to them and speaking. Good. That was sensible. He was organizing a search party. They would find Frances before long.

Peters walked up and said to them, "This young lady—Mädchen—she was here only twenty minutes ago. I went for cigarettes, and when I returned, she was gone." Peters snapped his fingers. "Just like that."

They hadn't understood him, naturally, and their expressions hadn't changed. They stared while the boy nodded and then talked on in his throaty baritone.

Peters looked at the others. Before, they had seemed an indefinite number . . . a small cluster of figures, several of them alien, and the boy from Milwaukee. But now, as he stared, they were indeed individuals. There were, in fact, only two women, an older man, and this boy. Peters halfheartedly tried to sense a familial relationship among them, but it was puzzling. For one thing, the women were both considerably older than the boy, and so was the man. They were all nearer forty, but the boy seemed hardly twenty.

Still, his actions toward one of the women were scarcely filial. She was the taller of the two women, with fiercely sunburned skin stretched as tight and shiny as rubber from a toy balloon across her wide, hard cheekbones. She was wearing a bikini, and her backbone stood out. When she glided away from them, Peters could see it grinding under her tanned skin. The thought made him shiver; and yet her body was very sexy, even if her breasts did sag low. She almost waltzed when she walked, and Peters thought that she must have been walking like that since she was ten or eleven years old. Then he wondered why he had thought this. All in all, she was a cruel-looking woman, and she had half closed one eye when she drew on her cigarette and stared at Peters.

Actually, he didn't notice much about the other woman, who seemed vaguely dowdy in an old cloth bathing suit similar to that once worn by Hitler's mistress. The man had a mustache, and Peters remembered that he could hear him breathe while they had been standing there together, wondering how to communicate.

The boy was called "Franz" by the tall, evil-looking woman. He was shining his flashlight all around the blanket, looking for something. It really wasn't that dark, and Peters sensed that Franz was still enough of a boy to love shining a flashlight, just for the sake of moving a beam of light like a magic wand.

The group remained silent, and for an instant Peters wondered if they had understood, or if they simply didn't care. For God's sake, he didn't know anything about this lake! He didn't know where Frances might have gotten it in her mind to go. For one thing, what American thought of wooded lakes when he thought of Germany? The strangeness of the whole situation was beginning to grow on him.

That was the thing that had attracted Frances and him here—the remoteness, the difference. It had intrigued them. They had been sitting in the back of a taxi one evening, after a dinner of spaghetti and zinfandel, and they had tried to invent a unique and exciting vacation. Once, Peters had known a man who had sailed the lakes near Berlin. So they had considered it, and after a while Frances had recited meditatively, "A summer spent sailing on a German lake. It has quality to it, Peters." (She had always liked to call him by his last name, mingling an arch mockery in her voice with a deeper sense of comradeship.)

"Indubitably," he had answered, in the expected way. She had once told him that she liked him to use "professorial" words, since he was a professor. She liked him to dress professorially. On his last birthday, she had bought him an umbrella—very slender and tightly rolled—which would jump open sturdily at the mere touch of a button near the handle. She liked him to wear tweeds.

"You're in love with a cliché," he had told her once.

"How do you spell it?" she asked.

"C-r-e-t-i-n," he had enunciated.

"Self-depreciation," she said. "It becomes you."

This conversation was typical. She had studied him too hard, and it had made him uncomfortable. Peters, now standing with his feet half-buried in cold lake sand—*on the shores of a German lake*—realized that this quality had been so aggressive that it had kept him from really knowing her.

Franz pivoted back, with his hand cupped beside his mouth. He called out something, and Peters heard the word "heise."

"Frances!" he shouted. The boy looked puzzled, apparently thinking that Peters might be shouting his own name. "Sie heise Frances!" Peters called again.

They all stared at him silently for a minute, then turned away.

"Where are you going?" he asked a few seconds later. "What are you going to do?"

But they were walking in a cluster down the shore—already a hundred yards away—and only the evil woman turned around to look, while Franz —the American boy who spoke only German—was walking alone, far ahead of them.

They went about it in a halfhearted manner, he was thinking. And how could they cover the woods grouped together like that? But they weren't even looking at the woods; they were looking at the lake. Peters felt cold goose pimples roughen the backs of his legs, and the sudden taste of nausea in his throat.

It hadn't occurred to him that she might have gone back in swimming. She had seemed too tired, after the sailing that afternoon, and the swim not over an hour ago.

Peters suddenly felt the need to talk to someone. He looked around, but by now it was quite dark. And the area wasn't well populated, even during the day. All of the cyclists they'd seen earlier seemed to have camped elsewhere. Isolation was one of the appeals: "Something that isn't just done by everyone," Frances had said.

Things had shifted dangerously. It was like cargo in his mind, shifting still, and threatening in a deep, disquieting sense. It all seemed to be a matter of ballast, suddenly. And he remembered with a sense of mockery the self-conscious way they both had (had had?) of going about things— collecting incidents, details, and characters to be re-created later into the stuff of anecdotes and drama. And whatever its character now, it would eventually have to be worked up into something that they *could laugh about,* or it would be untellable. It had occurred to Peters that people take vacations to stock up on frozen weird laughs, to be defrosted later, and served a thousand times to people who could duplicate them, some- how, with similar wacky experiences.

It all tasted bitter to him now. Suddenly, he felt intensely alone. It was surprising how much noise Frances could make, how much looking she could demand, how she could monopolize his mind. She left a wake, like a luxury liner, and when he was alone for a few minutes, even—going to the toilet or buying cigarettes—he would be filled with her (neither pleas- antly nor unpleasantly) until he returned.

But now, suddenly, she was gone. And the evergreen trees had turned as black as boot polish in the time you could smoke a cigarette. And the only four people in sight were just a little bit odd and not quite depend- able. Besides, they didn't speak English . . . or even a decent, formal Ger- man, for that matter.

He had an impulse to go out to look for her. But he decided that it would be best to stay right where he was. After all, she might come back; and what would it be like if he weren't there waiting? It would be horrible, Peters thought, not altogether in a flash of egotism. Horrible.

Then he decided to shout her name as loud as he could. He stood up on his toes, cupped his hands and shouted "Frances" in all four directions. From one, a faint echo came back, and at that instant, Peters thought the fresh, cold lake breeze smelled like a foul mephitis from a deep cavern.

Not even the "search party" answered. And Peters hadn't yet heard them calling. Maybe they had simply wandered off, or given up. Maybe they hadn't understood in the first place.

After a few minutes of shivering, he put on his navy blue sweat shirt and decided to look for some logs so he could build up the fire. Whatever you thought of Frances and the silly way she had of trying to *contrive* her experiences, she had a good heart and a pretty good head, even if it was full of errors and high-class clichés. Whatever you said about her, she was a good girl, and she deserved a bright, roaring fire when she came walking back to him over the sand that was so cold in places it made your feet ache.

He went back to the edge of the woods and found some sticks. He broke them into two-foot lengths and laid them neatly across the fire. They were pine, and soon they were crackling and bubbling in their frying sap, and the bright flames were standing two or three feet high in the darkness.

By now, Peters could see well enough to find the stick he had put in the sand, indicating where he had buried their last four bottles of beer. He dug down into the cold sand, clasped a bottle by the neck, withdrew it, and carried it back to their blanket near the fire, where his trousers lay in a roll. He got a can opener out and flipped the cap off. He drank half the beer in the bottle and then stared out through watery eyes and a gust of smoke at the lake. The moon was up, now, and he could see the waves glinting at myriad evanescences of light.

He looked at his watch. It was nine o'clock. Three minutes after. Franz and the wicked lady and the other couple were as good as dead and gone. Peters took another long drink from the bottle. They had been gone at least a hour.

"When they carried her up," something deep in his mind recited, "she was completely white in the moonlight. I hadn't the least idea she had gone in swimming, and naked, too. Of course in Europe that's no big deal. Still, it was quite a shock seeing her naked corpse lying there on the beach in the moonlight. It's something I'll never forget!"

There was no laugh in that story, but it would be a good story to tell. A good story. Gothic, bizarre, exotic. God, what a setting! And the mysterious young prince, the wicked lady. . . .

The only trouble was, as Peters knew too well, the best person to tell this story to was Frances. God, how she would have delighted in it! Peters was never so eloquent as when he really—I mean, *really*—had something to tell Frances. She would get this completely zany look of raptness on her face, her eyes almost crossed and her little foxy tongue stuck between her dazzling, fluoridated teeth.

Tears stung Peters's eyes, then, for it was damnably cold; and here he was alone out here by a German lake, not speaking much of the language. He could hear the whirr of the pine trees as they dragged against the wind, combing it with their thick, sharp needles. The moonlight glinted on a thousand wavelets, and the shore lapped in blind hunger at the water. It could almost have been Minnesota or Ontario.

"Frances!" he shouted, standing up suddenly. "Frances!"

His voice was sounding boyish, somehow, for he was straining it to its limits, and men—he thought—never gave themselves fully. He had heard this equation once: that a man should always keep a little of himself back . . . always hold a little in reserve, retain a little secret power, even in the things that mattered most: love, ideality, hate. Maybe it was his father who had told him twenty or thirty years before: "A good farmer will never buy a horse that's pulled its hardest."

But that wasn't quite right, either; and what did such formulas have to do with Frances?

For God's sake, what had happened to her? Where could she have gone?

He shouted her name again, and this time, an echo—as tiny and impalpable as the boy Franz's flashlight beam—glanced past: a strange, elfin sound out of the cold, hollow blackness of the lake.

Then he heard the startlingly different sound of a voice. There were the mere fragments of words spoken by a woman, and then a clear sound of soprano laughter.

It was from the direction opposite to that in which Franz and the others had gone. Peters set his bottle carefully on the sand and stared into the darkness, listening. Then he stood up and took a few steps in the direction of the laughter. Now there was silence, until Peters heard the crunching of several bare feet in the sand, and then the blinding stare of a flashlight in his face.

When they got closer, Peters saw that it was indeed only the same four who had left. Obviously, they had circled the lake. Franz said something, and Peters got the sound "forlorn," which he knew was the German word for "lost."

Franz said something else to him, not acting at all concerned, and then shrugged his shoulders. The women were getting their things together and rolling up their blankets.

They're leaving me, Peters thought.

And indeed they were. Quickly, efficiently, they started trudging up the beach toward their car, the only other car there besides the Volkswagen Peters had rented. For a few seconds, Peters listened to their footsteps munching at the sand. Then he called out, in a strange, toneless voice, "Danke."

But they didn't answer, and they might not have heard him at all.

"They must've been drunk," Peters said, half aloud, staring into the fire. And then, as if summing up something in German to approximate his meaning, he uttered the single syllable, "Schnapps."

By now, he was afraid; and he admitted it to himself. He didn't know of what . . . aloneness, perhaps—the unknown. But he had slept out in the woods before, alone. And he had faced up to danger before. He had always behaved moderately well in situations calling for courage, and he had always vaguely thought of himself as a somewhat courageous man. At least the kind of man who can rise to courage—the kind of man in whom courage can grow . . . even to heroism, perhaps.

But here it was, the simple fact: he was afraid. The muscles in his legs jerked and trembled . . . from the cold, partly, but from fear, too. He sought out another bottle of beer and pried the cap off. The moonlight lay over the beach—crowded like a neat, narrow alley between the thickness of trees and the lake—as pale as frost. Peters sat down and took a long pull from the bottle.

He tried to think of a poem to recite, but he could think of nothing. Nothing in German, nothing in English. A song, maybe. Something to sing out loud.

He stood up and called Frances's name in all four directions, and then sat down, feeling weighted by a terrible grief, a feeling so profoundly heavy that he stared at the fire for five or ten minutes, unable to move . . . dimly aware that it was almost out.

So he had waited this long, then. The fire had burned down, and the moon was high in the sky (*there* was the title of a song, recorded by Chaliapin). Time had passed, after all. But the great terrifying vault of the night still lay ahead of him. If Frances had been with him, why . . . .

And then a song came to him: "Du Kannst Nicht Treu Sein." And he started humming it in a horse, quivering bass that almost made him laugh, it was so toneless. He ended by drinking from the beer bottle, but when he put the bottle carefully down on the sand, the song stuck with him, like a brier in his mind.

Suddenly he stopped, and he understood why he was so afraid. *It was the thought of her dead body lying silent and motionless at the bottom of the lake.*

The image came to him with something of the violence of recognition, for obviously it had been there at the edge of his mind ever since the four bathers had started walking away from him, looking—not toward the woods, but toward the lake. And in this mute signal of their tragic suspicion, they had been at that very instant walking away from him, to circle back in mockery, it is true, but even then to leave . . . not once having said a word he could really understand.

It was the thought of her body, lying silent and motionless at the bottom of the lake.

The contrast between this vision and his memory of her at her most vivid moments—avid for information or ideas from him, prompting him, hungry for all of himself he could give—this contrast made him seem to tilt as if he were on some kind of carnival ride . . . only now, the beach tilted, the moon, the lapping waves (which lapped in German, ignorant of the feeling in his heart, the yearning for a simple, silly girl who had been trapped by sophistication merely because she was intelligent, but not quite intelligent enough . . .).

"I spent the night there, wrapped up in a blanket," the inner voice went on. "And I swear, I couldn't stop trembling. I kept seeing Francey's body floating there in the goddam black water, you know, and I couldn't get it out of my mind. . . ."

No, that wasn't the story he would tell. It was the truth, but there really wasn't the least sign of a laugh there. Nobody would laugh at a thing like this, especially the way he would have of telling it. Maybe someone would cry; maybe Frances would have cried. But who else was there who could really sense the awesome vacuity of fear in a situation like this?

"Oh God!" he groaned aloud.

He gritted his teeth and swallowed the tears in his throat. Then he washed his tears down with the last taste of stale beer in his bottle.

He stood up and called again. But there was no answer.

"Forlorn," he said aloud. "Forlorn."

There was surely something he could do, someone he could notify. But the thought of leaving was horrible. He should have tried to explain to Franz . . . tried to explain that the boy should notify "the authorities," whoever they were. But he had been muddled from the start. At first, a kind of adventure (as if they had been subconsciously planning it all along), and then suddenly—too abruptly—a tragedy so dire, so deadening, that he wasn't able to think rationally. The difference, he reflected, was somehow precisely that between the sweet-smelling, thick pine forest— where he had at first thought she had gone—and the deep, cisternlike lake.

The thought of the lake held him now as fear holds a man in a nightmare. The fire died before his eyes and within minutes the cold grew up around him. He thought of putting his trousers on over his bathing trunks, but he decided to leave them off. The cold was something he could feel and recognize. It was a discomfort that he thought he had in his power to end at any moment, merely by putting his trousers on.

After a few minutes, he walked up to the Volkswagen. As he approached, even it looked alien and ghostly in the moonlight, dead, unrelated to recognizable human needs. He stuck his head inside, and was met with a warm whiff of new-car upholstery, mingled subtly with the stale odor of cigarettes. The odor reminded him of his need to smoke, so he stood outside, flipped his lighter, and ignited a cigarette, while a stronger breeze from the lake ruffled his hair and whipped ghostly wreaths of smoke into the moonlight in crazy zigzag patterns.

As he smoked, tears began to roll down his cheeks. He was not really weeping; it was just the cold, perhaps . . . and that hellish vision of her body lying there at the bottom of the lake.

The image wasn't even real now. It was ridiculous; and for several minutes Peters couldn't even think of what she had looked like. For so long, you love someone (although you might not really know it, and that's the truth), and then when she's gone, the mind slips, like an old defective

movie projector, and suddenly she's no longer there on the reel of memory . . . is no longer available to you; it's as if she herself is cheated of the
existence a loved one should have in memories and dreams, even after that
part of her which is tangible is destroyed.

He went across the beach again to the blanket by the dying fire and
felt around blindly for his trousers. He slipped them on, his cigarette in
his mouth, burning his wet eyes. Then he walked up to the tree line again
and gathered some more kindling.

He rebuilt the fire, humming "Du Kannst Nicht Treu Sein" in his mo-
notonous bass (sounding like a stupid stranger watching him suffering
there). When the fire began once more to blaze brightly, the light glowed
warmly against his sweat shirt. The smoke smelled sweetly of pine pitch,
and it too burned his eyes.

Once again he yelled Frances's name as loud as he could, and he was
surprised that he had gotten hoarse. He had yelled a lot more than he
realized.

He sat down and buried his face in his hands. He was warm, now; the
sweat shirt, the long trousers, the roaring fire all warmed him. But inside
he felt sick and cold. He kept thinking of the silly way she had looked
when she was brushing her teeth.

Finally, he lay back in his blanket, looking up at the stars. The sight of
them so far away made him dizzy, so he turned over and buried his face
in his arms.

And eventually slept. He had no idea how long, although it was getting
light when he awoke. There were men's voices in the distance, sounding
clear in the morning air, and before he could look up, he knew they were
near the Volkswagen. He raised his head, and there were two men in some
kind of uniform, flanking an odd, tiny figure wrapped in a blanket and
picking her way barefooted over the parking area gravel toward him. The
two officers were very solicitous toward her.

When she got to the sand, she started running toward him, even drop-
ping the blanket on her way. In that instant, he saw that she was carrying
the camera, and he could hardly believe that he could have missed such an
important detail last night.

The men were very polite, but it was clear they were determined to
verify the story Frances had told them. So he nodded at everything she
said, and the two officers finally shook hands with him, saluted, and
walked away.

She told him she had seen a deer drinking water on the shore of the
lake, and she had wanted to get a picture of him. But he had run a short
way back into the woods, and she had followed; and then he ran another
hundred yards, and she had followed, until she didn't know which way to
turn. She had wandered all night, and had been cold and terrified. She

said she had forgotten everything she had learned as a Campfire Girl, but she had a feeling that he, Peters, would somehow know what had happened, and get her out of it.

"Of course, it's all right," he soothed her, rubbing his hands up and down the small bones of her back as he hugged her.

She got dressed, and they stood together watching the sun rise over the lake. "It's lovely," she said. And the birds sang as if they were mad with joy.

Then they lighted cigarettes, got into the Volkswagen and drove to an inn four miles down the road. They ordered black sausage, poached eggs, sweet fruit rolls, and a pot of coffee. As they ate breakfast, they studied each other's eyes and noticed how tired they were, how circled with fatigue lines, and how full of the dark echoes of tension. They began to chat as they ate, and gradually both became lightheaded. It was almost like being tipsy from wine, she said.

They were each on their second cup of coffee and had lighted cigarettes. Their bellies were full and their eyes burned, but they were warm with the morning sun and the morning breeze, cool with the smell of water and bright with sunlight, which whispered through the curtains of the windows.

Before them was the larger lake, sister to the one they had visited yesterday.

Frances told how she had twisted her ankle "in the black shadows under the trees" (she laughed at the triteness), and how she couldn't help thinking about Hansel and Gretel, and the witch who lived deep in the forest. After every sentence, she paused to whoop with laughter, blowing warm smoke all about, her eyes actually beginning to sparkle.

And Peters told her about the wicked woman with the pebble spine, wearing a bikini, of all things, and the boy from Milwaukee who refused to speak anything but the most rapid, most bewildering *umgangssprachlich Deutsch*. And the silent gloomy man and woman who accompanied them, sinister. . . .

Frances's enthusiasm flamed; she stuck the tip of her tongue between her teeth, opened her eyes wide, and *listened*. Peters told her how the moon looked when seen through a German beer bottle. It was surrealistic, she said. And she mentioned that she could hear the birds rustling in the tree limbs at night.

Before long they were laughing at the old bugaboo myth of the night, and saying to each other, "Just wait until they hear about this!"

FIRST THE LEGS
AND LAST THE HEART

I turned down Cosgrove Street, and right there at the corner, I saw Dad standing inside a telephone booth, looking out upon the traffic.

By the time I could get stopped, the traffic was pressuring up behind me, and I couldn't see Dad or even the telephone booth any longer, so I turned the corner, circled the block, and miraculously found a parking place in front of a twenty-four hour laundromat at the corner of Elder and Cosgrove. When I got out of the car, my heart was beating hard, and I started swallowing a lot, the way I do at such times.

I turned on the sidewalk of Cosgrove Street, and felt (or imagined I could feel) the hot wind from the traffic as motorists sped home, tailgating so hard they were almost bumper to bumper. They were all so tired, so jaded, so intent upon their first martini or Heinekin's that they probably didn't even notice Dad as he stood there in the phone booth, looking out. Or if they did notice, maybe they thought he was simply waiting for a call.

I began to slow down as I approached the booth, because I didn't want to startle Dad. I didn't want to come upon him all of a sudden, silently in the general roar of traffic, and appear without warning only two or three feet away from his elbow. I didn't want to flush him; I didn't want the crazy old bird to take flight.

But he was facing the street, which was only three or four feet in front of him, and I couldn't very well approach him subtly on this side, so I decided to cross over, if I could get a break in the traffic.

I stood there, about fifty yards away from the booth, waiting. He probably wouldn't see me, probably wouldn't even turn his head; but if he *should* do so, I would be far enough away not to surprise him. He would just think: "Well, there's *Frank!*" And he would think it was simply one of those coincidences. Dad didn't put things together the way most people do; you could depend on that.

Eventually, there was a break of about seventy or eighty yards between cars, and I sprinted across the street, smoothed down my hair with my hand (it had gotten mussed with my running), took a couple of deep breaths and then commenced walking on the sidewalk up that side of the street until I was directly across from the phone booth. I glanced over, and there the old Scout was, still standing there with a peaceful, friendly look on his face and gazing upon the madness of people enclosed in their cars, gliding and roaring by.

He didn't seem to see me, so I raised my hand and waved, and called out, "Hey, Dad! Hey, old Fellow! Look over here. It's me, Frank!" I called out for a long time . . . maybe three or four minutes, waving as hard as I could. But Dad didn't seem to hear or see me either one. He simply stood there looking as calm as a Bishop or a Judge.

Well, I soon realized that I was going to have to risk surprising him, because it wouldn't do to leave him standing there in the booth like that. Some harm might come to him. Some hood might come up and rob him, or maybe a bunch of kids would come up and make a spectacle of him, and soon they would be pointing and taunting him, and dogs would be standing there and barking at him, and God knows what all would be happening.

Yes, I would have to rescue him. That was clear; but before I decided on crossing the street once again, it came to me what Dad looked like standing there: he looked like one of those contestants in the quiz shows years ago. He had the same inert, far-away look, and you could almost hear a surge of music, and see the door swing open, and see Dad step out and give the answer that the silver deposits of Potosi, in Peru, were discovered in the year 1545.

I was still cautious about surprising him. I didn't want him to come out of there on the run. I didn't want to have to chase him down the sidewalk along Cosgrove Street, with his coattails flying, and me yelling, and my hair flying all over like that of a madman. Not that I couldn't catch him pretty quick.

So I decided to walk about twenty or thirty feet up the curb, and wait there for a hiatus in the traffic. Surely, my darting across the wide street would attract his attention as he stood there, keeping watch.

Within a few minutes, I had darted across once more, and now I was walking up the yellow curb toward the phone booth, where Dad stood waiting. His eyes were still mildly and peacefully directed toward the street, watching the traffic passing by.

I walked up and stood directly in front of the booth, which was surrounded by spikes of dry, dirty grass, poisoned by the exhaust from speeding cars, and waved, saying, "Hi, Dad." His eyes looked at me with their old kindly expression, but they were a little more alert, now. He didn't wave back or give any sign that he recognized me as his son.

Then I opened the door, and said, "I'm here, Dad," and he looked at me and said, "Hi, Frank."

"Are you ready to go?" I asked.

"No, not yet," he said. "It's not time yet."

"Yes it is," I said.

"No it isn't," Dad said.

For a few minutes we stood like that. I was blocking the doorway, because he's very quick in circumstances like this, especially for such an old duffer.

"Lot of traffic today," I said conversationally.

"Yes," he said, nodding. "Quite a lot." Then he looked at me, still nodding, and said, "Your hair's all mussed up, Frank."

"I suppose it is," I said, rubbing it flat with my hand. "I just ran across the street."

"Why'd you do a crazy thing like that?" Dad asked.

"I saw you in the phone booth."

"Oh. It's a nice enough place. Not bad."

"No," I said, "not too bad. Although it smells like stale urine in here."

Dad sniffed and said, "You know, it does at that."

"Crummy kids and drunks," I said. "They come along here and piss in the phone booths all the time."

"Yes, it does smell like urine," he said. "Strange. Maybe they think it's a urinal."

"They don't think, period," I said.

"Well, can't cry over spilled piss," he said.

"No, nothing to cry about."

For a few seconds we just stood there, Dad looking over the traffic as it whipped by, and me watching him for signs of cooperation. He seemed awfully contented, though. He had his hands in his pockets, now, and he was rattling change with them. It was beginning to look like it might be a long wait.

"They've jerked the phone off the hook, too," I said, breaking the silence. "So now this phone booth isn't worth a damned thing."

"Nice place to stand, though," Dad said.

"How can you say that? It's *hot* in here. And the traffic fumes are poisonous; they come in through those broken windows on the other side. They're even killing the grass around the booth. Look how brown it is. I bet you didn't notice those little windows were broken, did you?"

"Oh yes, I noticed," Dad said.

"Come on," I said. "I have to get home. This is a crummy place to stand."

"I sort of like it," Dad said.

"But there's no *reason* to stand here!" I cried.

It wasn't smart for me to cry out like that, and I realized it immediately. Dad's eyes flickered nervously, and I knew he might decide to take off if I talked like that again. I braced myself in the door.

"No *reason* to be *anywhere*," he said, his voice so low it was almost like a whisper. But I could hear it, even above the traffic. I thought of the old joke: *"Everybody's* got to be *somewhere."*

"Everybody will be wondering where you are," I said. "You can't do things like this all the time. People have a right to know where you are."

"Tell them I'm here."

"But I mean, they have a right to know that you're all *right,* and everything."

"Tell them I'm right here and I'm all right."

I turned toward the street, then, and cast a look of appeal at the passing cars, but of course they were homeward bound, which is what I wanted to be, and they probably didn't even see us, let alone take notice of the impasse we were in.

I decided right then that there was no point in nagging at him, so I said good-by and walked over to the laundromat and went inside. All the time I was walking, I imagined that Dad just might be watching me, wondering if I was going to give up that easily; but I seriously doubt if he did. I imagine he maintained his old posture, looking out upon the traffic, his mind filled with God-knows-what thoughts, memories, and expectations, oblivious to my interruption.

The laundromat was empty, so I went inside and walked over to the window, where I could see the telephone booth. God, how I wanted a drink! But obviously I couldn't leave Dad out there like that, so I decided I would wait here for him.

Well, if I couldn't have a martini, I could have a candy bar and a cup of coffee, so I went over to the two machines that stood side-by-side at the rear, put in my coins, and got a Hershey Bar and a cup of coffee with cream. I stood at the window, eating and drinking as I looked at Dad. When I finished, I sat down on a wooden bench and started leafing through an old rumpled copy of *Modern Romances.* I started to read one of the stories, about a lonely telephone operator who accepted a proposal over the phone of a man she'd never seen, and thus began a miserable married life; but I soon lost interest and threw the magazine aside. There wasn't anything else to read, so I just sat there for a while, drumming my fingers on the torn vinyl seat beside me.

Of course, now and then I would go over to the window to look out and see how Dad was doing. He seemed to be doing all right, especially for such an old Geezer. Once again I marvelled at his endurance, and felt a faint mixture of pride shoot through my general mood of being damned irritated and imposed on by the beloved old Screwball. (Mother claimed that wackiness came in the family, and that it was bound to show up in any of us, anytime. But of course, she'd *never* understood Dad.)

In spite of his physical condition, the strain of unrelieved standing would have to get to him before long. Even if he were thirty years younger, the simple damned dumb gravity pulling on his heart and vascular system, without the relief of movement, would tire him out. How long had he been there already? How long could he stand? I shook my head and blew my lips like a horse.

Ten minutes later, I went back to *Modern Romances* and tried to get involved in another story: this one had to do with a high school dropout (girl), who ran away with the football coach after a torrid love affair, consummated two or three times a week (if I got it right) in the coach's private office. The story was titled, "Why Did I Leave With Him, When I Knew He Wouldn't Stay True?" The title was more interesting than the story, which you can see is saying a great deal.

When the girl got pregnant and the philandering coach accused her of having messed around with the offensive team, I threw the magazine aside once more and went over to the window. Dad was still there, looking from this angle like one of those old-time street car conductors who stood isolated in their little cubicles as they piloted their cumbrous vehicles through waist-high traffic.

Well, hell, it was obvious by now that I would have to call my wife and tell her I would be late for dinner because of Dad. "What's he up to this time?" she'd ask, and I would have to supply lies, or at least euphemisms, so that she wouldn't start in again about having him probated. I'd tell her he'd sprained his ankle and couldn't move. I'd tell her he'd met an old friend, and wanted me to wait and take him home.

Anyway, whatever story I thought of would be as poor as any other, but it would keep her off me, because she'd have to *pretend* to believe me. It was clear I would have to get to a phone so I could call.

As if hearing my intention, a thin, strained-looking woman in jeans and a man's baggy gray shirt came in, and threw a laundry basket up on the table in the middle.

"Excuse me," I said, "but is there a phone around here I could use?"

"There's a phone booth out there," she said, pointing her hand vaguely in Dad's direction.

When she said that, I had to think quick. I didn't want to tell her the phone had been torn off, because she might happen to see Dad out there and wonder what in the hell he was doing. So I said, "I know, but it's occupied. Isn't there another one around?"

"Not that *I* know of," the woman said, digging down into her laundry basket. Her tone was one of dismissal; it also suggested that to her way of thinking even one phone booth was too many.

"Well, I guess I'll just wait, then," I said.

I sat down once more and returned to *Modern Romances*. I began to read a story about a woman whose husband wanted to swap her for a friend's wife, but she had always been religious, and besides she couldn't stand the other man, who had a dirty-looking skin. Her husband had been in a near-fatal auto accident, and seemed to feel that she owed him something for going through so much pain and suffering. He was an electrician, she said, who made a great deal of money, although he didn't buy her a nice house with it, but squandered it on such things as fishing trips and expensive box-seat season tickets to the Baltimore Oriole's home games. This reference was the first I saw of the fact she was living in Baltimore, but then maybe I wasn't reading well. One thing I *was* doing, though: I was beginning to hate this woman as much as I had the lonely telephone operator and the high school trollop.

I laid the magazine down halfway through the article and went to the window. There was the old Champ, as upright as ever. Son of a bitch, but the old guy could stand! I shook my head admiringly, and went back to sit down. What would I do? How would I get in touch with my wife? What would she think had happened to me?

"Is he still using that phone?" the skinny woman asked incredulously.

I jumped a little at the sound of her voice, but then I looked at her and nodded reluctantly. I shouldn't have brought the subject up; I could see that. The skinny woman had a profoundly resentful, even angry, look in the eyes, as if she shared the rudeness that was keeping me away from my call.

"Why, he's been in there almost a half hour," the woman said. "If I were you, I'd go up there and knock on the door and let him know I wanted to use the phone."

"Oh, I can wait a little longer," I said uneasily.

"Well, *I* certainly wouldn't," she said. "It seems to me you've waited long enough, and I don't think it's right to have you wait any longer! Honestly, the nerve of some people is beyond understanding!"

"It certainly is," I said, happy to find an area of general comment upon which I could agree, and thus distract her from the issue of Dad. Actually I was a little fearful that she might come to the window and see him well enough to detect that he wasn't actually using the phone at all, but just standing there.

So to verify my patience and unconcern, I went back to *Modern Romances,* and began reading a story titled "When Will I Ever Learn About Men?" This was about a woman secretary who was fired from her job because she was too attractive. I had gotten to the part where her most recent boss said she had to accompany him on a business trip to Atlantic City, when the skinny woman in jeans, who had gone over to the window, said, "Do you know something?"

"What?" I said, putting the magazine down just a beat too quickly. But I did refrain from glancing toward Dad.

"I've been looking at that man in the phone booth, and he isn't even *using* the phone!"

I looked up and said, "Are you sure? It's getting pretty dark out there."

"It isn't *that* dark," the woman said. She had a real gift for indignation, that was evident. Staring at her face for the merest instant convinced me that she seldom laughed, and *never* smiled.

"Well, it's still kind of hard to see at this time of evening," I said. "I mean, the shadows confuse things, you know?"

"Don't tell me what I can and can't see," she said. She was older than I had first thought. There were wrinkles all over her face, even though her shiny brown hair, luxuriously piled on top of her head, looked like the hair of a young girl. It was pretty hair, fine-textured, clean, and smooth; it seemed to me to deserve a better face.

"I'm sure he's almost through," I said.

"You don't seem to *care*," the woman said resentfully. She circled the table, shaking her head. I noticed that her clothes basket was empty, and one of the giant driers was whirring warmly, containing her clothes, no doubt. Why didn't someone else come in to break the trajectory of her thoughts? She was a frightening woman, I fancied, because her mind was empty most of the time, and whenever a notion *did* get into it, it echoed and reverberated like the yell of a lunatic boy released into an empty gymnasium after hours of boring classes.

"What?" I said.

"What do you mean, *what?*" the woman asked. She was leaning with the heels of her hands against the edge of the table. It was a mannish posture, and revealed the little peaks of her shoulder blades.

"You're on *his* side," she said. "And here I thought you really wanted to use the phone."

"I *do*," I cried passionately.

"Well?" she said.

When I didn't answer, she continued, "Before long, I want to use the phone myself to call my husband and have him come and pick me up. He'd better be finished by *then!*"

"He's almost through," I said.

"How do *you* know?" she asked. "And through with *what?* I tell you, he's not even *using* the telephone!"

"I'll go out and see," I said, charging toward the door. The woman irritated me so damned much, I knew I'd have to get out or else kick her in her skinny, jeaned ass. In fact, as I strode angrily and swiftly toward Dad's phone booth, I began to see her merge with the lonely telephone operator, the school slut, the unwilling wife of a wife trader, and the prurient secretary of doltish bosses in continuous animal rut. In fact, I imagined them all occupying the lighted windows of a building to my right, sitting there framed in the yellow electric shine (faces dark, like hands pressed against velvet) and regarding me silently, mockingly, alertly, with the malevolence of an abidingly critical obligation.

Yes, I was getting low on blood sugar and could see it all now: they were all skinny, and their breasts had shrunken to knuckles jutting out from their washboard chests. The eyes had gotten large and unsleepy, and they chewed burning flavors of gum with tiny feral teeth; and behind their working masseters, their damned ears pointed like arrows toward the moon.

"Hang on, Dad," I cried. "Stay in there, old Buddy!"

Of course, Dad couldn't hear. But when I was about fifty feet away, the light went on in the phone booth (or was it just at that instant dark enough for me to notice that the light was on, and had been on all this time, since the door of the booth was open?).

When I got up to him, I was panting. I swung around to the open door, and stared at him. He looked back at me and said, "Hi, Frank," as if he didn't remember I'd been there earlier.

"Hello, Dad," I said, grateful for his perseverence. I took his hand and shook it up and down. "Hang in there, old Fellow," I said heartily. "Don't give up."

"I don't know, Frank," he said slowly, after a pause in which I heard my heart beat three times.

"What's the matter?" I asked.

"I'm not as young as I used to be," Dad said, nodding at the dark stream of cars going by, following the false beams of their headlights. "No sir, not by a long shot."

"You can do it," I said.

"I don't know, Frank. I don't know whether I can or not."

"You can't give up now, old Scout!" I cried. Then I grabbed his shoulder and shook it. Dad kind of grinned, then, but there were pain and fatigue in the grin.

Then, after another pause, he said, "It's my legs, Son. It's the legs that go first. I remember that's what Ruby Bob Fitzsimmons used to say. The greatest fighter that ever lived, and he never went over 168 pounds. Had a blow that could fell a horse. In fact, one day a sportswriter brought a horse up to him at his training camp and bet him a hundred dollars he couldn't knock it down with one blow, but old Ruby Bob took him up on it and knocked that damned horse down on its knees, like it had been hit with a ball bat. Ruby Bob was a freak, he could hit so hard with his fists. Both hands, like a hammer. Not many people know that story, but I used to know the sports writer. A man named Phil Plattley. Phil was born without a thumb on his right hand, but believe you me, he could write like an angel. Yes sir, like a recording angel, Phil Plattley was!"

"Listen," I said, "there's a woman up there in the laundromat who's just itching to pry you out of this damned thing. Don't let her do it. Do you hear?"

"It's the legs, son. The legs let you down, first. And then it's the mind, strangely enough. First one end, and then the other. You keep your grip pretty long, though. And shoulder and back strength. But do you know what the last is?"

"What?" I asked.

"The heart, Frank."

"I figure it's possible the mind went first," I said, musing.

But then I wasn't so sure; maybe Dad was right and it *was* the legs. After all, he'd gone through a hell of a lot in his long life. He'd witnessed things I'd never witnessed, and seen things that no one else had. There was a firmness about the Old Fellow that never failed to impress those who watched him long enough and close enough.

Still, there was the problem of those astonishing acts produced by the busy brain machine. Sometimes it would start producing things not programmed in it at all (or not *knowingly* programmed . . . things the brain didn't know about itself), as if an auto assembly line started turning out lamps and air conditioners. (And what if the mind existed in the legs? If the eye turns images upside down, so that we're always walking on ceilings and don't know it, why can't the mind be located below the kneecaps, scuttling up the leg to safety in the event of amputation?)

The fact was, as you might detect from this sort of questioning, I was in bad need of a martini, and beginning to feel a little bit crazy myself, and began to surmise for the first time in my life that maybe old Dad had some pretty good ideas after all. The real problem was, they didn't translate into words very well. For example, I couldn't conceive of ever being able to explain him to the skinny secretary in the laundromat.

"You want to take over, now?" Dad asked.

"Well, I guess I could," I said. My mind was chattering like the monkey cage at the zoo, but what the hell.

"Traffic's not so heavy now," he said, raising his head as if to see it better. "Shouldn't be so tiring. I guess I could go someplace and rest awhile. And maybe get me something to eat."

"There's a laundromat right up there," I said, pointing carefully. "And you can get a candy bar and a cup of coffee there, while you're resting and waiting. It'll give you energy."

Dad sort of looked around, even though I don't think he saw; but he nodded anyway. He always did know he could trust me. "Sure," he said.

"I'll stay here," I said. "And if that woman up there asks you anything, tell her I'm making a call."

"Sure," Dad said.

Then he edged past me, and I edged past him (like a man stepping off a dock, exchanging places with another man in a boat, so that it doesn't float away), and Dad walked up to the laundromat. I watched him for a while. His moves were those of a man coming home from work—tired, but satisfied, kind of, and full of a realization of something accomplished and fulfilled, too deep for expression, and, yes, too deep for words.

THE PROJECT

The nearer he got, the crazier the whole trip seemed. The first sign came when Ziegler had boarded the jet and sat there in a window seat with his overcoat piled in his lap like a desk, looking out over the wing.

Suppose they were highjacked, and people found out why he was on board. What people? Well, that didn't matter. An investigation. "Tell me, Professor Ziegler, what was the purpose of your trip? Where were you headed before your flight was diverted? Were you thinking of visiting your estranged wife?"

He tried to imagine who might approach him with such silly, nightmarish questions, but the face remained blacked out somewhere in the back of his head. And then the stewardess was asking about his coat, and he thought she was asking about his seat belt. Solemnly, he lifted the coat to reveal that he was securely buckled down, according to regulations.

"You want to keep your coat in your lap?" she asked, nudging her whole body forward as a fat man passed in the aisle behind her.

Instead of answering, he simply nodded and put the overcoat back down. There was a brief searching look in her face that seemed to be her sole alternative to a smile. Now she would be suspicious. Professor Ziegler—a tall, hook-nosed man with burning eyes—was a security risk . . . or perhaps on a secret mission. Ridiculous!

After takeoff, he was sure that one of the stewardesses was watching the back of his head, and the thought made him uneasy. He decided to fix his mind on the project itself, and forget how he had tried to manipulate people to get air fare to Chicago, so that he could go ahead.

"Something like this," he'd said to a dozen of his colleagues—in meetings, in the lounge, in the hall, in DeLong's office—"has to be approached very delicately. We know what his mother was to him. Did anyone *ever* have him in class without having the mother come to visit at least once or twice? If anyone did, *I* certainly don't know about it. As for my classes, she made at least six visits in each course. I got to know her as well as my *own* mother!"

Although this argument had become virtually formulaic, he had gotten to feel a little uncomfortable about the last part: the fact was, Mrs. Springer was almost his own age. (Maybe the exact age of his ex-wife.) And her wide, pretty face was truly unforgettable, for it had a mad, secretive, sweet look quite unlike any face he had ever noticed. She was a widow in her forties, splendidly dressed . . . a little chubby, with heavy, sleepy eyes that bulged out ever so slightly, held in place by glassy lavender eyelids. Her lipstick was a startling red. The only thing her boy possessed in common with her was the faintly exophthalmic look, and a slow, lazy voice.

Of course, it really had to be done. That was the thing. And he kept telling himself this more and more often as the plane approached Chicago. Really had to be done.

And yet, it was astonishing. He had built up in his imagination the whole project, entailing a couple of hundred in department funds for the trip and expenses . . . built up the whole thing with the conviction that everyone would resist him. Consider the project unimportant, or eccentric, or irrelevant. Fight him all the way.

But really, there was no resistance at all. Everyone agreed that, yes, it was *precisely what should be done.* This immediate agreement triggered something irrational in him, and he found himself boorishly insisting upon the project anyway, reciting his arguments in the lounge, the hallway, the chairman's office. If he had still been married, he would have argued the whole case over with his wife.

"Yes, hell, yes," DeLong had said. "The money's available. And you're right, Fred, it should be done. And no question, you're the man who should do it. You knew the boy better than anyone else."

"Well, he wasn't exactly a boy," Fred Ziegler had replied fatuously, groping for the comforting pressure of dissent. "He was twenty-six when he died."

DeLong had just stared at him then, and Ziegler had said, "But, of course, that's irrelevant. And I know it. Goddammit, thanks."

Lake Michigan gleamed suddenly through the clouds ahead, and then his window pushed upward slightly as the plane tilted, showing a great unrelieved expanse of blue sky.

At this instant, he felt obscurely betrayed, as if they had all known he would make a fool of himself by approaching the boy's, that is, *the dead man's* mother with such a project.

But the truth was, he had been teaching for over twenty years, and never had he done anything quite this selfless, this idealistic, this inspired. The two hundred dollars be damned.

And the one, inescapable fact, which he had been almost afraid to admit into his mind, was that the dead boy, the dead young man, Jeff Springer, had been a genius, if the word still has any meaning left.

As if to reconfirm himself in this truth, Fred Ziegler silently intoned the lines:

> Or if these thoughts should ever glow
> and catch the flame of passion, like those wands
> small girls hold in their summer hands at night,
> then will you know the love that's burnt my mind;
> and yet you'll breathe that smoke and be sustained.

The department's two hundred dollars be damned! It was all worth it.

He closed his eyes, and a few minutes later, the wheels drummed heavily upon the runway at O'Hare, and Professor Fred Ziegler opened his eyes as if he knew exactly where he was going, and why.

When he was settled in the taxi, once again with his overcoat in his lap, he tried deliberately not to think of the sort of house she must live in, and what she might say to him (for she was expecting him, with no precise idea of what he had in mind; he had kept his mission vague for much the same reason he had assumed that his colleagues and "the department" would resist the project).

But the act of blocking this out from the stage of his mind merely caused it to shine brighter from the wings, as it were, occupying his attention with a morbid insistence.

The fact was, he told himself, the whole thing might be silly. And then he argued that it was silly to think it was silly. "What if triviality were excluded from our lives?" he asked himself rhetorically and a little hysterically. Then the answer came thundering down about his head: "We would all be paralyzed!"

But the voice sounded unconvinced, and he forced his eyes to take in the features of the four-lane expressway that led through the city to the suburb where *she* lived, and where *he* had lived for almost twenty years, growing the sensibility of a poet like some beautiful morbid inner cancer that would eventually choke out his life.

For the present it was good he could keep such a thought to himself, and let it have its say in the private studio of his mind. You'd never catch Fred Ziegler gushing like that in the classroom or the lounge. Still, the feeling was there.

The thing was, there was no accounting for the astonishingly elegant— at times, almost *mandarin* voice of the young poet. Could his mother give any insight into this curious fact?

Well, that was one more sanction for the trip. It *was* damned important, even if it *did* seem willful and eccentric to others in the department. (God, how his ex-wife would have misunderstood!) But if the book ever came about, husbanded carefully by Ziegler himself, with the help of the dead boy's mother . . . then, there would be no doubt of the wisdom of the project.

The taxi veered right, and then descended a long ramp into a neighborhood of brick ranch houses. Judging by the trees, the neighborhood was between fifteen and twenty years old. He thought of asking the driver if they were almost there, but then he decided not to. Control was achieved by dominating one's small actions. Ziegler nodded, and then recommenced nervously tapping the desklike surface of his folded overcoat with his fingers.

Still, this neighborhood didn't look a damned bit right. He'd pictured (unable to control his imagination) a very old, sedate, once-genteel neighborhood. Something to fit the lines,

> That dog wakes and circles once again;
> the moon follows in a mimic of its cry;
> What both mute bodies want is this:
> to circle through a sleep until they die.

God, the lines still thrilled the muscles in his back like a kind of fibrillation!

He thought of the dead boy's faintly bulging eyes, and the hair that lay like a stern cap slanted across his forehead. Of course, as he had often said, nothing was more certain than that the boy, Jeff Springer, would kill himself: his poetry was full of it.

"I, too, have been half in love with easeful death," Fred Ziegler murmured, thinking of that *other* doomed boy.

And then the cab pulled over to the curb, its meter ticking like a bomb, and the driver said, "This is it."

Professor Ziegler lifted his eyes and saw a long, low ranch house of blotched and faded redwood. At its side was a patio, with a broken gate ajar. It all looked terribly lonely, staggered by disuse.

"What can I say to her?" something inside him cried.

But actually he was standing with his coat thrown over his arm, paying the driver. Somewhere in the distance, the wind was blowing wind chimes in a sudden spasm, like the spilling of a xylophone down an abandoned staircase.

Now, in the sanctuary of her own home, there was an almost impressive formality, a certain cautious and subtle remoteness that he wasn't prepared for. This wasn't at all like the pudgy, charming woman with the fuzzy hats who had attended class with her boy, to the awe and amusement of students and faculty alike.

She greeted him politely, with the slightest hint of a crooked little smile (as if only one side of her mouth remembered the ceremonies of human warmth). She was dressed in a light gray slacks suit, with a red berry necklace. Her wide pink face was without make-up, the lavender sacks that held her eyes a little shiny. Her gray-blonde hair was neatly packed about her head. Everything was tidy inside the living room, making Fred Ziegler think of the broken gate to the patio, creaking in the wind.

Her face seemed astonishingly familiar, and when he first gazed into it, Ziegler had the curious impression that he really knew this woman much better than he had ever realized, but he wasn't quite sure what this knowledge was.

She offered him sherry (which seemed to fit something; he wasn't sure what), and then invited him to be comfortable in a chair before the gas fire that curled upward in graceful parentheses around an asbestos log in the fireplace.

After stating his mission, clearly and simply, Fred Ziegler picked up his glass of sherry (which he hadn't touched before), and sipped at it. Only then did he allow himself to look at the widow . . . well, that too, but the bereaved *mother* in the face. Her expression was uncomfortably vague, like that of someone resisting a sneeze, or about to cry.

"It's really a great honor for him," he said.

"What?"

"For a book to be gotten together. As I explained, I've already had a meeting with the director of our university press, and he's gotten several readings of poems I'd kept from Jeff's work, and there's absolutely nothing to stop us. No one doubts the power of your son's gift."

"I suppose it *is* an honor," she said. She didn't have a glass of sherry, and for the first time Fred noticed this. She was sitting straight in her chair, with her hands on the arms. Her eyes were a little distant, and a little mad, as if she couldn't focus upon anything as close and real as her room, or Ziegler.

"You see, most publishers would be unwilling to bring out a book of someone who's . . . well, no longer living. That is, unless it's somebody like Sylvia Plath, whose reputation was already made. Then a commercial publisher can really exploit her death, in a way. I don't mean that in a bad sense, but the simple fact is, she became an even more romantic figure after she died. But you see, Jeff . . . well, he didn't publish anything at all. In fact, he didn't even send any of his poems out to magazines, no matter how hard I tried to persuade him to. It was strange, really: he seemed a little detached, even indifferent to this truly incredible gift he had."

"That's strange," she said, "about publishers. Why won't they publish the work of someone who's dead?"

"I guess it's because they want to promote their writers. They want a whole career, a promise of a future, the hint of endless masterpieces . . . God knows what it is!"

He was sorry he'd said that; it sounded ironic, and he didn't want it to sound that way. But Mrs. Springer seemed to be dreaming at his face, like someone trying to see what he must have looked like as a small boy by examining the evidence now.

"It seems cruel, somehow," she said.

"Kindness isn't what they're about."

"No, I suppose not. But if someone is no longer alive. . . ."

"I know, I know," Ziegler said, shaking his head and frowning as if he didn't want to consider the thought further. He finished the sherry, but she didn't offer to refill his glass.

He was about to repeat the central question when she answered it. "Yes," she said slowly, "I think that's the right thing to do. I'm sure *he* would have been pleased. Yes, he would have been very proud. . . ."

She ended the sentence more as if breaking off, more as if she had been about to say, "proud *of*," but then she swallowed and began to pick at a button beneath her chin.

For an instant, Ziegler was very tired, and he closed his eyes and thought, "God, how lonely she must be!" Even this thought had been prepared for; he had first conceived of her as being lonely, distraught, bereaved (even if the boy had been dead for almost eight months), and then he had corrected this image: *no* one is that alone. His ex-wife collected people everywhere, constantly—this trait, considering his own gift for total immersion in his work, had been one aspect of their general incompatibility; and surely in the case of Mrs. Springer, there would be eccentric middle-aged women friends, brothers, friends remaining from her dead husband (he didn't know when Jeff's father had died, or how—this was something he had to find out . . . in time, of course, and with great delicacy).

But at this moment she seemed as lonely and as pathetic in her self-control as he had first imagined. No one *remained* for her; the broken gate on the patio (a place of sunlight and *fun*) was an indication of that.

Maybe all she had was Ziegler himself now . . . eight months after.

"Would you like another glass of sherry?" she asked.

"Oh," he said, looking at the glass. "No. No, thank you."

"Are you *sure?* It's getting cold out. And windy. Sherry warms you up."

That was the friendliest she'd been, and Ziegler agreed to another glass promptly, afraid to break the fragile little spell of vitality that seemed to have fallen like an accident upon her.

When she left the room, he closed his eyes for a moment and thought about the situation. Everything must be handled prudently, skillfully, judiciously. Had he made it clear that he himself would edit the book and write the introduction?

"I have edited several other books," he said, when she returned carrying his filled glass. "And I would like your formal permission to undertake this project as well. I think you'll find I'm qualified." He reached in his breast pocket and withdrew a thick envelope. "Here is a Xerox of my personal data sheet, my curriculum vitae. Actually, I'm under contract to edit a book of essays on English First World War poets, but I'm willing to put it aside to start on this. I can keep them both going, actually. The other book's almost done, and this . . . well, I don't mind admitting to you that it will be something of a labor of love."

"You were that fond of Jeff?" she asked, raising her eyebrows in delicate inquiry.

He sipped the sherry and frowned. It was no wonder he was so tired lately. He was straining too hard to be careful. First the unnecessary fandango he danced with the department, and now this whole delicate mess, which made him profoundly uneasy. But still, it must be made clear.

"No, it was not the boy himself," he said. "You must understand; this is nothing personal, not at all. The fact is, even though I knew Jeff better than I know most students, we don't really get to know any of them. We have too many, Mrs. Springer. They all begin to look alike after ten or fifteen years. That's a tragic fact, but it's an unavoidable one. We don't know what they do in their dormitories at night, or what dreams they have, what myths they try to live out. And the counter truth to this rather sad one is even sadder: after awhile, we don't care. They have their lives, we have ours. I suppose it's always been that way. When we come together in the classroom, it's a meeting of strangers, of emissaries or generals from alien armies, hardly speaking the same language, and not at all sure what their orders are, or whom they are serving, or why."

God knows what he was doing, or why he was going on like this. She listened patiently, but a little remotely. When he finished, she seemed to be looking over his head at something very distant . . . perhaps the memory of her dead son.

"It was his work, then," she said. "A labor of love in *that* sense."

He was going to say, "Of course," with a note of indignation in it, for what else *could* he have meant. But instead, he only nodded, and said, "Yes, that is what I meant."

"The poetry is really that very special, then," she continued.

"Beyond any doubt. If your son had lived . . ." but then he stopped, aware of the cruelty of such a speculation.

But she still didn't seem to be listening fully. At that instant, it occurred to Ziegler that the woman might really *be* a trifle batty. In spite of all the sweet reasonableness of her behavior, every little gesture, every little intonation, had a subtle oddity built in—as if there were some deeper intelligence behind the woman, prompting her in her actions, enjoying their consequences, and tirelessly presiding over what she did.

"Well, I'm very pleased that you consent to the project," he said, twirling the empty sherry glass in his fingers. He studied the glass, suddenly aware that he had emptied it. "And I understand that you agree that I will edit it. Is that right?"

"Oh, yes. I think so. I know it must be a great opportunity. And honor."

He started to say, "The honor is ours," but such an Edwardian gallantry seemed a little false . . . or it might set her to thinking of an unthinkable alternative, so he remained silent.

"Would you like some more sherry?" she asked.

"No. No. Thank you." He said this firmly, intent upon not being distracted from the remainder of his obligation.

And then, out of nowhere, he was struck by the desperate old-fashionedness of the woman. Surely, this might in some way explain that faintly archaic diction and cadence in her son's poems. Obviously, being the only child of a widow, and having that woman breathing on him day and night as he grew up, he would imbibe more of her than was healthy or normal; and she, conversely, would live herself *into* him, entwining her inflections and graces and tragedies in the sinuosities of his mind.

He set the wine glass down and clapped his hands once, as if to dispell the ghosts of speculation. To the business at hand. There was much that needed to be decided and—even more importantly—established. Like understanding and trust.

"I'm delighted you agree," he said. "Now this brings us to the next thing. I'm sure Jeff left a great number of poems, letters, notes, notebooks, manuscripts around. And I'm sure you've kept them."

The vagueness in her look made him uncomfortable. This was another thing that made him think she might be deranged: she had this expression on her face of a high-school girl listening to a transistor radio in public—autistic, dim, guarded.

When she didn't answer him, he repeated the question more succinctly, and she said, "Well, yes, there might be some things around."

"I seem to remember his keeping a notebook," Ziegler said slowly. "And of course I kept all the things he did for my classes . . . things he didn't ever bother to pick up."

"Yes, I think there might be something lying around."

"Would it be possible for me to look at whatever it is?" he asked. "I mean, I certainly don't want to pry or anything, but the memory of all human events is terribly fragile, terribly evanescent. I can't emphasize too much the importance of getting all we can down in writing, in print, filed away carefully. We need to protect whatever records we can find. Our university library would like to have his papers—the librarian, Dan Ritter, will be getting in touch with you about this, but he knew I was coming, and wanted me to mention his interest. The fact is, this would help me a great deal in getting the book together."

"I don't know," she said. "It all seems so terribly unreal. And sad, in a way. I can't express it, but *sad.*"

"Yes, I understand," he said. But he'd said it too quickly, and in the little silence that followed, the lines came to him:

> Sun is the heart, the heart, the deep red heart,
> And it beats in the yellow hay and river;
> It beats in my love but sucks it like a rain
> Back into the darkness of that sun, forever.

"Maybe I can lay my hands on something," she said, rising from her chair and leaving the room.

She returned in a moment, bearing a thin sheaf of papers, and a photograph of Jeff Springer.

"This was the last picture he had taken," she said, laying everything on the coffee table before him.

Ziegler looked at the picture a moment, and then leafed through the papers. "Surely, there's more than this."

"I don't know," she said. "I was never one to save things, the way a lot of women do. Sometimes, I do, but not often."

Ziegler hoped that at least one of those occasions had been the boy's leaving his papers and manuscripts around. He hoped that she had saved much more than she realized. A thick feeling of despair arose in his mind.

She got up once again and left the room. When she returned, she was carrying two large photograph albums. "Of course, there are *these,*" she said uncertainly.

She handed them to Ziegler, and he spent the next half hour looking at picture after picture—almost all of them showing simply the woman and her genius son together. They were standing in front of historical buildings, bridges, monuments, scenic mountain views, lakes, and seashores. Always they were alone, standing side by side, staring either soberly or smilingly back at the camera (held in God knows whose hands). Their lives together were thus chronicled in standardized images, showing them growing together—the one into middle-age, the other into young manhood. Changes in clothing fashions, hair styles, and even those less evident changes wrought by time were all shown here . . . but shown as if superficial variations upon an abiding and unchanging truth: this mother and this boy, locked in some deep mystery of affection, need, and imprisonment.

After looking at the pictures, Ziegler felt he understood less of the boy than ever.

The return flight was bumpy, but Ziegler managed to sleep part of the way, secure in the realization that he had succeeded in what he had set out to do.

Now there was the work of editing, collating, writing the introduction and commentaries . . . the whole job of getting the manuscript together, somehow, in between classes and committee meetings and student conferences and preparation for his courses. But the prospect of so much to do was comforting to him, and his brief nap on the plane was simple and uncluttered.

Back in his office at the university, he pulled out his desk drawer and withdrew his Springer file. He laid it carefully on the desk in front of him and then opened it. Before putting the additional material he had gotten from the boy's mother in with the rest, he leafed through some old manuscripts he had kept from Jeff's earliest student days, convinced already that the boy had a miraculous gift and it would be prudent to keep anything he wrote. For some reason, the boy had seldom bothered to pick up his themes and creative writing assignments.

Beyond any question, Ziegler had known him better than anyone else among his teachers, but this fact seemed to mock him in some obscure way. There was so much that remained to be known. For example, the boy's three in-class themes Ziegler had assigned for his Introduction to Poetry students almost five years ago. The writing was adequate, but uninspired. The word "perceived" was misspelled in the predictable way (!); and yet the longer he studied the pages the more certain he became that there were a few touches there, a few observations that might be said to hint at the sensibility that soon produced such lines of both cosmic and existential guilt as,

> Listen, where were you when it came about?
> Did you know we were waiting for you?
> Did you hear the excuses that we made?
> Did you feel our polite but suffering breath upon your skin?

Of course, the themes had been done in haste, between glances at the wrist watch, and in the pressure of saying it all in fifty minutes. There were greater mysteries than this.

The bell rang beyond the heavy oak door, and Ziegler folded the new material in with the old. This task would have to wait, for he had this very course to teach in ten minutes, at the second bell. No point in following dark trails at a time like this.

So he went to class, climbing up the stairs from his office in the basement (eye level with the ankles of coeds as they walked swiftly past his window). He lectured for half an hour (his thoughts only occasionally troubled by the vague ghost of the boy); and then he invited discussion.

There were twenty-three in the class, mostly sophomores, with a few juniors and one senior. By the end of this hour, they knew something of Yeats's ambivalence toward the political issues of his time (and they also knew the word "ambivalence," although most had probably known it before this), and Professor Ziegler gathered his notes and books together and followed his large hooked nose out of the room in search of the stairway that led back down to his basement office.

On the way, he stopped at the old wooden mail case and withdrew three letters and a publisher's brochure. One letter was from a high school in the state, and, putting it up to the light, Ziegler knew that it was a recommendation form sent by a former student. The second letter was from his wife's attorney, notifying him that his alimony payment was overdue. But Ziegler had sent the check only yesterday, so in a spasm of irritation he crumpled the letter up without opening it, and deposited it in a wastebasket in the hall.

But the last letter was the one that stopped his mind: the name in the upper left hand corner of the envelope was Dolores Springer.

Back in his office, he put his things down and carefully slit open the letter. He read it and then leaned back in his chair, looking out his window at the feet of passing students. He read the letter again. There was no room for hope; the boy's mother had changed her mind about the project. With apologies for any inconvenience it might have caused him, she explained that she had decided there should be no book of her son's poetry. It was too personal, she said. It was too much a thing of the past. It was too heartbreaking for her to contemplate. She asked that he return the materials she had given him, along with anything else that might have once belonged to her son.

For a brief instant, Ziegler fancied he could hear a gust of laughter from the faculty lounge, far above him on the third floor.

He turned his mind to other things. In fact, he so immersed himself in editing the book of essays (it was to be titled, *The Entrenched Muse: Studies in the English Poets of the First World War*) that, after a brief flurry of letter writing, he finished the project off and mailed the manuscript to his editor. Somewhere along the way, he himself was inspired to write a paper, "The Poet as Soldier," using surplus material he had gotten together for the book's introduction.

So he had the manuscript typed and mailed it to the chairman of an English conference, whose papers would later be collected in a publication of modern studies, and was notified within three weeks that his paper had been selected for one of the meetings, and he was asked if he would consent to read it there.

Of course he was delighted, and he wrote immediately saying so. The meeting was to be held in Chicago, on February 10 and 11, almost a year since he had visited Mrs. Springer.

Ziegler wrote to her before Christmas, informing her of his visit to

Chicago to read a paper at the conference, and asking if he might once again come to talk with her.

There was no answer to the letter, and Ziegler was forced to assume that she had not changed her mind in the least about the book; for surely she would have known immediately why he wanted to come there. There could have been no other reason: he was still haunted by the boy's ghost. But apparently she could not bear to face it again. Or had exorcised it permanently, so that it could not be brought back, even if she had consented.

Ziegler buried himself in other tasks, and waited for the February meeting. To hell with her. She was crazy, anyway. It was probably a good thing she had killed the project at the beginning. It might have proved a nightmare to him, if he'd gone ahead with it.

But maybe she would die soon, for some reason. That is, die before Ziegler did. They were not very old, but they were getting there, and one of them had to go first. And if it was Mrs. Springer, then Ziegler would be waiting.

It might have been that it was he alone who was aware of the boy's staggering talent. Of the incredible accomplishment performed before he had blown his brains out in a motel room at the age of twenty-six.

But precisely as these dark thoughts were formulated in his mind, Ziegler began to entertain others that were even darker. In one sense at least. He scarcely allowed them to surface. Rather, he busied himself with the details of his profession, and brooded on other things. One of these was another book of essays on the idea of the Romantic poets as "student activists." The idea was no longer topical, but it appealed to him; and even though it would be taking him out of his professionally franchised territory, he was soon thinking very seriously about it.

Such thoughts as this kept his mind away from those darker speculations having to do with Mrs. Springer. Even as it was succeeding, this strategy impressed him with how multiple and subtle the mind is, how splendidly bureaucratic; and how—with enough practice—you can think just about anything you want, and even control reverie to a large extent.

His paper was scheduled for 9:30 on the second morning—a bad time, generally, because there would be some of the conference people who couldn't get up that early, others who would be groggy from sleep or hangovers, and still others who would simply stay away in order to save themselves for the 10:45 session.

Still, there was a good turnout, and the discussion afterward proved that Ziegler's paper had been well received. Nat Benchley of Northwestern and Cecil Babchek of Minnesota came up to him and suggested they go have some coffee before the next meeting. Babchek asked about his wife, and Ziegler had to explain for the five hundredth time that they were No Longer One.

It was when he was leaving the room that Ziegler saw Mrs. Springer. She was standing in a heavy blue coat, with her gloved hands folded in front of her. A fuzzy white hat, like those she used to wear when she accompanied her son to class, was pressed down low on her head (maybe the wind out on the street was too strong to allow it to rest gracefully). There was what seemed to be an apologetic smile on her face. In short, everything about her was reminiscent of that earlier time, when her boy had been alive and she had intruded into his life and classes, looking fragile, diffident, a little wacky.

Ziegler told Benchley and Babchek to go on, that he would try to join them later, and they nodded and left.

"Well," he said. "I didn't expect to see you here."

"No," she said, shaking her head. "I didn't want to interrupt the program, so I waited outside."

That explanation didn't explain anything, but Ziegler nodded anyway, and asked if she'd like to go down to the hotel snack bar and have a cup of coffee.

"That would be nice," she said.

So they walked together to the escalator, and then descended silently, like figures in a pageant, to the high-ceilinged lobby. He started to take her arm as they crossed to the snack bar, but then he decided not to. He owed her very little, it turned out; not even presumption.

When they were settled in a booth, and the waitress had brought them cups of coffee, she said, "I didn't answer your letter. I guess I should have."

There was nothing to answer to that, so he blew on his coffee.

"The thing was," she said, drawing something invisible on the table with her gloved index finger, "I didn't want you to have to make another trip out there for nothing. And yet, I didn't know how to say it in a letter."

"Say what?" he asked. But he'd spoken too abruptly. He saw a flicker in her eyes, even though she was looking down at her own finger, watching it move on the mirror-black surface of the table.

"Oh, that there was no use to it. I thought it would be better if I, you know, came here to the hotel and told you. So you wouldn't have to make a special trip. It's a long way to where I live."

"I know," he said, sipping his coffee. "But that's all right. You could have told me in a letter."

"Well, maybe," she said.

"It's all right, though," he said.

She looked up at him, full in the eyes, to see what he might be thinking.

"All right?"

"Yes."

"You mean about my not answering your letter? Or about the book."

"Both. All three."

Again she looked at him, and then her eyes moved warily aside, and finally settled on the back of a waitress as she walked behind the counter.

"God knows, I was always too protective of him," she whispered suddenly. He might not have heard, but he did.

"It must have been very difficult," he said, nodding.

There was no answer adequate to that, so she lifted her cup and sipped. And in that instant, he was sure she, too, must have felt something like a strange wistful sort of communion between them.

"I don't suppose I have to say anything else," she said. "Do I?"

"Not unless you want to," Fred Ziegler answered.

"I had no idea it would turn out like this."

"No, of course not. How could you have?"

"I know. It seems so incredible, somehow."

"Yes, it does seem incredible."

"I did everything for him. He was my whole life. You see, my husband left me. He didn't die, although he might be dead now. But Jeff was all I had. It was like I had to live through him, or not at all."

Ziegler nodded and then suddenly loosened his collar with two fingers. The movement was almost spasmodic. Her gloved hand was trembling above the surface of the table, the index finger still extended as if she were afraid to touch anything hard.

"He was all there was left," she said lugubriously. "And sometimes I wonder if I didn't, you know, *cause him to be afraid, somehow! Crowd him too much; you know, take over for him in too many things.* Or maybe it wasn't that bad; maybe I just caused him to be ashamed or embarrassed. But as I told him, there wasn't any reason anybody would ever have to find out. And of course, neither one of us could have predicted that you would, you know, *like* them so much."

"I understand," Ziegler said. "At least, it makes some kind of sense. I can't say I understand, of course."

"No, I don't think you could say that."

"Well, it's all over with now. Or is it?"

"What do you mean?"

"Do you still write poems? Have you written anything since he died?"

For an instant she was silent, and then she shook her head. "No," she said finally. "No, there doesn't seem to be any reason to, now. I can't quite explain it, but it's like it was all said then. And after he died . . . oh, God, how he must have *hated* me. *All those years!*"

She looked as if she were about to cry, but she didn't. Instead, she sniffed and drank some more coffee.

Ziegler nodded thoughtfully. If the story ever got out, he'd be considered a fool of monumental accomplishment; and yet, he found that he didn't seem to care, really. He didn't know exactly what he *did* think. Nor was he clear about how great a loss the poetry was, now that he knew it was empty, a mocking show of words upon the mind.

Of course, what did the matter of provenance have to do with it? Poetry *was* words, and if this rather silly and pathetic woman had somehow, in some totally incomprehensible way, been the occasion for these words coming into being . . . the fact of her cheating, or *thinking* that she was cheating, had nothing to do with it.

But such a view was too platonic and too specious for Ziegler to believe in it. He had been misled, used, fooled. It was his own obtuseness, his own readiness (after twenty years of teaching) to have a gifted student, that had conspired in this monstrous forgery of the mind.

"You must think I am a monster," she said, surprising him by the statement, as if she had momentarily been part of his thoughts.

"No," he said.

"When I think of all the trouble you went to, I just . . . well, I don't know what to say."

Ziegler was nodding, and then he let his vision stray a little to the side, looking at the door that led back into the lobby.

"You have to go back, don't you?" she said.

"No, I don't have to. Not if you're not all right."

She looked at his tie and said, "I'm all right. You don't have to worry."

"Are you sure?"

"Yes. Positive. Only I'm embarrassed and . . . oh, I don't know what all. I've been such a fool."

"We all have," Ziegler said, getting up from the booth. "But then, maybe there isn't much else *to* be, is there?"

She stared at him a minute, and then held out her hand. He took it, and they shook hands briefly and slowly, before he left the booth and returned to the conference upstairs.

THE GIRL AT THE WINDOW

This was the old house we had bought: a vast and cumbersome island afloat upon the land, towers and cupolas and gables rendering the sky complex with their anfractuous horizon of darkness that galloped against the rose pink of twilights. Deep and heavy walls of liver rock held this circus of wood afloat, but one could see where the impossible weight had sunk even these rocks waist-deep into the clay. Weeds and grass and wild roses thickened everywhere about the house, the smoke-colored sheds and the roofed well.

A double wagon track was worn like a paradigm of memory into the depths of the yard. Otherwise, all was overgrown and blurred with desuetude and the brainless vigor of an inhuman and unwanted growth.

But it wasn't the house itself that was the secret; rather, this house was only the vessel of—not simply the secret, but the inner vessel of life; and it was life that was the secret, only this particular and induplicable form of life.

On the third floor of the house, there were rooms complicated with the detritus of a century—old shawls draped over the backs of cold and dusty love seats, clothes forms made in the shapes of young women long turned to air and loam, scrapbooks containing the portraits of staring, somber faces without names . . . high-topped shoes, bent stiffly at the ankles, books and magazines, rolled-up blinds, clothes hangers, broken oil lamps, chairs with burst cane bottoms and splintered arms, chests heaped with diaphanous black garments and flowered hats, as strange as extinct birds . . . all of these things, covered with the oat-smelling dust of soil and time.

For three days, we cleaned and rearranged these objects, and there was such a multitude that after a while they all began to look alike—the books and the letters, the chairs and the photographs.

But not quite. There was one photograph—at least a century old—that caught my attention. Not at first, for I was sorting out different papers, and it merely lay among them; but later the thought of it came back to me so strongly that I returned to the room and looked for it. (The room was like the others—slanted beneath the gable and dim with a light that seemed peculiarly adapted to the thought of a long distant past.)

I found it again, and this time—holding it in my hands—I was troubled by the elusive strangeness before me. The photograph dated surely from the 1850s or 1860s, and it was simply the photograph of a large building. Apparently an apartment building. There were no human presences that I could detect in the scene, and yet the immanence of something human was as certain and palpable as an odor. Indeed, there was no tangible life in the picture at all, except for a sorry-looking horse standing in harness before a quaint little carriage. The head of the horse was blurred, obviously from a sudden movement in a day when photographic exposures required seconds rather than fractions of a second.

What was there about the picture that magnetized my attention? I stared at it in the darkness of that room until my eyes blurred and the everyday sounds of the world subsided into something half-unreal and half-silent. Then I closed my eyes and concentrated upon the scene that remained fixed in my mind.

The more I thought, the stranger it seemed. And yet, I was close to experiencing some sort of recognition in it. In some way the photograph seemed to be meant for me alone, in a sense that was obliquely mysterious. This photograph had been waiting for me, and for no one else.

Although I was not able to define this unsettling power, I did in fact learn something from all that thought: whatever the mystery was, it had to do with the windows.

In spite of this fascination, I had to put the photograph aside for several weeks while we settled in the house and made it fit our family the way new shoes or a new suit is made to fit the body.

But eventually I sought out the photograph again, and sat before it and stared into that strange scene of a building that had existed in an unknown city at least a century before, and was now undoubtedly disbursed into soil, mud, brick dust and air.

I decided to take it to a room in the basement, which I had set aside as my darkroom, where I intended to develop all my own photographs. I proposed to make a negative and enlarge it. I was aware of the problems, of course, and scarcely hoped to learn much from the photograph, for the techniques of that distant time were impossibly crude, and upon enlargement, the details of that scene would undoubtedly be lost in the hypertrophied grain—elements of vision that had an atomic absoluteness, and would wax thick and gross, like anonymous golf balls of gray and white inhabiting the expanded view.

But this was not so. For I was astonished to discover upon my first enlargement that the grain did not expand with the view, and that the images of people appeared in the windows of that building.

I did not really study that first enlargement at all. Someone watching me might have thought I was simply impatient, or in a hurry. All I did was throw the photograph aside, after that first discovery, switch out the light, and leave my darkroom to go upstairs and join my family.

The children were sitting around the television, eating peanut butter and banana sandwiches. My wife was preparing supper. Everything was normal, and as it should be. I went into the kitchen and fixed drinks for my wife and me. The children were laughing in the other room, and the TV was turned up too loud, as usual.

I have sometimes pretended that the people you meet in recurring dreams have an independent, suspended reality during the intervals between their appearances in your dreams. Not suspended entirely, perhaps, but only as actors. That is, I have fancied that between their appearances in dreams, they might live an existence as divorced from their roles in your dreams as it is divorced from the reality of everyday life. That they actually might meet for rehearsals somewhere, in some totally unknowable realm, and discuss the terms of what they will do on the stage of your next dream, memorize lines, and strive to control and predict certain effects upon the audience. In this situation, it is the dreamer who (like an audience) is the only unpredictable element, the only unrehearsed participant in what happens, the only uncertainty, as of jury or God.

It was this way with the people in that photograph. While I turned back to the daily affairs that called for my immediate attention, those people whose faces had just begun to emerge sat back in their darkened rooms and waited for me. They were waiting for that quiet and secret moment when I would come back to them, and enlarge their images until they became cogently human in the text of my attention. Perhaps they talked with one another, and lived lives beyond the scope of my imagining, imprisoned as they were in the crepuscular rooms of an ancient building . . . which in turn existed only in the flattened image of the photograph of a dead, past time.

Still, everything that could be said to be *there* once had access to the light, and this suggested to me that it was somehow accessible to the understanding. It might *not* be beyond recall. It was possible that the people in those rooms continued to exist with their own lucidity, no matter how intangible this lucidity might seem.

It was a week or ten days before I found time to go back. It was evening, and when the children turned on the TV, I descended the steps and went into the darkroom. I enlarged the upper right section of the photograph, showing one window completely, and two half windows to each side. When the image began to come forth, like something emerging from the deep water of time, rather than from the tray before me, I saw that there was the face of a young girl to be seen in the room beyond the window. It was perfectly clear; and the eyes of the face were fixed intently, unmistakably, upon mine. That is to say, upon the lens of the camera.

Whoever had been taking that photograph over a hundred years ago, he had been watched by this young girl. Probably without knowing it.

In the two half windows that showed at the side of each window, there was nothing at all. Merely the darkness of unlighted rooms.

I studied the face of the girl. It was a beautiful face, but somber. She must have been only nine or ten years old; but already, I could imagine, there was something old in her features.

I could see dark combs in her light hair. Her chin was slightly raised, and one hand was cupped softly on her throat, almost in a theatrical gesture of surprise or fear. Whatever it was, the emotion on her face was clearly one of some force. There was something of unease upon it, but there was fascination, too.

It occurred to me that she might not have seen a camera before this instant, and she was staring out through the window at a man leaning over, seeming to peer absorbedly into nothing but a shrouded black box.

Nevertheless, she probably knew what the camera was, even if she had never seen one. Possibly she saw something else that disturbed or frightened her.

Then I considered the strange impossibility that she might have seen into the lens, into the camera itself, and even into that very future to which the camera would bring her image. In other words, that she might be looking at me, just as I was looking at her.

A whimsical idea, which I put out of my mind immediately. Then I studied her face closely for several minutes before going back upstairs, having had enough of such communion for a while.

But of course I returned, and enlarged that single window with the girl in it. There was surely some revelation in that face, if it could be brought closer. The closer it came, I was thinking, the more lifelike it would be. And I even fancied that I might eventually see the face grow to life-size, and feel something like a breath on my hands as I worked with it.

Ridiculous, of course. But all of this was part of the hypnotic effect the photograph had upon me. And my wild fancies were not discouraged when I found that, upon this latest enlargement, the girl's face actually began to show something almost like color. As did her hair, which might have been a pale gold with slight rednesses in it.

The eyes, of course, were even more lifelike. And behind the girl I could now identify an asymmetrical shadow. This was the back of a man who appeared to be stooped and leaning forward with his face in his hands, weeping. It was impossible to see clearly, but he appeared to be elderly.

Whatever condition he was in, or whoever he was, the girl continued to stare in fascination out upon the world, and into the camera lens, and even (as I have suggested) at myself, as if I were a voyeur god gazing upon her over so great a distance and so much time.

Beyond the man, there was something else, a long horizontal shadow that he seemed to be facing. But at this stage of the enlargement, I could not tell what it was. Still, I studied it very closely for a long time, and then I looked once more at the man. I was almost certain that his hair was silver and long, curling over the collar of his dark coat.

And when I finished studying these two things, I looked back once more at the face of the girl as it continued to gaze at me. I am sure I imagined it, but the face seemed older. The girl might have been as old as twelve or thirteen. It was very difficult to tell.

And there was a slight mole on her right cheek. No larger than the tip of a lead pencil, but there it was, clear before my gaze. I was sure it was not a defect in the photograph, but an actual mole on the girl's cheek.

With the next enlargement, I discovered that the long shape beyond the old man was a casket. No figure was visible in it, but the ornate satin upon the lid glowed faintly in the dim light, and the shape of the lid was unmistakable.

Therefore, the photograph had caught this old man in a moment of grief, weeping into his hands before a loved one who had just died. And it had caught the girl, too.

However, the girl had happened to turn around and look outside, where she had seen something that surprised or puzzled or terrified her, so that she had clutched vaguely at her throat while the shutter opened and closed, fastening their image permanently by the witnessing of light upon a chemically treated plate.

But what was it the girl saw? What precisely was the landscape of her fear or grief? That window she was staring through was not so different from the lens of a camera, I told myself. Nor so different from the images I busied myself with, enlarging them without either attenuating or fragmenting them, in contradiction of all law. It was as if one could increase the power of a microscope without destroying the surface appearance of that which he regarded, but only rendering it clearer and more unmistakably itself with each enlargement.

Only in this, the mystery grew with each enlargement, precisely as the human discoveries increased, defying all expectations.

And yet the girl's face was no different; merely more human, in its strange way, and perhaps still a little older than even that second discovery had suggested.

There was something else, however: her lips were slightly parted. The realization was beyond question. Her lips were open just a fraction of an inch, and I realized that the camera had caught her in the act of speaking a word.

But how could this be? The camera of that day had disastrously slow shutter speeds, as I have said. The horse harnessed to the cart outside the building gave evidence that this was so, for his head was blurred. So why didn't I conclude that the girl's lips were simply parted . . . from an adenoidal condition, perhaps, or because of something else? But no. This was not so, and I could see it was not so. Although I could not have proved it to anyone else, I was certain that the girl had been caught in the act of saying something.

Possibly something to the old man behind her. Her grandfather, perhaps; speaking a word of consolation to him as he stooped before the casket weeping for the loss of a loved one.

But this would not do either. The girl was looking out the window. Her eyes were focused. She was looking at the anonymous cameraman, at the camera itself . . . at the lens, at me.

And she was speaking a word. Not only her lips, but her eyes gave testimony to the truth of this hypothesis.

It was the next and the last enlargement that conveyed to me the final revelation. And this was the revelation I had been waiting for, although it might in itself seem arcane and impossibly ambiguous. For the answer is really, in one sense, a nonanswer. But even a nonanswer is an answer of sorts . . . or it can be, as when it signifies that no categorical answer is possible because the terms of the question are wrong, or the implications of the question are somehow unthinkable.

This happened on the very next night, and I was excited when I descended the steps to my darkroom and prepared my enlarger.

When the image grew before my eyes, it was almost like the entrance of someone I had known all my life. The girl's face, looking still older than I would have thought possible the first time, appeared between my hands, and her lips were now so clearly parted that no one could have doubted that she was in the act of speaking a word . . . as no one could have doubted the deep, unequivocal focus of her eyes upon the person who gazed upon her.

As I studied her image, it came to me—suddenly and irrefutably. I mean, the word she was speaking (whispering, I think, so that the old man behind her could not possibly have heard).

The word was, "No."

That was all. "No." Nothing else at all.

For who else might have seen this possibility, or might have understood the burden of her prescient fear? What strange Cassandra was this girl? And what dreams might she have had before and after this one instant, when she stared outwards into time as well as into space?

These are questions that undoubtedly deserve nonanswers. Whatever they might have led to, however, I decided that evening to destroy all my enlargements, along with the original photograph.

Good and evil had nothing to do with it. Although it seemed to me to be an act of cleansing, as well as liberation. I mean the act of destroying everything that had to do with the photograph.

Sometimes I wake up in the night and wonder about the girl, and fear for her, and feel pity for her.

Did she, I wonder, worship the future, or the judgment of the future, as a kind of God? Was she, in short, as poisoned by this error as we are? (I speak of the error of believing that the future is wiser, or more nearly infallible, than we are; an error that is an inevitable corollary to the myth of progress.)

Was I like a god to her, to the extent that she guessed at, or imagined, my presence? Consider this: if she were mad, she might have dreamed that some unknown man was staring at her through a glass, and that this man lived a hundred years beyond that instant. The man might have been her great grandson, or the great grandson of people she had never known. All would be the same to her.

What I am asking is this: if one might have a glimpse of the future, might it not occur in such a manner as this? Wouldn't the camera still seem to her in that day a marvelous, a magical invention? And if something of her could pass through the lens of the camera in one direction, might she not conceive that something, or some vestige of someone, pass in the other direction?

But it isn't simply the girl who is at the heart of this mystery (although God knows she embodies enough!). For I am thinking of all those other windows. And I am thinking of the poor horse and the strange little carriage it was harnessed to. I wonder if they belonged to the photographer.

And the photographer himself. What was he like? Who was he? And the camera. I would have liked to have a photograph of this man. I would have liked to see him as that girl saw him.

As it is, I only conceive of him as huddled behind the old camera, his head covered with the stiff dark cloth that kept out all the adventitious light of day. He is gazing into the lens before him, and the building he sees is inverted and upside down. All the windows are upside down. The horse and the carriage are upside down. The horse moves his head, but the girl speaks the word "No," and already the picture has been taken.

ELMA

When Elma Krouse's mother started talking about how much Elma and I were suited for each other, Mother seemed not to hear; she changed the subject—started discussing her marigolds or the squirrel nests in the drainspouts; or she drifted off into a mysterious silence with the thoughtful expression on her face of a child sucking hard candy.

But Elma's mother was never to be put off. She was such a fool you almost had to respect her. Absolutely nothing cut her down. She was a big woman with a lantern jaw, a smile of maniacal innocence in her eyes and a single-minded dedication to mating me with Elma.

I suspected that it was not so much respect for me as a young man as it was a recognition that I was an essential part of Elma's childhood, therefore the most fitting husband imaginable. I seem to remember Elma's mother plotting our marriage when we were still going out on Halloween to ring doorbells. Elma and I tried to get even with her in a quite simple way: we hated each other.

At least we thought we did throughout high school. Her mother's contrivances to keep us constantly facing each other across gin rummy or Chinese checkers kept us sullen and intractable until we learned that if we smiled, we could say spiteful things to each other, and Elma's mother wouldn't notice. This gave us both a perverse pleasure. Elma called me "Ugliest," and I called her "Sour Krouse" and "Elmer."

Elma was not an attractive girl. She was large—not fat, but actually brawny in a kind of super-feminine way. By the time she was fourteen, she had a spectacular chest and hips that worked massively under her shorts when she walked. Whenever she strolled away from me, I would go "boom-te-boomp; boom-te-boomp," and watch the back of her neck get red. Her mother never seemed to notice; she was always too busy planning our next get-together, or talking on the phone. Or she simply thought it was all in good fun.

It was inevitable that Elma's mother would see that Elma attended the same college as I, when the time came. So naturally, I chose a man's college. It was a hot August morning when Elma's mother heard about it, and she marched over to our house and talked with my mother for an hour.

It was an odd thing about the woman that she always smiled. The smile was physically a part of her face; but on this day, I could tell she was furious. She told Mother specifically how to persuade my father to change my mind. She knew that in our family, at least, it would be my father who ruled. It really hadn't occurred to her that he would back me in my present decision, without question.

And of course he did, albeit he was never really challenged by Mother. She had tried to throw Mrs. Krouse off by mentioning that our chrysanthemums didn't look promising that year. She even got her mysterious look; but Elma's mother didn't waver. She talked for an hour straight, and when she had finished, Mother took her into the kitchen and got her a drink of water. Elma and I were on the screened porch, glaring at each other (it was an insufferably hot day, and there wasn't anything more interesting to do) when they came into the kitchen. Her mother stood with her legs apart and drank the water down like a tired lumberjack. Then she stared at me out of her meaningless smile and said: "Do you know how it's going to hurt Elma if you go through with this thing?"

Elma jerked upright and hissed, "Oh, Mother, shut up!"

But her mother had already turned back into the house. As she often told people, she never listened to what the children said. They never knew their own minds anyway.

In spite of all her mother could devise, Elma and I went to separate colleges. The last two or three weeks we had together at home were almost amicable; we were soon to be free of each other. I dreamed of a girl who was small, dark and intense, with flashing eyes, and she probably dreamed of meeting a boy who was half a head taller than I.

I hadn't been away over three weeks when I received a letter with her name and address neatly inscribed in green ink in the upper left-hand corner of the envelope. Her writing was tiny, scriptlike and absolutely vertical.

Her letter suggested in a manner that was half plaintive and half chummy that we correspond with each other to satisfy her mother, who would know from my mother if we didn't write. It seemed that Elma's mother had already started nagging her to write to me.

The letter made me furious. I went to the post office the next afternoon, bought a post card, and wrote: "Absolutely not," in the biggest, angriest scrawl I could manage. I signed the card "Ugliest," and mailed it to Elma.

The card must have been effective because I didn't hear from Elma for the rest of the year.

In my second quarter at college I received all "A"s. When I got my grades, my first reaction was that this would really surprise Elma. She had always pretended that she was smarter than I. Whenever she could, she tried to prove me wrong. I had often gotten the impression that it was the only reason she ever bothered to listen to what I said.

Well, this would impress her. It was odd—although I didn't realize it at the time—that it was Elma I thought about when I got the grades. I had no desire to see her or to write to her. But I kept thinking of her face and of the angry glint that would flash in her pale eyes when she heard about my success.

I had never felt so confident. A week after the grades were out Mother wrote, saying that Father and she were immensely proud of me, and—wasn't it a coincidence?—Elma had gotten all "A"s in her second quarter, too. Mother mentioned that Mrs. Krouse couldn't get over the coincidence. Obviously she took this to be merely another sign of the inevitable rightness of a union between Elma and me.

But if Mrs. Krouse was confirmed in what seemed to be the central conviction in her life, she was not able to enjoy this confirmation long.

It was on a bitter, cold day late in March that I received a telegram from home saying that Elma's mother had died suddenly of a kidney disease. It was a shock to me. The telegram suggested that I should come home for the funeral; and I knew in my heart that I should. Instead, I sat down and wrote a brief letter to my parents, saying that I had mid-term examinations coming up and I couldn't possibly miss them. This was a simple lie, but I knew that Mother would make the appropriate excuses to all concerned.

The least I could do, I was thinking, was write a letter of condolence to Elma. And once or twice I sat down to do so, but I wasn't able to write the letter. I seemed to realize that I was behaving strangely, not to say rudely and childishly. I realized that what I was doing was inexcusable. But I simply didn't care.

On the night before her mother's funeral, I had trouble going to sleep. For some reason, I was filled with a shimmering hatred for the dead woman. It seemed to me that she had cheated me in dying before I could have somehow convinced her that I despised Elma. Although there was more to it than that. I remember that before I went to sleep, I experienced deep feelings of sorrow, shame and simple bewilderment. There was no focus to any of these feelings; they seemed to blow through me like the wind. I was sure of one thing only: I did not want to see Elma.

During the rest of the school year, Mother mentioned Elma occasionally in her letters. But the tone of such references was remote, and when I arrived home for the summer vacation, I learned that Elma had come home the week before. Mother said she had visited her one afternoon and they had drunk iced tea and chatted about school, Mother's flowers and mutual friends.

"She's improved," Mother commented.

"Is that right?" I said. I found myself wondering briefly in what way she had improved; actually, I knew that it had never been Elma herself who had caused trouble.

Mother had me out in the yard, pulling some dead climbers out of the trellis. She stood back, watching me intently (there were live vines in the trellis, too, and she was mortally afraid I would damage one of them); it was almost as if she were discussing Elma's visit merely to keep the conversation going.

"She's certainly an awfully *quiet* girl," Mother was saying. "I don't think I ever realized what a quiet girl she is."

"Is that right?"

"This trellis certainly needs painting," Mother said, dusting her gloved hands together.

I tugged at another blackened cord. It gave a little. Then it came loose, and I pulled it out, hand over hand. I looked through the vines at the Krouse's back yard. It was empty. Empty of people and somehow empty in another, more subtle way. I stared for a moment before I realized that there were no flowers. Mrs. Krouse had died in March, and there had been no one to plant the long borders beside the fence and back by the tall elms.

"Will you paint it?" Mother asked. "When you have time?"

"What are you talking about?" I asked.

"The trellis. I just said that it needs painting badly."

I refocused my eyes on the trellis in front of me. "Yes," I said. "I'll paint it one of these days."

"That will be nice," Mother said.

When I had finished pulling the dead vines out, Mother stepped directly in front of me and looked into my eyes. I was suddenly aware that she was not facing me precisely as a mother faces her son. There was uncertainty in the look . . . a kind of delicacy and regard for me as for someone she couldn't quite understand but was willing to respect.

"Don't you think you should go to see her?" Mother asked.

"Elma?"

"Yes."

I picked up the rake and started scratching the scattered vines together in a pile. "Sure. I probably will one of these days," I said.

"I think you should do it soon," Mother said. "She's always thought a lot of you. And with her mother dead, well. . . ."

The next day I saw her once. I was sitting idly at the piano, playing chords, when I saw Elma walking through the back yard. It was almost as if she hadn't changed at all, as if we had never really been apart. I remember that at that precise moment I had a powerful sensation of Mrs. Krouse . . . I could almost see her cast-iron smile, smell her perfume! I could almost hear her speaking to Mother.

That evening, Mother asked me to burn the vines we had cut out, along with some other trash. I stuffed newspapers in a basket and carried a grocery sack filled with wastepaper back through the yard to our incinerator by the garage. The spiraea bushes were thick, but I could see the Krouse's back door through the limbs. Elma's father went into the house, and I supposed that they were about to eat a late dinner. I balled up some newspapers and threw them into the incinerator. Then I set fire to them and stood back, watching the white smoke roll up, slide away in a gust of warm air and filter through the spiraeas toward the Krouse's back yard.

It was almost dusk. I stood there watching the fire burn and feeling the brittle heat dry the skin of my face and arms. It wasn't soft and warm, like the heat from the earth and the evening sky . . . there was something fierce in it. I could feel the hot sweat gathering on my chest and pressing out into my T-shirt, but I didn't move back. I stared at the fire in a kind of dream.

Then, suddenly, Elma appeared. She was wearing shorts and a dark blue sweat shirt with the name of her college on the front, raised high by her large bosom.

She said hello, and I returned the greeting. Then she put her hands behind her back and stared at the fire. She was barefooted, and I noticed that her toenails were painted a thick red. It occurred to me that I had never seen Elma wear lipstick. I looked at her face; she had a good tan and her eyelashes looked bleached, like stiff, white threads.

After watching the fire a few minutes, Elma sat down on the ground, drew up her knees and clasped her hands around them. In the dying fire-light I could see a look of concentration on her face. I was aware that, suddenly, all conventions had dissipated and we were facing each other—not as children again—but as two humans so intimately related that an almost dreamlike communication was possible, perhaps even inevitable.

She started talking about the shallowness of her friends at college, and then she stopped and said: "You know, you've gotten better looking. You're almost handsome. That's not true of me; I haven't lost a damn pound."

I was embarrassed, and a little surprised at her language (somehow it didn't fit Elma), so I said nothing. I took a stick and stirred the fire. I was also flattered, because I was basically aware that I wasn't really handsome . . . at least not in anyone else's eyes.

"You've gotten taller, too," she said nodding for some reason. "I noticed it when I walked up."

"That's because you're in your bare feet," I said.

"No," she said. "I took allowance for that. You're taller."

"You know," I said, "I'm on the freshman wrestling team, 135-pound class. The coach said that I might be varsity next year."

"I think that's fabulous," Elma said intensely. "Honestly, I think it's just great."

We were silent for a few minutes. I rummaged around and found a few more scraps of paper to throw into the incinerator. It was strange to realize that we were no longer *expected* to be together.

The night breeze, cooling the perspiration against my shirt, now carried the deep, sweet odors of grass and new leaves. The full moon shone through the tangled limbs of the Krouses's weeping willow tree. Deep shadows lay like spilled sleep on the lawns and tree toads screeched all about us. I heard a car honk far away, then there was once again only the loud night silence.

I found myself searching for something to say, but the harder I thought, the emptier my mind seemed to be. Elma sat staring into the dying fire with her arms crossed heavily.

She must have sensed that I was staring at her, for she looked up. It was then that I saw something that almost made me jump: Elma smiled at me, and it was the identical smile of her mother.

"What's the matter?" she asked. "Is there something wrong?"

"I've got to go in," I said. "I have a date tonight."

"This late?"

"That's right," I answered, scooping up the empty basket.

So I went inside, leaving her sitting there. I took a shower, put on clean clothes, and went to a movie alone. All the time I thought of Elma, sitting in her empty house, reading. I wondered if she had ever once had a date. I told myself that she had a personality like DDT. What male in his right mind would like to spend an evening competing with her, being riddled by her questions, and then facing that cast-iron smile—inherited complete from her mother? And her looks—sometimes she reminded me of a giant caryatid just salvaged from the sea, and at others like a sturdy palomino filly, aggressive and cussedly unbroken.

When I got home, all the neighborhood was dark, except for our porch light and the light in Elma's bedroom. The latter cast a pale rectangle on the Krouse's back lawn. As I was undressing in my bedroom and staring meditatively at this square of light, it went out. Elma had put her book down and was now going to sleep.

I made the wrestling team that year, and I was shamefully proud. In high school I had been a nonathlete, and thus a nobody, except maybe to Elma and a few others. But now I walked with a self-conscious spring to my step and stood straight and tall.

In the middle of the winter quarter, I received a letter from Elma. In it, she said that she loved me and had loved me for as long as she could remember. The farce we two had always acted out underneath her mother's eyes, she said, had been a bitter mockery to her and had almost broken her heart. But she had always acted sarcastic with me because she knew that was what I had wanted. She understood how much her mother had made me suffer with her talk. Only now she couldn't pretend any longer. She hoped that at least I had an affection for her, but even if I hated her, she couldn't help it. She said she would do anything for me. She would die for me.

I read the letter again and again. I even studied the precision of her handwriting, as even and neat as italics. I folded the letter and put it in my pocket. I went into the bathroom and rinsed off my face in cold water. Then I put my jacket on and walked for an hour or two on the campus, even though the sky was black and spitting sleet. I missed dinner that evening and had to settle for a candy bar and a cup of coffee from the cafeteria.

I got my varsity letter in February at the sports banquet. I dated three girls during the spring, but I was always uncomfortable with them. They were essentially selfish and narrow; but to me, they seemed very sophisticated. I had picked up the habit of laughing in a high, nervous bray. It was sickening the way it would jump out of my mouth when I least expected it, and then I would try to compensate by staying aloof and silent for fifteen or twenty minutes. Elma would have pounced on me, asking what the trouble was. She was unflinching about such things. But these girls merely looked bored or dismayed.

Nobody seemed to notice my letter. I guess they all knew it was for wrestling, and most of the girls had never seen a wrestling match. All they could talk about was basketball.

But I still hadn't written to Elma. And this bothered me. Did I always have to let her down? I thought of the time her mother had died. She had loved me even then, she had said; and I hadn't been with her.

And now, I didn't know what to say. I couldn't say that I loved her, but I couldn't say that I didn't. It was confusing enough just realizing that she loved me, and there wasn't anything particular I had done—or was now expected to do—to earn it. It was just there—a fact in Elma's life, like her looks and personality.

That year I was runner-up to the league champion in the 135-pound class. There were a few notices in the paper, and I wrote my parents telling them the news. Otherwise, there was little attention given to the fact. Except for Elma, who wrote me a long letter of congratulations, saying that she had been cheering for me all the way. Had I felt her cheering?

Had I felt her cheering? The question didn't sound like the girl I had always known. It didn't fit the direct stare and the cast-iron smile. I laughed at the phrase, listening to myself laugh; then I thought of it that night in my bed until I went to sleep.

The next week, another letter came. It was delicately scented with a perfume that spoke to me mystically of a slender woman with dark eyes. Along with the letter, there was a picture of Elma, with long hair and false lashes. She looked half languorous and half puzzled, and perhaps she felt just as she looked.

I showed the picture to my roommate, and he said, "Not bad!"

I looked at it again; in fact, I studied the picture, trying to see it through new eyes . . . trying to see Elma as a woman, not as a brattish, childhood friend who a few years ago could punt a football farther than a lady should be able to punt. But I seemed to see nothing but Elma, playing dress-up, perhaps, in adult clothes that were just a little too small. And yet the picture troubled me.

A week after that, Elma wrote to ask me to come to the Sadie Hawkins's dance on their campus. I read the letter two or three times and looked at her picture.

That night, ten minutes before lights-out, I placed a long-distance, person-to-person call to Elma. I told her that I would really like to come. I sounded like someone else talking, and so did she. We weren't the same people; I could sense that.

And I am sure Elma understood this too . . . in a way her mother, for instance, couldn't have begun to understand.

GLUCK,
THE SILENT ORACLE

Early one morning in November a sixty-four-year-old widower named Gluck decided that he would never speak to another person as long as he lived.

The early winter sun scarcely invaded his dim living quarters—two rooms that he rented above a printing shop. In fact, the rooms were never well-lighted, and there had been times when Gluck had had the feeling that he was only an obscure image, inhabiting a faded photograph.

But on this particular morning, his sense of liberation over his decision left no room for any other thoughts. He stepped naked on the bathroom scales he kept in the kitchen and saw that, predictably, he weighed exactly 122 pounds. His mind buzzed like a fat bee over the implications of his contract and decision for silence as he filled the saucepan with water for his morning tea and set the pan carefully on his electric hot plate.

While the water heated, Mr. Gluck put on his clothes. Then he poured the boiling water over the tea leaves in the pot, and ate a small can of apricots while the tea steeped.

There was only one incident of any consequence on Gluck's way to work: a sixteen-year-old boy, who had once delivered newspapers to his door, greeted him . . . and of course received no answer.

Gluck was a jeweler. He was intelligent, and he knew that he had never been very good at his trade. He thought it was because he had learned to resent cramping his vision into such tiny perspectives, upon things so cold and intractable as precious stones. God might have felt this way if he had had to look at the moon through a jeweler's eyeglass for eight hours a day, over a period of forty years, and had never during these hours been able to gaze upon Jupiter, for example, shrouded in methane, or upon that more distant and glorious frozen sneeze of lint, the Milky Way. Gluck was an imaginative man, upon occasion, and he often found himself wondering what things must look like to God, who naturally could not share the defects of diminution which characterized the vision of jewelers and men.

The shop where he worked was called Tempko and Son. The old Tempko had died of a stroke right there on the floor of the establishment twenty-one years ago, while his son—still young and slender at the time—had looked on.

Now, that son was gravitating marvelously into a replica of his old father. He had thickened all over, his head was now as round and bald as his father's had been, and he stared out patriarchally upon customers and employees alike through thick horn-rimmed glasses. His expression always seemed to suggest disappointment at an imminent human error—a mixture of anticipatory compassion and anger.

Mr. Tempko was, however, a fair employer. His was the burden of an imperfect world, deriving from his own unspoken consent to be a victim of the weaknesses of others. Perhaps he thought he was strong enough to ingest their frailties and still prevail.

At any rate, he conducted the business of the shop with even more efficiency than his father had done. He had frequent headaches and would pop aspirin into his mouth several times a day. He had a high, ringing voice that must have hurt his head fiercely every time he said something, for he was incapable of modulating it. There were employees who had been with the firm three years who couldn't remember an occasion when Mr. Tempko had either smiled or spoken in a voice less resonant than that called for by the lead tenor role in *Rigoletto*.

This, then, was the man for whom Gluck had worked for twenty-one years, Gluck having been inherited by that son along with the business itself, two middle-aged clerks and an aged female secretary named Miss Barnes (all now deceased), and an estate assessed at $176,000.00

But there was no crisis this morning when Gluck entered the shop. Mr. Tempko merely raised his head as the older man passed the counter, and sang out, "Good morning, Gluck," and then ducked his head back to some receipts he was studying, without waiting for an answer.

But a little after ten o'clock, Mr. Tempko came back to the cage where Gluck sat fiddling his life away on infinitesimals and said: "Gluck, Mrs. Thompson called about her watch. You got it done yet?" Silence.

"Gluck. You hear what I say?"

Gluck methodically, and with a very calm hand, reached out and picked up a small pair of tweezers.

"Gluck!" Mr. Tempko sang (so loud that three customers and four employees lining the cases in the front of the store turned their heads to stare).

"Gluck!" Mr. Tempko called again, blinking at the detonation of his own voice.

For approximately half a minute, Gluck toyed with a spring in the watch, listening to Mr. Tempko's stomach breathing beside his arm. Then Mr. Tempko grabbed the arm of the old jeweler and shook him—not hard, but experimentally.

Another thirty seconds of heavy breathing and silence. The employees and customers were head to head again, examining small and precious items in their hands. Then Gluck heard Mr. Tempko's footsteps pad slowly away on his expensive patent leather shoes.

A few minutes later, he saw Mr. Tempko's round lamp light of a head by the water fountain, and saw his reproachful look behind his glasses as he took some water from a paper cup, tossed two aspirin into his mouth and swallowed them with an angry nod.

Mr. Tempko tried again at a little after eleven-thirty, with approximately the same results.

And then, shortly after lunch, he tried to phone Gluck. Gluck saw him pick up the receiver in the front of the store and dial. Then he heard the phone beside his elbow start ringing. But he did not budge. He had never been so calm in his life. There had been times in the past when he had jumped at the sound of that phone ringing at his elbow, but now it didn't bother him at all, because he knew that he would never again answer a phone as long as he lived. His silence had rendered him inexpugnable. The phone was like the outworn menace of the fearful dream, considered by a person who has finally come fully awake.

The phone stopped ringing, and Gluck heard Mr. Tempko call out: "Gluck, are you deaf? Gluck! I'm calling you."

Mr. Tempko was shouting from the front of the store with his hand still resting on the telephone. Maybe he was afraid to come any closer.

Naturally, this couldn't go on.

And at about three-twenty, Gluck saw Mr. Tempko writing a note on the front counter. His face was very white—Gluck could see that from where he was working in back.

And he could see Mr. Tempko give the note to one of the women clerks, and then ostentatiously brush the palms of his hands together with the dramatic sweep of a cymbal player.

Gluck heard, without watching the approach of the woman clerk, Mr. Tempko's note folded in her hand. The clipped sound of her high heels on the marble floor increased in volume until Gluck saw her hand thrust the note through the half-moon slit before his work bench. (This slit was a vestige of the day when old Tempko had worked there as his own jeweler and handled the payments too. This was all that was left of those days.)

Gluck unfolded the note and read it. It was restrained, as he knew it would be. But it was definite.

And at four o'clock, Gluck went to the cashier and received his two weeks' severance pay. In the corner of his vision, he could see Mr. Tempko's face, glowing like a moon of sadness . . . of consternation and misery.

And when Gluck pocketed the money, Mr. Tempko rushed up to him and grabbed one of his arms with both hands. Gluck didn't look, but he knew that there on Mr. Tempko's sausagelike third finger glowed one of the largest, most handsome diamond rings he, Gluck, had ever seen. He fancied he could almost feel the warmth from that ring through his suit coat.

Gluck tried to keep moving, but Mr. Tempko pulled him to a stop. The other employees were shuffling around in the background, a little embarrassed and perhaps a little alarmed at what had happened to Gluck and what was now happening to Mr. Tempko.

"Gluck!" Mr. Tempko sang, his voice almost breaking.

Gluck stared dumbly into the glass door, waiting.

"*Mr.* Gluck," Tempko went on. "For God's sake, what has happened? What have I *done* to you? Haven't I been a fair employer? Just answer me. Haven't I?"

Mr. Gluck looked neither to the right nor the left. But waited.

Tempko took three or four rapid breaths, like a man about to dive into water. "Isn't the salary all right, Gluck? Just answer me that. Salary?"

In the silence that followed, a heavy truck ground by on the street outside, rattling the windows of the store and leaving an even deeper silence in its wake.

"What is it, Gluck? You sick or something? Maybe a stroke, like Papa's? Is that it?"

"Should I call a doctor, Mr. Tempko?" one of the women asked.

"No, wait a minute. I don't think he's sick. His color looks good to me, and his pulse is okay."

Sure enough, one of Mr. Tempko's hands had slid down and two of his fingers were unobstrusively pressing Gluck's wrist at the base of his thumb.

Now, Mr. Tempko was gently trying to pull Gluck back to the cashier's desk. "A vacation," he was saying. "Just a vacation. He's not fired. You got that?"

The cashier said, "Yes, Mr. Tempko."

"You hear that, Gluck? You got a two-week vacation. And that money in your pocket is to spend. A paid vacation. It's an advance on your next year's vacation. Okay? November's a good month. Florida is just great now. Sunshine is good for a man."

Several of the employees walked out the door in front of him, and Gluck could see his image flap back and forth with the swinging of the door until it came to a stop, and there he was—still standing there—the face he had known for sixty years, and Tempko was still holding on to his upper arm with one hand and his wrist with the other.

"Sick leave!" Mr. Tempko announced in a tone of ringing affirmation. "Our insurance will cover it. You'll still have your vacation next year, Gluck. Okay? Salary okay too? Hey, buddy? Good salary?"

Mr. Tempko was patting him on the back, now, and his voice was vibrating with good fellowship.

But this didn't last long, either, and Gluck could hear Mr. Tempko breathing again. Somebody switched off the lights, then several more employees slipped out the door. Then the cashier said goodby in a sick-room voice and left. Now, Gluck and Mr. Tempko were alone.

"Jesus Christ, Gluck!" Mr. Tempko suddenly cried. "*Say* something!"

Gluck opened his mouth. Tempko gasped. Then Gluck sighed. And another truck rumbled by outside.

Tempko's hands were now kneading the old man's arm.

"Mr. Gluck," Tempko said. "You were a friend of Papa's. Isn't that right? Papa? Remember Papa? Dying on the floor right there, while we all stood around and watched him? You remember that? Don't you, Mr. Gluck? Say you do. Just say it. Say: 'Yes, I remember'."

But Gluck said nothing . . . merely shifted his feet. He didn't even look bored. Clearly, it was something else altogether.

"Look," Tempko said, releasing the old fellow's arm and walking around behind him. The store looked beautiful in the evenings, with the lights out, Gluck was thinking. Like an enchanted cave of exquisite glass, shot through with planes, squares and curves of muted light . . . as if they were waiting in passion for a single, unmistakeable call to break into silent and cavernous spires of flame.

Tempko was swallowing audibly, and senselessly repeating the single word, "Look," as he paced around behind the old jeweler, snapping his fingers nervously. "Look. Look Look."

Finally he stopped, and said, "Mr. Gluck. Remember when I was just a college kid? You were already Papa's most dependable employee. I used to come in here, and you used to smile and ask me how things were going at college, and I would sit down and smoke a cigarette and talk with you while you worked back there at the bench. And Papa would smile and say, 'Al, don't keep Mr. Gluck from his work. He's an important person around here, our Mr. Gluck!'"

"Remember? He used to call you, '*Our* Mr. Gluck!' What a warm and friendly old guy Papa was to us all!"

Silence. Suddenly, the sound of a dozen unidentifiable clocks heard ticking like mechanical bird beaks against glass, measuring the dimensions of the store's deep silence.

"Remember?" Tempko asked again.

Gluck turned around and stared over Tempko's head at the electric store clock (the silent and most efficient clock of them all), which was set in the wall at the rear. He could sense that Tempko was watching him with something like the yearning of a despised and ignored child.

Then Gluck turned back to the door and stepped toward it. He heard the palms of Tempko's hands slap tiredly against his trouser legs in a signal of defeat as he stepped silently out of the door into the cold November wind.

It so happened at this time that the weather turned wintry and the heating system in Gluck's rooms went bad. Gluck toyed around with the two radiators, sticking pencils as far as he could down the pipes, and then a clothes hanger that he had straightened out. But whatever was thrombosing the old pipes was beyond the reach of a pencil or clothes hanger, and the rooms began to turn waxy with a damp, motionless cold.

Gluck couldn't have been happier. This was clearly some sort of test, for he could easily have gone to the pay phone in the hall and called his landlord, demanding repairs.

The landlord was a little afraid of Gluck, for the old jeweler had been living there eleven years, never once missing his rent or making a tardy payment. The landlord hadn't even been able to rent the rooms for a year or two prior to that. And now his enormous good fortune in having a renter like Gluck made him twist with servility, jump at the least suggestion of a correction or repair (especially since Gluck seldom complained of anything) . . . and once or twice, when Gluck had encountered the man on the street and had shaken hands with him, the old jeweler had wondered at the look of apprehension and worship upon the landlord's face, and had considered it possible that the money-crazed old fellow (he was seven years older than Gluck) might even kiss his hand on impulse, while he stood there pumping it up and down and whispering, "My dear Mr. Gluck, my dear Mr. Gluck; what a pleasure it is to meet you like this by accident!"

So Gluck, with a sense of power equalling that of an infinitely potent, if discredited, demi-urge—knowing that he had merely to drop a dime in the telephone and call the landlord, speaking one sentence . . . but knowing that he wouldn't do so, because of this sacred and compelling contract with himself never to speak to another person again as long as he lived . . . so Gluck put on an extra pair of underwear, an extra pair of socks, and his overcoat, and proceeded contentedly to make a pot of tea.

A few days later, the letters from Tempko started coming daily. They began with the expected exhortations for Gluck to return to work, even if he chose to remain silent (they would furnish him with a note pad and sharpened pencils, Tempko said) . . . and then going into inquiries about the extent of his, Tempko's, responsibility for this tragedy.

But after a week had passed, Tempko seemed to forget about Gluck's problem. By now, the letters were long and involved analyses of Tempko's own problems. There were intimate glimpses into Tempko's family life—sometimes there were whole pages of dialogue between his wife and himself.

Then a few days later Tempko's confession that he had a mistress, whom he absolutely hated but could not possibly give up or ever forget. And in another letter there was a mention of his youngest son, who seemed too effeminate to Tempko; he feared that the boy was a homosexual, and if he found out that this was true, he said, he would send him away from his house forever, and never speak to him again.

And of course, Tempko's Papa soon came upon the stage. That dear, beloved, infinitely kind and patient father still lived on, padding through his son's dreams, referring to "*Our* Mr. Gluck" and tapping the cigar ashes of memory upon the glass cases and the marble floors of the store and upon the thick pale hands of his dutiful and anxious son.

And then naturally the old fellow couldn't help dying there on the floor, as if that one hideous act had established a habit that would repeat itself as long as his son lived . . . happening in pantomime, while the ghost of that slender young man, idealistic and just out of college, stood bound and gagged by fascination and fear, imprisoned in this fat, bald man they now knew as Tempko, looking on.

All of these things began to appear in the letters, which came daily, confessional and anguished, to the sprung and torn metal mailbox outside the printing shop where Gluck's mail was deposited. The letters waxed thicker and thicker, until they bulged like pancakes about to spill through their crusts, lined with stamps whose profiles all faced the same way and remained almost as silent and inscrutable as Gluck himself. By the third week, Tempko had altogether stopped asking Gluck to speak. He no longer seemed to think that Gluck was diseased or odd. In the letters there were hints that Tempko had found something in the puissant depths of Gluck's withdrawal that he had been seeking since his father had died twenty-one years before, circled by son, employees and customers.

Gluck, on the other hand, had faced his second decision: whether or not to write an answer to Tempko someday. But he decided that writing itself was a kind of speech—the most lasting and damning kind, when you thought about it—and his decision against speaking to others had nothing to do with the simple mouthing of words and making sounds, but with speech itself.

So he did not answer, and his stony, godlike reticence apparently inflamed something in Tempko, who began to send salary checks to him, "until the time you feel like coming back to work," he explained. Gluck noticed that he had not said, "feel well enough," but "feel like." There was significance in that careful wording.

The weather turned very cold, then. Gluck lived on, swaddled in extra clothes . . . sitting like a convalescent before his window and staring at the winter through his jeweler's eyepiece. His shape was monstrously altered by the extra clothes he wore, and his head got so cold at night that he started to wear an ancient golfing cap to bed with him, lying there twisted and bound by a dozen different fabrics of varying thicknesses. His nose and ears began to glow permanently red from the frosty air of his two rooms, whereas the skin of his forehead had turned glassy and pale, with faint highlights of a diaphanous blue you see sometimes in precious china.

Gluck had discovered very early in this new life of his that the mere sur-cease of talk had liberated him in subtle and entirely unforeseen ways. For one thing, now that his ideas could not in any way escape him in speech, he felt no desire for things and no restlessness. It is talk that makes us mad, he thought.

And thinking this a dozen times a day, he ensconced himself even more deeply in his own silence.

Furthermore, he was eating less. A couple of cans of fruit a day, two pots of tea, a can of sardines, and honey spread on bread kept his belly full. But of course the belly itself was simply shrinking to accommodate his new life, and above the swollen and grotesque corpulence of his mani-fold clothing, Gluck's neck and face stretched up, stringy and gaunt.

He couldn't altogether forget about Tempko, however. He even felt sorry for the man, in a remote way. The fact was, Gluck had become a kind of mirror of Tempko's hallucinations, and his haunted employer couldn't resist dancing in front of that mirror like a child drunk with mad-ness, making faces and flailing his arms, and dancing with all the grotes-queries conceived by a nightmared heart.

Who could have dreamed that Tempko was so odd, so full of tricks, so nearly undone all these years . . . hiding as he was behind all of those aspirin, the tired and tolerant visage and the furious *bel canto* of that tenor voice?

Then one day the letters stopped.

Gluck was hardly aware of the fact, for he had never done more than merely accept the letters—never expected them, for instance, much less anticipated them with anything like pleasure.

And then, about a week after that, when the weather had turned warmer, but Gluck was still thickly wrapped in all the clothes he could get on, there was a knock on the door.

Gluck opened it, and faced the landlord.

"My dear Mr. Gluck," the landlord said. "I have heard of your mis-fortune. Please let me step in for a minute!"

Gluck nodded and stepped aside.

The landlord held his hat in both of his hands and said, "You wouldn't tell me what it is, would you, Mr. Gluck?"

Gluck didn't answer, and the landlord said, "Of course, it's not any business of mine. Is it, Mr. Gluck?"

Then he turned all around. "Say, it's awful in here, Mr. Gluck. Why it's *freezing*. I'll see to that furnace right away. Meanwhile, I would like to ask if you've somehow forgotten about the rent. I hate to bother you, because your splendid record of taking care of the rent speaks for itself. But you haven't paid this month, you know?"

Silence.

"Of course, you'd simply overlooked. I knew you had, Mr. Gluck, *Knew* it, Sir!"

The landlord stared at his own hat for a moment.

"There's something else, too, Mr. Gluck. I told you that I had heard about this terrible thing . . . this catastrophe, so to speak. Well, the fact is, Mr. Tempko's wife called me. He's in the hospital, you know. Suffering from a severe case of nerves. Very ill indeed, they say."

The landlord hummed in misery for a moment, unable to bear the silence of Gluck's sober regard.

"I knew you'd be affected by the news," he said, finally. "And especially when you heard that Mr. Tempko has been asking specifically and constantly to see you. To *talk* with you, as a matter of fact. I went to see him; did I tell you that? Well, I assured him, Mr. Gluck, that *you would come to see him.* It seems awfully important to the poor fellow. Mr. Tempko is a terribly sensitive man. You can just feel it. He must be a wonderful person to work for. Wonderful. I can just feel that he's wonderful to work for. Right? Right, Mr. Gluck?"

The landlord furiously twirled his hat around in his hands and looked worried.

"When can I tell him you'll come to see him, Mr. Gluck? Just name an hour." A pause. "I see. Could you write it down on a piece of paper then."

The landlord had suddenly become terribly agitated. Eventually, he actually sobbed out loud, and withdrew a handkerchief to hold to his mouth as he stared at Gluck with frightened eyes. Then he gasped once or twice, rattled the door loudly as he bumped into it (it was as if he were trying to crowd out of the door along with three or four other panic-stricken people).

Gluck stood and listened to the old man's footsteps as they scuttled down the stairway. Then he felt the soggy floor of his room hiccup gracefully as the big press on the floor below was engaged and started printing with shuckelling sound. Although it was warmer outside, the air was very dark. And Gluck noticed that it was starting once more to snow.

Perhaps the landlord was the only one who knew exactly how many days had passed. Tempko was beyond the cares of time—a skinny version of himself, dressed in a bathrobe striped like a barber's pole, pacing back and forth in his private room, singing out instructions and complaints about headaches in lucid, bell-like tones. Apparently the headaches were hallucinatory, for Tempko was kept as near the shores of sleep as was deemed safe . . . kept there by a whole battery of ataraxic drugs, whose administration to the patient left the doctor in charge wondering at how Tempko managed to keep up all of that pacing back and forth.

Gluck, meanwhile, sat in his chair by the window and stared out at the street through his jeweler's eyeglass, which he had remembered to bring with him from Tempko and Son, Jewelers.

And when the police finally evicted him, he refused to look at them, except through the eyeglass—his other eye squinted as tight and blind as a navel that had grown monstrously there in his face. Naturally, too, he did not answer any of their questions. And when they carried him bodily out of his rooms, and down the stairs, and put him on his feet in front of the printing shop, where the press was shuckelling away in its old, compulsive meter . . . when they placed Gluck on his feet, the old fellow merely started walking away like some kind of mechanical doll—his eyepiece still fixed in his eye and his hands folded comfortably behind his back.

Obviously, they couldn't let him go around like that, and after due legal procedure of probating, he was confined to the very hospital where the skinny remains of Tempko resided and suffered.

And as a matter of fact, Tempko saw Gluck as an attendant led the old jeweler down the hall. It had been a mistake, letting Tempko have a room with an opening in the door.

Gluck didn't glance at his ex-employer, however . . . in spite of the terrible cries of recognition that came from the cell.

Instead, Gluck was led to an open ward and placed in a chair, where he stared at the wall through his eyepiece. He could still hear Tempko crying out from his room down the hall: "Gluck! Gluck! I've got to talk to you, Gluck!"

After a while, Tempko was silent, and Gluck assumed that he had been put to sleep with an injection.

Gluck was very comfortable that first night. And the next day, when he was led into the ward, he heard the news that Tempko had hanged himself the night before with strips he had torn from his robe.

When he was told this news, Gluck was aware that several of his ward companions were watching him. Somehow, he knew that they were generally aware that he and Tempko had known each other.

For a few minutes, Gluck was silent. The attention of the others was on him . . . they were compelled, somehow, by a magnetism deep in the heart and mystery of this silence.

At that instant, Gluck was aware that silence can draw everything to it, and it renders the will of others impotent.

Gluck grabbed the eyepiece and screwed it more deeply into his eye and started to speak . . . to say: "Amazing what you can see through one of these things!"

But no sound came out. In fact, it was more a yawn than speech.

Another immate saw the gnawing of the old jeweler's mouth, and huddled closer. "He's trying to speak," he said. "Look at his lips moving."

Something obscure but essential had been forgotten. So that Gluck realized that he had been enormously, incredibly successful. Few men could carry a thing through to the end the way Gluck had done.

The eyepiece then fell out of his eye, jostled loose by the reverberations of the old man's effort to speak. And when that one sensitive eye looked out upon the unfiltered surroundings Gluck now found himself in—the plastered walls, dented and scarred from ancient attacks of thick spoons and shoes and fingers, and dappled with stains of hurled coffee and blood from suicidal head-first lunges . . . when the eye perceived all of these things, undeluded, it rounded in terror.

Then it closed. Gluck shuddered all over, and the eyepiece, which had fallen only into his lap and lodged in a fold of his robe, was shaken loose and fell to the floor.

LOVE SONG
FOR DORIS BALLINGER

As he sipped coffee, his eyes focused upon the front page of a newspaper, held up to conceal the face of the man on the next stool. There was a picture at the top of the page. The portrait of a beautiful, smiling woman.

The picture troubled him. He drank his coffee slowly and shook his head no when the waitress asked if he wanted it warmed up, by which she meant filled.

Then he walked out of Gaetz's, temporarily forgetting the picture, and started back to his office. The snow had stopped falling, and now the sun was out, turning the slushy streets into strips of dented and battered tin, burning fiercely with reflected sunlight.

The thought of the picture came back to him, however, and he decided to stop and buy a newspaper. He paused in the middle of the sidewalk and stared at the woman's face once again, nagged by something trying to move into the face. Then he looked at the caption, hoping that it would prompt his memory and make the face pulse suddenly clear:

MISSING WOMAN SOUGHT

And in the text following was the name, "Doris Jensen," a girl whom he had known as Doris Ballinger years before, in high school. It was impossible for him to conceive of her as missing, because it seemed at that moment that he had not even thought of her as being in any way present since graduating from high school twenty-six years before. How could anyone like that be considered *missing?* Or what other state was possible? How could a Doris Ballinger work her way into a position to be missed?

Now he abstracted himself from the street, letting his distant cold feet find their own way through the melting snow upon the sidewalk. The snow was pockmarked from the heels of pedestrians, each heel print a saucer of cold water . . . tiny puddles that shone like the broken-off bottoms of pop bottles, faintly green with the memory of sand that cheap (or old) glass retains. The sun had not really warmed the air.

Doris Ballinger, he was saying. A man ahead of him turned to the side and spit a gray ghost of phlegm arcing onto the rugged snow tire of a 1965 Buick.

Then he saw her in her last (or at least her most memorable) posture: she stood high upon the stage with her hands folded before her, tiny chin raised and mouth open. As yet, in the arena of his mind, she was silent—as if physically and helplessly waiting for the inventory in the inscrutable memory of a forty-three-year-old man, who had once (at this precise time of her interruption) been a member of her graduating class.

Because he wanted to be sure this was the authentic and living Doris Ballinger. As the seventeen-year-old girl stood up there on the stage, open-mouthed and paralytic with unreality, he noticed the bulging, muscular calves and the earth-goddess breasts that had impressed him then. Four great physical facts that designated her fate and sometimes turned her cheeks red with shame. For her delicate and fragile spirit was not meant to be saddled so suddenly with such an excess of womanhood and flesh.

Pale blue eyes, perfectly arched, and a beautiful, pious face. Then he remembered even her handwriting, and remembered that she had dotted each of her i's with a meticulous little teardrop. She was a member of student council and the Dolly Madison club, where all the girls sat in a circle in the Home Ec room, doing needlework and sewing, as if preparing for the long matronly years ahead.

An instant's silence, as if time were crouching and hunching its muscles, and then the piercing brilliance of Doris Ballinger's soprano voice, as she hit the high note in *"Spargi d'Amore il Pianto,"* which she sang in Italian, exploding each syllable, so that there were blinks of silence within a single word that someone could have sneezed in.

But no one did, for this was a solemn event, and Doris Ballinger was the most solemn, upright, religious, tender-hearted, big-titted, honorable, dependable, victimized, prudent, judicious, mature, domestic, practical girl in the whole high school. Which was something of a record.

How could a Doris Ballinger disappear?

Contra Naturam. Better contemplate the possibility of a squirrel's attacking cats, or of crab grass being blown into balls of twine and unravelling in the air like dancing, hissing snakes. Better consider the possibility that milk would start oozing from the cracks in brick walls, and the snow that lay upon the distant roofs, as remote and irrelevant as unheard music, might burst forth into black and purple flames, whose smoke was composed of the echoes of lost children, crying.

Because all of these anonymous evenings, when a passing car's horn was blown, interrupting the figures on the television screen (less real than the memory of Doris Ballinger), and interrupting his wife in the kitchen, smearing peanut butter on Ritz crackers and lining up uneven tumblers of cold milk for the kids (so that she would call, "Is that someone honking for us?" and he would call out, "I don't think so," without even looking) . . . all this time, Doris Ballinger was preparing for an exodus. If not her mind, then her great warm breasts—fat kennels of nourishment—or at least her lineman's calves, insidiously preparing for the time they would carry that monumental woman, dismayed, away from whatever destination her eyes thought was before her, waiting.

He stopped, slapped the paper with the back of his hand, and turned around, searching for an interested face. Only an old woman approached him, her cheeks heavily rouged and her legs—as brittle as glass straws—probing her swaddled body forward, her face gazing down from above with alarm.

So, in a vastly different weather—and still damp and warm with the colony of flesh she had borne with her from high school, and the scattering of flowers—so had Doris Ballinger's legs betrayed her; hers, by walking her body out of public life, family life (as from the warmth of a television tube); while this old lady's, by walking her irreversibly into the bewildered suburbs of old age, where a man might turn around, slapping his paper, and say,

"She herself might have been in that car!"

"What is that?" the old lady might ask, looking up; and in looking up step on the edge of an ice saucer, so that the heavy frozen slabs of sidewalk would spit her legs heavenward, and she would fall, cracking like an icicle tightly bundled in furs, while on a distant rooftop a carnivorous squirrel prepares to jump to its death down the back of a dead drummer boy, frozen upright.

Which of course did not happen, and the old lady edged herself sideways (as if the sidewalk were trying to tilt her toward the street, and send her like a BB down the sewer hole; seven old ladies down sewer holes, by tilting the whole town, and the demi-urge wins the game), and cranked herself into the candy store that was exhaling odors of popcorn and caramel over his newspaper.

"I was speaking of Doris Ballinger, who is missing," he continued, now that the lady was inside the candy store, and there was no possibility of a misunderstanding.

Doris Ballinger would of course have been the very one to pass by one's house, her husband pressing the ring of the horn as a dark dog skittered before the headlights, causing one Ritz cracker to wait a fraction of a second longer before being immured in peanut butter.

And at such a time, there would have been no camera, no screen, upon Doris Ballinger, for her husband would have been thinking of his impending lawsuit, concerning title for an apartment building that a corporation he had formed was trying to buy. While Doris Jensen, *née* Ballinger, sat dreamy and unreal (missing already, in this interval—a preview of coming distractions; for being seen is part of existing)—as the car glided down a residential street (darker than a forgotten canal in Venice), the heater before her knees pouring out a balmy and susurrant stream of warmth upon her magnificent, but aging shins, while somewhere within her expensive hair-do, a nervous seventeen-year-old girl still stood on a stage, exploding sounds in fabricated Italian over the head of a boy whose name she had forgotten, or would forget.

The back seat was empty.

By this time, he had returned to the office, and the missing girl, who was now a woman, was forgotten, so that she was—without knowing it—further ensconced in mystery, insofar as even her *missing* was now missing, and conceivably, if all those who knew her, or had once known her, forgot about her simultaneously she would have gone up in a puff of smoke, at the end of a frenetic drum roll, the magician's wand scarcely warmed by the muted flash of her exit. So much probity and tenderness excised from the world by an instant's neglect, a second's impiety!

Was this what happened?

Always somewhere in the penumbra of his preoccupations, Doris Ballinger stood waiting, as if for a cue—or else paralyzed by the irrelevance of her presence, until this man brought the camera of his attention around, and at the very instant of its focus upon her raised picnic-ham breasts, her clasped, white-knuckled hands, the explosion of that brilliant soprano, translating melodramatic words about flowers and graves into thrusts of aural needles in the pincushion of a single man's attention.

No music ever dies, and if a pure-hearted girl is ever found to be missing, she must be resuscitated in memory according to the memory of each one who has known her, so that there are these multitudes of girls waiting to rehearse and be heard.

The newspaper story was vague. It gave her age, forty-three, and the business of her husband, real estate; and the fact that the couple had no children. Her husband was referred to as wealthy, and beneath her picture was his. She had presumably been returning from an appointment with her physician, driving her new model Buick alone.

Somewhere, on one snow tire, a silver strand of saliva clung. But of course, that was not so.

What was so, was this. Doris Ballinger was missing long before her husband, the wealthy realtor, reported the fact to the police. Not simply in the sense that she was missing according to him—and worse, unthought of; but missing according to at least one girl standing abandoned on a great stage, before an empty auditorium—the echoes of a foreign song only vaguely transeunt, like the breath of a god no one can quite believe in. Like all of us, Doris Ballinger had abandoned the child she was; and to that child, was missing.

Such might have been the moment of nearest perfection for this strange girl who did not complain, even though she might even then have guessed what awaited her, but stayed nice and kind and thoughtful anyway. This would warm at least one man, twenty-six years later; although it would do no good to what had become of that girl—the frozen corpse in the car, for instance, fallen sideways in a swift gesture of stoney giddiness from a secret aneurysm . . . in a place where the woman it had once been had pulled the car to the side of the road, to let traffic pass. She would not have wanted to disobey the law, or obstruct traffic, while dying.

On the waxed and slippery roof of that handsome new car, a squirrel skated precariously after a fallen hickory nut, while the windblasts from the swift traffic passing by beat like a drum upon the silent upholstery of this car. On the TV screen that evening, a middle-aged woman's picture was flashed briefly before ten thousand faces of local citizens, between the major national news reports and the latest scores of local high school basketball games.

Many who might have recognized her are dead; many who had once known her did not recognize her because of the passage of time, the metamorphosis of the girl, and the changed name.

Ten thousand more newspapers lay crumpled about, in various rooms and in various postures of disuse. Each one holding Doris Ballinger's face, folded already into the past.

Why didn't she have children? This, too, was a shame.

Snow fell from the roof of the third house down, startling a dog who had just raised its leg to wet into the black shadow of an arbor vitae.

He walked home, slapping the newspaper against his leg as a car turned left at the corner, its headlights gliding over him like the beacon from a lighthouse that was itself sliding carefully and inevitably into blackness.

Beyond this stage, another looms; a dark car is parked crookedly against the curb on a little-traveled road.

Beyond that stage, is a higher one, where a girl stands with her hands folded. There are tears in her eyes, and the world is beautiful and important for her; and she wants, above all, to be loved and to love.

He clears his throat and spits toward a parked car, whose parking lights are on. The parking lights are visible after-thoughts—warm and muted, like congealed globules of chicken fat in a bowl of darker gravy. The car has a cracked left front window; the glass is most essentially itself where it is cracked.

In the distance, one can almost hear a muted drum beat; and if he listens closely, an echo from this beat. A mirror of sound, accepting what it is.

Even farther away than that, a lonely woman suddenly and for no apparent reason, thinks of a boy she once knew years ago; and with a strange wistfulness that she cannot understand or even bother to admit (in the factualness of where she is waiting her turn), she now wonders where he might be waiting, and what coins might be spilling from his hands as he cups them together, lifting water to the doe of her heart, and saying, "Look, I remember. I remember."

THE DESCENT

The lights phased off and on in a slow dim pulse, and Emeritus Professor Claridge squinted his eyes and looked up from his book. There was a sudden movement in the shadows of the far carrel as a boy and girl untangled themselves from an embrace and walked away, ignorant of the old man's presence.

Dr. Claridge smiled indulgently, but there was no one to notice. Only three evenings before, he had come out of the library at closing time, as usual, and had almost stumbled over a couple in the dark. They were wrestling together, *in flagrante delicto* almost, when they had sensed the presence of the old man on the walk, and they had stopped in a sudden spasm of surprise and fear. Professor Claridge had a brief impulse to tap them with his cane, and bid them get on with it. They had no right to assume he was against their passions merely because he was old.

The lights in the library dimmed again, then brightened. The second warning. If he was going to make it to the door in time for closing, he had better start down the steps immediately. He cranked himself up from his chair in the carrel and gripped his cane.

He edged his way around the staircase that rose like raw vertebrae through the stacks, and was about to take the first step when he felt a sudden rush of wind on his left side. Instinctively, his hand had gripped the rail, and now he felt the rail throb as a boy ran down the stairs. The boy was wearing tattered shorts that were too tight, and his legs were completely bare. He wasn't even wearing socks, and his white tennis shoes were turning golden with age.

Professor Claridge blinked and smiled down the stairway, so the lad would know it was all right . . . that the old gentleman didn't mind his jumping ahead of him like that, racing down the stairs that would take him almost a full minute to descend.

Then there was another boy next to him. Professor Claridge felt the boy's breath on his cheek. He was standing there looking down the steps after the other boy, and he was waiting for the old man to step aside so he could follow. At that instant, Professor Claridge realized that the two of them had been racing, and the first one had slipped ahead of him just in time, but the second had had the bad luck to arrive an instant too late.

Dr. Claridge smiled and looked up at the lad; but he was still staring after the first boy, and waiting for the old man to go down the steps. He had already made the decision to wait, and he was not looking at Professor Claridge at all. Several years before, he would have insisted that the boy go ahead; but now he wasn't even sure the boy would hear him if he said anything. He could feel the boy breathing on him heavily; the young rascals must have been running all over the stacks.

While the boy waited, he started toiling down the stairs, and when he came to the last step, he felt the rail lurch under his hand as the boy vaulted past him towards the mezzanine.

Professor Claridge paused at the circulation desk and started to say good night to Mrs. Berryman; and then, with a distant, little flowering of surprise, he remembered that Mrs. Berryman had moved to Seattle. She had been gone for several years, in fact; Professor Claridge couldn't remember how long.

He did nod and say good night to a young girl, however. He didn't quite recognize her; but then her face wasn't completely strange, either. He had lived so long that almost every face he saw had some sort of antecedent. And all the words he could hear through his hearing aid came to him like echoes of words spoken long ago.

Did the girl see him? He asked if it was still raining outside, and for an instant the girl's eyes seemed to flick over him—the way a woman will notice a picture that she doesn't remember hanging in a vaguely familiar room . . . or a lamp, that seems to be in a different place.

Then there was a kind of laughter, like wind blowing through dry leaves. Somewhere, a door slammed; a draft of warm air blew against Professor Claridge's bare hand, and he remembered that he had forgotten to put his gloves on. Far above his left shoulder, a clock ticked. The familiar sound comforted the old man. He had listened to that sedate and measured sound for many years. He turned halfway, to mention this old clock to the girl, but now she was gone.

Surely it had only been an instant since he had asked her about the rain; but now it was as if she had evaporated. It occurred to him then to wonder if she had really been there, or if through the telescoping of time, her image had simply been superimposed upon some emptiness behind the circulation desk. That in the instability of his senses, her ghost had fallen casually onto the screen of his viewing, like a tossed playing card that carries a lifeless image of a cardboard queen with dead eyes.

Never mind. (What was the scholarly joke he used to tell his students when he was discussing philosophical dualism? "Never mind; no matter. No matter; never mind.")

No matter. He smiled and gripped his cane more tightly and turned in another half circle, his mouth easing open from the weight of his chin. He was now breathing through his mouth, tasting the old must of paper, the aura of learning and the vague mephitis of the anonymous academic absorptions of years.

It was then he came awake to the fact that there was no one about. The lights were still on, but darkened—like light in an old photograph. Ahead of him, an announcement of some sort, on blue paper, rattled in the draft from the big registers. Or was a window open somewhere, and was this summer?

This was of course a humorous oversight. He fixed his mouth in a smile, so that if someone came up to him as he edged his way out of the building, he could share the joke with them.

He let himself down the steps, one by one, as he approached the large doors of the main entrance. Beyond the doors, the night glowed with the blackness of deep water. It was splattered, here and there, by the faint yellow of the lampposts that lined the campus walks.

As he approached the front entrance, Professor Claridge told himself it was probably still raining. He was glad he had worn his rubbers and raincoat. But what about an umbrella? Had he brought one? Where had he laid it? It had been fifteen years since they had lined their umbrellas along the wall, in a spirit of communal friendliness that was part of the casual, intimate college life they had shared in those days.

And as he tried to remember about the umbrellas, he began to wonder if he had checked a book out after all. His wife would chide him, sometimes, for taking books out. His eyesight was really too poor to enable him to read, but the habits of a lifetime could not easily be broken. And it was as unthinkable for him to leave a library without a book or two under his arm (even if he could manage to read only the table of contents), as it would be for him not to visit the library at all.

Turning around, he gazed back into the dark, upward tunnel he had just descended, wondering if he might climb the steps and find a book on the counter, duly checked-out by Miss Berryman. Or was she the one who had gone to Seattle?

As he looked up the stairway, it seemed to shrink until it was as small as a toy room in a toy building. Professor Claridge could well remember the time he had first driven a car, frightened by the optical illusion of the road's narrowness, as another car approached and he mentally calibrated the distance between shoulders and the swelling magnitude of the approaching car.

He began to climb the steps, but stopped after the third or fourth, because he had forgotten what errand he was on. What duty was to be performed. "Old age hath yet his honour and his toil." Or was it "duty and toil." No, honour. Spelled in the English manner, with a "u"—to be spoken by a firm young man wearing glossy mustaches.

Here, there was a door, and when he opened the door, there was a sudden splattering of bird sounds, falling like cool rain into his hearing and his face. And a freshness, as of a garden early in the morning. His wife was there, wearing a large hat against the harsh rays of the sun. She was holding a sprinkling can, and she smiled and said, "Did you bring home *another* book? You, with your poor eyes almost blind? Why do you persist this way, my dear?"

"Because," he said. And then he forgot what the question was.

And suddenly it was dark, and an ancient locomotive stood looming in the distance, a building of metal, lights glowing from a thousand indentations in the gigantic wall of an unstable superstructure. And the land moved away from the train, which grew smaller and smaller until it was a small frog, grunting under a damp slab of stone.

All about him, there were rabbits and moles, fumbling like warm mittens in the grass as they mated, and a whole civilization of insects—mostly crickets—singing, "Illicit, illicit, illicit." He raised his cane and tried to brush away the cobwebs about him. But, foolishly, he discovered that they were not cobwebs at all, but the stars themselves. And his cane would not reach.

Before him there was only a heavy brass door latch. The one he had heard crack only a few minutes before, as the two racing boys had sped out of the building and into the night.

It was not raining. It was not cold.

The door latch cracked downward as he leaned upon it, and he was spilled outwards into the soft dark air that smelled of flowering lilacs and leafing trees. The campus lights glowed solemnly in their prudent silence. Overhead, the red light of an airplane pulsed on and off as the plane approached a landing field that would look as small as a boot sole in the darkness.

As he descended the steps outside, left foot first—edging sideways down into a still warmer air and the closeness of the grassy campus floor, a boy and a girl moved slightly to let him pass. He once more had the impulse to tap them with his cane and tell them to go ahead. But he did not do this. For one thing, they hadn't asked him. For another, they didn't even know he was there.

All that sacred foolishness could do would be to lead them down into this, or into something else.

The crickets kept up their singing, "Illicit, illicit, illicit"; but of course the two of them didn't hear that, either.

POLLY SUE AND
THE ST. LOUIS DODGERS

"You come walking in here after midnight," Polly Sue whispered with a withering inflection, "drunk like this, when that lawn hasn't been mowed for three weeks."

Ned drifted over to the mantel and groped for a pack of cigarettes. Then he turned around and faced her.

"Didn't you hear me?" she asked, lowering her voice. "The lawn! The lawn hasn't been mowed for three weeks, and my party's tomorrow!"

"We haven't had very much rain," he said, skating over the words.

"Just listen to the way you talk!" she said, thrusting her tiny fists down into her bathrobe pockets so hard, the neck of the robe separated. "If my friends saw you like this . . . oh, god!"

He fumbled a cigarette loose from the pack and squinted his eyes at her. "Big deal," he said. "Big loss, your distinguished friends. You oughta pay me to get drunk, just so they can come over to see me."

"Oh, shut up!"

"Shu' up yourself."

She took her fists out of her bathrobe, shook them in front of her stomach and made a humming sound.

"Oh, hell!" he muttered half-heartedly, lighting the cigarette.

She stopped crying, because there was still a big point to be made about the lawn.

"Do you know the neighbors are *talking*?" she asked, pulling a curler back from where it had come loose and bounced against her nose. She glared at him as she fixed the curler back in place.

"I didn't think they knew how to talk," Ned told her. "I thought they were deaf mutes and just walked around measuring how high the grass is in people's lawns."

"Oh shut up," she said. "It so happens that this is a respectable, decent neighborhood. And respectable, decent people will keep their property looking nice. If they don't, it hurts the whole neighborhood."

He pulled his cigarette out of his mouth and spread his legs, as if to brace himself. "Goddam it," he shouted. "To hell with the stupid sons o'bitches! I don't give a damn what they think of me or the St. Louis Dodgers or whatever goddam sport they're always talking about, or their goddam cars they manicure all the time or what their stupid goddam wives bid in their stupid bridge games or how much they pay for hamburger or whatever in the hell they grill in those buckets out in their backyards or how much they pay for dancing school for their snot-nosed daughters or if daddy coaches little league for their brainless snot-nosed sons, or. . . ."

Suddenly, for no evident reason, he stopped talking. He fumbled the cigarette to his mouth and puffed on it.

"*Well!*" his wife said after a moment's silence. "*Well!* That takes care of *us* in the neighborhood. *Everybody* on the block must have heard you!"

"Serves em goddam right." He puffed rapidly at the cigarette, and squinted his eyes half-shut in a smug and canny look.

"Well!" his wife said again, "That certainly does do it! Now I'll *never* be able to look them in the eye." She started to weep once again.

"They ought to have more than one eye," he said. "All those people and just one eye."

She didn't hear what he said, because she was now making the sound of a distant electric shaver.

"Of course, I'm not surprised," he said. "They can't see anything beyond their car and barbecue grill—if that's what they call those buckets—and their goddam lawn. All you need is just one eye when that's all in the hell you care about. That and the goddam stupid St. Louis Dodgers. And the goddam programs with doctors and spies walking around acting like God almighty."

"Oh, you're so intellectually superior," she said.

"And I forgot the cowboy shows. All these idiots in the neighborhood are good guys with shiny new cars. I forgot that."

"The only reason you resent the attention they give to their cars is that you're just too lazy to even wash ours. And too cheap to take it to a car wash. And you say we can't afford to buy a better car. You *know* Daddy'd give us a good price on a newer one from his lot!"

"You're quite a psychiatrist, aren't you?" Ned said suddenly. "You know, I've never realized before what a wonderful psychiatrist you are."

"Oh, shut up!" she said, and started to weep again. "You make me wish I were dead."

"Well, why don't you take the hint, for Christ's sake? Promises, promises, that's all I hear!"

He honestly thought that was kind of clever. He went to the screen door, opened it, and flung his cigarette cartwheeling out into the lawn.

A little skyrocket of fire for the ever-watching neighbors to enjoy. Another Fourth of July.

He stared at the lawn a second, and then turned back into the house.

"Well, are you still hanging around?" he asked.

She screamed in a high wail of hysteria and ran upstairs. Ned heard their bedroom door slam, then the baby start crying, and the door whapping open again as Polly Sue thumped down the hall to the baby's room. After a minute or two, he heard the crib start to shake back and forth as she tried to coax the baby back to sleep.

She lay in bed, stiff with anger and anxiety—vowing that she would leave him tomorrow and sue for divorce. And if he had the gall to come to bed with her tonight, she would get out of the bed and go downstairs to sleep on the sofa.

It was all over between them, and she had no more tears to give her grief.

She turned on her bedside lamp and looked at the clock. It was five minutes until three. She couldn't hear him downstairs any longer. He was a restless reader . . . he would never read over ten or fifteen minutes, before he would have to get up and walk around, still carrying his book and losing himself in it, the way other men watch baseball on TV or talk about cars and normal things like that. He would move about the house reading like a sleepwalker, looking like he had to raise a belch, never answering her questions at such times . . . just bumping into things and turning pages.

It must have been about three o'clock when she heard the repeated, shimmering call of an owl in one of the big trees in back. The blackness was intense, because clouds had curtained the sky, promising a cooling rain.

Suddenly, the silence of the night was burst by the sound of a power mower starting up. Then she heard the heavy drone as the mower was guided across their back lawn, guided beyond a doubt by Ned, who couldn't possibly have seen his hand before his face, it was so dark.

She ran to the window and pulled the venetian blind cord. Naturally, she couldn't see anything, but she couldn't help *trying* to see, by crowding up next to the screen and peering out into the darkness through a little tent made by her hands.

By the time she got to the window, she could tell that he had moved over into the Johnson's yard, next door, and was pushing the snarling mower around in their lawn. Good Heavens, what was he doing? He might have sliced off some of the roses in Mrs. Johnson's flower border. The man was absolutely crazy!

Then the sound of the mower was still farther off, perhaps even as far away as the Tabor's house, beyond the Johnson's.

At that instant, the Tabor's powerful backyard lights flashed on, revealing Ned mowing diagonally, and at a brisk rate, back toward the high maple trees that bordered the rear of their lots.

Suddenly, he turned the mower around with a swift, reckless sweep and started trotting with it directly toward the Tabor's house, as if he intended to run it down. His mouth moving open and shut, and she knew he was probably singing some dirty song at the top of his voice, the way he had done several times before after she had finally gotten him to mow their own lawn. Although he said nobody could hear him singing, she was always afraid some of the neighbors could read lips.

Now Ned was shoving the mower right into the bushes that bordered the Tabor's property and the old retired couple's property next to it . . . she couldn't think of their names for a minute—wait, it was the Hemsleys. They had also flashed their backyard lights on. Polly Sue couldn't see Ned by this time, but she could imagine what the Hemsleys thought of him out there, zig-zagging crazily through their lawn at three o'clock in the morning, drunk and singing bawdy songs.

The last straw! The Hemsleys were wealthy, and Mrs. Hemsley had once commented that she had never seen Ned in church, and Polly Sue had felt her face burn with shame, as she mumbled something about his love for reading. "The Bible and inspirational things," she had added, telling a white lie, because Ned had once shocked her terribly by saying that the Bible was the biggest and filthiest pack of lies that had ever been collected.

Now what would Mrs. Hemsley think? Polly Sue ran downstairs and went outside on their darkened patio so she could see better.

Strangely enough, no one dared to come outside. They would just switch on their lights as Ned pushed his power mower every which way through their lawns—spoiling the mowing pattern of each lawn, and slipping off showers of daisies and nasturtiums and roses and barberry everywhere he went.

She knew that every time he pushed the thing into twigs, little fragments of wood must be shooting out like bullets from the powerful rotary blades. And she found herself praying that one of them would strike him in a mortal spot.

But none did. And Ned's sojourn through his neighbors' yards ended at about 3:18 when a police cruiser came up and two policemen arrested him for disturbing the peace, while Ned argued with them about freedom of speech and civil rights in general. One of the policemen brought the power mower back to Polly Sue, and she wasn't able even to look him in the face.

She cried all that night, she was so humiliated.

She and her baby went to live with her mother and father, who was a prosperous used-car dealer in a nearby small town. He was a redfaced man with a mustache and a gift for angry opinions of a conservative nature.

Polly Sue had always been awed by her father, who had loved to spend his evenings at home when she was a child, telling her mother the things he had said to people during the day to straighten out their opinions. He had once read a book on economics, written by a retired Army officer, and he took the book with him to his car lot.

Polly Sue's father had a way of signaling for silence by a swift intake of breath that could interrupt the loudest conversation. Polly Sue and her mother heard it frequently after Polly Sue and her baby returned.

Usually Daddy said, with reference to Ned: "I could never understand how anybody could be such a nut!"

Polly Sue and her mother would nod silently and respectfully. Because if Daddy couldn't understand, the matter was clearly incomprehensible. And if Daddy called someone a "nut"—the strongest and most insulting term in his vocabulary—that person was hopeless. He used the word for Communists, Washington spenders, modern artists who wore beards, foreigners, Negroes, Jews, Catholics, Protestants, atheists, liberals, literary people, pacifists, one-worlders, people who bought foreign cars, people who rented cars, people who didn't keep their cars washed and waxed, etc.

"I can't understand why you had to marry a nut," Daddy would say, cracking his paper open and chewing on his teeth. When he did that, his thin mustache would wiggle like a strange little insect. It had always fascinated Polly Sue; it was one of the little things she loved about Daddy.

"Now, Daddy," Mother said. "Everybody makes a mistake sometime in their lives. It's just human nature. And that fella"—this was the only way she could bear to refer to Ned—"was Polly Sue's mistake."

Daddy lowered his paper and thought a minute. "You know," he said in a slow and judicious voice, "That's the truth. Everybody makes a mistake in their lives. It's just human nature."

One day the veneer of Polly Sue's happiness was chipped somewhat by her receiving a telegram from Ned, who was working on a railroad section gang in Montana.

"Congratulations," the telegram said, "You have just given birth to a 180-pound baby."

That's all it said. Daddy was so angry he called up Western Union, demanding to know what they meant by letting some nut send such a wire. All the man told him was that there weren't any objectionable words in the wire, and Daddy slammed the receiver down and said to Polly Sue: "Actually, there weren't any objectionable words in the wire, when you come to think about it."

"That's true," she said. "But it's so *wacky*. It's just like him to do something like that. And *you* know. . . ." Polly Sue stopped and made a futile gesture of dismay.

"Well, it can't be helped now," Mother said, repeating her favorite consolation.

Later that day, Polly Sue asked her Daddy how much he weighed, and he told her 176 pounds, dripping wet.

The next telegram from Ned said, "Congratulations to your mother on her golden wedding anniversary."

"Why, Mother, you've only been married twenty-seven years," Daddy said.

"I know it," Mother said, with a worried look on her face.

Daddy called Western Union again, but the man there said that *they* didn't have any way of knowing how long a woman had been married. He said that they didn't know Mother, or they would have undoubtedly realized that she wasn't that old.

Daddy took a deep breath, but Polly Sue and Mother were already listening. "You know," he said. "These fellows at Western Union don't have any way of checking on the ages of people. They just get a wire like that, and they suppose the person is as old as the wire says."

"Why that's right," Mother said. "I don't blame those fellas at Western Union. It's the other fella I blame."

"Oh, I hate him," Polly Sue said. "You just don't have any idea."

"He's a nut, all right," Daddy said. "But that's all right, Polly Sue. Everybody makes one mistake in their lives." He patted her shoulder as he said this, and looked at Mother, who nodded at him slowly with her eyes closed.

Then the wires began coming just about every week, each one crazier than the last. "Plug up the leaks," one of them said, "the State is sinking." Daddy called Western Union, of course, and the man there said he thought the wire might have been in some kind of code.

"You know," Daddy said, after hanging up the receiver. "He's kind of a nut, that fella down there at Western Union."

Other wires from Ned were poetic, such as "They boy stood on the burning deck, a used car in his hand."

"Drunk," Daddy said, when he read that one.

"He certainly is a nut," Mother said, feeling cozy and agreeable because she had used Daddy's word.

Daddy thought a minute, and then said: "Yes sir, he's a nut, all right. A *drunken* nut!"

Soon after that, Daddy tore up the telegrams as they arrived, his mustache twitching. Mother and Polly Sue pieced the telegrams together, however, after Daddy left for the used-car lot, and read them.

They stopped coming soon afterwards. and Daddy had the idea that Ned had "moved on," although he didn't clarify what he meant by that.

Polly Sue, however, pictured her ex-husband as a tramp, riding the freights out west. Or she pictured him with a power mower, roaring through the states, cutting down all the things he hated: ranch houses, mortgages, telephone poles, wisteria bushes, normal people, soft drink plants, public schools, potato chip factories, electric fences, college students, service stations, ministers, old ladies, billboards, used-car lots, churches and Savings and Loans establishments.

But Polly Sue never heard from Ned again. Not even a telegram. And she was extremely happy at home with Mother and Daddy.

Only sometimes she would cry at the terrible mistake she had made in once marrying a fella like Ned, and Daddy would pat her on the shoulder and gaze in the distance, saying: "Never mind, Polly Sue, Honey. Everybody makes one mistake in their lives."

Daddy, Mother, Polly Sue, and her little baby lived happily ever after. And just about the only time Polly Sue ever thought of Ned was once a week, during the summers, when Daddy tenderly mowed their lawn with his shiny, well-kept power mower, whether the grass grew or not.

THE ETERNAL MORTGAGE

I was expecting him, because of his phone call almost two hours earlier. When he parked the green Mercury and got out, I thought of how exactly his appearance matched his deep, gruff, old-man's voice. He closed the door to his Mercury and just stood there a minute, stooped and bowlegged, then cranked his elbow back as he shuffled under his overcoat for a handkerchief in his rear pocket. When he finally got it out, he wiped the tears out of his eyes and then carefully blew his nose. He still hadn't looked up at my trailer. He was dressed all in black, with a thin brown tie against a white shirt; and his gray hair was shaved high against the sides of his head, making it shine like silver.

There was something uneasy, a little wrong, about him. Through the thermal glass and aluminum floral patterns of my storm door I watched him climb along the walk bearing an old man's expression of profound disgust at having been betrayed by his body.

I didn't give him a chance to knock, but just swung the storm door out before his foot reached the cement block step, and told him to come on in. He glanced up at my arm, but showed no surprise whatsoever. He looked like a man who'd outlived all surprise. His face was pale and heavily wrinkled, slightly twisted around the mouth, as if from an old stroke, with eyes peering out from under heavy brows. There was also something almost familiar about it, but I had no clear idea of what this might be.

"I'm the man that called," he said, shaking his head no. He smelled of witch hazel and cold damp air.

"Hello," I said, and motioned him to the only chair that wasn't cluttered with books or papers.

He stood there nodding in such a way it seemed to have a negative meaning.

"Go on and sit down," I said. "Would you like me to hang up your coat? Or maybe you'd like a cup of coffee. I've still got some left in the pot."

He sat down and said no thanks. Then he seemed momentarily dis-oriented, and with a worried expression started to chew on his false teeth. It occurred to me that he might have forgotten why he'd come.

I sat down on the edge of my kitchen counter, and he appeared to relax somewhat. "You mean to say you manage to conduct a book busi-ness *here?*" he asked, looking at the clutter all around.

"That's right. I've got four or five thousand books crammed into this thing. Usually, I sell by mail. Only now and then somebody will want something special and come to my trailer. Like you."

"Amazing," he said, shaking his head no. "Yes, amazing."

I said, "Well, I sell a lot. Keep turning them over. There are always books coming in and books going out. I move a lot of books. Only it's just a sideline for me, if you know what I mean."

"I know," he said. Right then, I thought he must be some kind of preacher. I had several boxes of old theological works—mostly from the Civil War period through World War I—that I had stashed away in the first bedroom.

"Are you interested in religion?" I asked.

He looked surprised then, and shook his head no. But exactly as he did this, he said, "Yes, but that is not what brings me here today. I have come for a different reason."

I nodded and waited; however, he wasn't even looking at me, but at an old hourglass-shaped wine stain on the carpet about two feet in front of his shoes.

I said, "Maybe you're interested in county histories. I've got a Wyan-dotte County, a Meigs, and a Washington. That's all I've got on hand right now, but if you want another one, just let me know and I'll keep my eye out. They can turn up any time. Even though they're getting to be awfully scarce. Still, I've got ways of digging them up."

He was once more nodding his head, and he said, "No, no. That's not what I'm after at all." I had him figured, now: when he nodded yes, he would say no; when he shook his head no, he would say yes. Old age had obviously rested its hand on him. "Well, what *is* it you're after?" I asked.

"I guess you could call them picture books. Photographs. There's a Latin word: *curiosa.*"

He raised his eyes then and looked at me with an expression that I thought might be almost mirthful. I decided to make sure, so I asked him if he knew exactly what sort of thing it was he was asking for; and he set his jaw and looked me right in the eye and said yes. This was the clearest thing he'd done yet, so I stopped trying to figure him out, slid off the counter, and said, "Okay, I'll dig up a few items. I don't collect that sort of thing myself, but sometimes I get them in a batch of books or a whole library, when I buy one. Most of these I'm going to show you right now came from a professor of mathematics at the university, believe it or not, who died about a year ago."

When I said this, the old man shook his head no extra hard and said, "Yes, yes. I meant to bring that part up. The chances are, the one I want is in there. The fellow who sent me here said he thought that Professor . . . Professor . . ."

"Becker," I said.

"Yes, Professor Becker might have had the one I was looking for."

"You mean you've been trying to track down one particular book?"

"Yes, a little book that was printed in Columbus back in 1938. You won't find a date on it, anywhere; but that was the year. Also, there are some photographs in it."

I told him to wait a minute, went back into the second bedroom of the trailer, and dug under the bed where I keep the *curiosa*. It's a box of about fifteen or twenty books . . . some of it pretty tame by today's standards, but some of it still properly taboo—*Fanny Hill*, Frank Harris's *Autobiography*, a couple of early Henry Millers, a book titled *Gruszhenka*, etc. And, indeed, a few books with photographs. There's a particular smutty quality to those early editions, with their slick dark snapshots of whores wearing their hair like curly wet caps close to their skull, and their fat white thighs puckered up under tight garters . . . there's a hot, ugly fascination to them that I don't think can ever be duplicated.

I pulled the whole box out and took it into the front room and put them on the floor beside his chair. He reached over and stirred his hand in the pile for an instant, and then pulled out a particularly grubby one in the old-time plain brown wrapper, titled *Lucy Lets Her Hair Down*. A really crude printing job, with some pretty gross photographs of a man and two women going at it in a variety of ways.

"This one," the old man said.

"Any others?"

"No," he said. "This is the one. How much is it?"

"Aren't you going to look at it?"

"I don't need to," he said. "Just tell me what the price is."

"Well, I said, "in New York, they're selling those things for fifteen and twenty dollars, believe it or not. But you can have that copy for five. I didn't pay much for it. And it doesn't mean anything to me."

"It does to me," he said.

"What?"

"You said it doesn't mean anything to you, but it does to me."

"What do you mean?" I asked.

Again he nodded, and then he said, "Never mind. It doesn't mean anything to anybody but me."

I was going to ask for an explanation, but he lurched to his feet, reached in his pocket, and pulled out a five dollar bill and handed it to me.

I took it and said, "Okay. But are you sure you don't want to look through some other things. You mentioned religion. I've got a lot of books on religion."

For the first time, he seemed to smile. At least, the corners of his wrinkled old mouth seemed to relax a little. He tapped the book in his hand with his index finger and said, "You mean, you expect me to buy *this* book, and then turn around and buy some books on *religion?* You must think I'm pretty odd to do a thing like that."

"In this business," I said, "you meet all kinds of people. I figured it wouldn't hurt to ask, would it?"

He nodded sadly. "No, it didn't hurt to ask."

He started toward the door, and I said, "Well, you come on back sometime, and maybe I'll have something else you'd like."

He stopped for a minute and stared at the floral pattern in the glass storm door before him. "If you should ever get another copy of this particular book," he said, "I'd appreciate it if you let me know. I'll always pay five dollars for it. You can't reach me by phone, but Fred Davidson can get in touch with me."

"I'll remember," I told him.

He nodded and opened the door. When he stepped outside I said good-bye, but he didn't anwer or even turn around. He just lifted his open hand to the side and walked slowly out to his car.

I went back into my kitchenette and poured the dregs of the coffee into my little aluminum sink. I turned on the tap and was just getting ready to wash out the coffeepot when I looked through the window and saw that the old man had fallen to his knees beside the open door of his car.

I hurried out the door and ran out to him. He was still kneeling there with his eyes closed, almost like a man praying. "What's the matter?" I said.

He didn't even open his eyes, but just shook his head back and forth. "I can't seem to get back up," he whispered.

I helped him up to his feet. The book was lying face down on the asphalt, so I leaned over and picked it up. "I hope you didn't get it dirty," I said, holding it out to him.

"That doesn't make any difference," he mumbled, not bothering to take the book from me.

I told him he'd better come back into the trailer and let me get him a drink of whiskey or something.

"No, I don't drink whiskey any more." He panted a little, and said, "No, not under any circumstances. In fact, not for many years now."

He was pale and woozy, and he didn't really argue; so he let me help him back into the trailer. When I got him seated, he accepted a glass of water, and I sat there on the counter and watched the life come back into his eyes.

"You gave me a scare," I said. "I didn't realize you'd fallen until I just happened to glance out the window, and there you were."

"I didn't fall," he said.

"Well, it sure as hell looked like it. Don't you remember I came out there just now and helped you get up off your knees?"

"I'll admit," he said, raising his voice, as if there were a great crowd listening, "that I might have blacked out, momentarily. I'll admit that I couldn't quite make it up to my feet without your help. And I want to thank you for your help. Yes, I want to thank you for that."

He went quiet after saying this, and a moment later I said, "You're welcome. But he didn't seem to be listening any longer. He didn't seem to be getting ready to leave, either . . . even though a little better color was coming back into his face.

"It almost looked like you could have been praying or something," I said finally.

He just stared at me and nodded. "No, nothing like that."

Right then I noticed that I was still holding the book, *Lucy Lets Her Hair Down,* so I handed it to him. He took it and shook his head no.

"I wouldn't want you to forget it," I said. "Not after all this."

"No, I wouldn't either."

Then he stood up, and I said, "You really were praying, weren't you?"

"No," the old man said. "I wasn't praying. I admit that I might have been pausing a second to give thanks, but I didn't intend to sink down on my knees like that."

"Give thanks for what?" I said.

For an instant, he just stared into my eyes, as if he recognized me for the first time as someone he'd known for years. "It was what you might call a prayer of thanks for finding another one, if you have to know that badly."

"Another one of *those?*" I asked, pointing at the book.

"Someday," he said distantly, "if I can only live long enough, I may get the last one that exists."

"Why are you trying to buy them all up?"

"To burn them," he answered, shaking his head no. "That's why."

"Buy why in the hell would you want to . . ."

For an instant I just stood there, and then I held my hand out. "Let me take a look at that book again, will you?"

He nodded and said, "No; if you've looked inside at those photographs once, you've seen more than I ever want anybody to see again. At one time, it was different. At one time, I'll tell you, I couldn't have cared less!"

His eyes glistened with an anger so intense there seemed to be something like pride in it, and he shook his head so hard that he lost his balance a little and caught himself with his hand on the aluminum floral pattern in the storm door.

I pointed at the book and asked incredulously, "You mean to tell me you were the *star* of that production?"

He nodded and glared at me. "There were others who did things just as bad," he said. "But what do I have to do with *them*? What do their sins have to do with mine? The fact is. . . ."

He paused, swallowed, and then said, "Twenty-five dollars. Can you conceive of that? *Twenty-five dollars!* Think of it! And then all those years later, when the time came that I understood that we are called to account for our infamy; that we must pay our debts to the dime and even the penny; that if man is not the son of God, he is nothing. And then there is nothing for us, nothing waiting . . . no judgment, no order, no names for the things that happen to us. And don't you see?"

He stepped forward and clutched my arm, shaking his head no. Evidently, he wanted some kind of answer from me. Fascinated, I also shook my head no, my head synchronized with his.

Breathing heavily through his mouth, he whispered passionately at me—the smell of his breath woefuly morbid and vile—"The son of God does not do what I did in those pictures!"

I heard a motorcycle roar by outside, and I glanced past him as if to see who it was; but such tactics were worthless, and, when I looked back, his violent old face was still trembling before me as he awaited some kind of answer.

"Sure," I said. "I mean, what the hell. I see what you mean."

"I was drunk, do you see? I was wild and drunk and mocking all the time in those days. Drunk and fornicating and forgetful. I think of those words day and night. They're like a terrible poem to me!"

"Why don't you sit down again?"

"Every time I find one, I give thanks. Because that's one more out of the way. The burden of just one more taken away from off my conscience!"

"How many were printed?" I asked.

"That printer ran off five hundred," he said. "It was just some dirty little shop on Goodale Street, part of what they called Fly Town in the Columbus of those days. They tore down all that area long ago to make room for throughways and apartment houses. Good riddance, I tell you! I suppose the printer's been dead a long time; he seemed like an old man to me at that time. I remember going into the shop with Bert Gordon, the man who'd written the book and paid to have it published, and I'll never forget how that old man looked at me the minute he realized I was the one who was pictured doing those things with those two women. You could tell he hated his job right then. I'll never forget that vomitous expression on his face! I'll never forget how he looked at me, and then looked at Bert Gordon, who had planned the whole thing. Bert was the one who'd paid me twenty-five dollars to have my picture taken with those two prostitutes. I suppose he made some money on the project.

I don't think the two women did any better than I did, but at least they got paid better than they would have for a regular night with a man. They didn't care about anything, anyway." He stopped and stared out of glazed eyes at nothing, chewing on his false teeth.

"And you know something?" he went on, "I didn't either, when I walked into that printer's office. There wasn't any reason to go there, but Bert saw me uptown, and he said, 'Come on, and we'll go see how our literary work is coming along.' It was a fine sunny day, so I said sure, and I went with him—he was driving a big, shiny tan Hudson, with a black metal tire case at the side, only two years old—and we went down on Goodale and walked into that printer's shop, and I was as cocky as a young devil could be. I remember I was smoking a cigar and just sort of grinning around it when I saw the printer adjust his glasses and take a long look at me. I knew right then he recognized me from the pictures. Bert knew it too and he laughed out loud.

"But the printer was nervous, because the police had been hanging around Goodale a lot. It was a high crime area. The printer motioned to the rear with his thumb and told Bert he could pick up all five hundred of the books in back, where they were all wrapped up in bundles, covered with old newspapers and tied with twine. So Bert and I took the Hudson down the alley and loaded every one of those bundles into the trunk and back seat. It's a shame we didn't run the whole thing off the bridge into the Olentangy River."

He stopped as suddenly as he started, and I could hear him breathing hard as he sat there in the chair. He was breathing like a man who had just climbed a long flight of stairs.

"I don't ever talk to people about that," he said, clasping his hands in his lap and shaking his head no as he stared out past my shoulder.

"No, I don't imagine you do," I said.

"But I told you."

"I know."

"As long as I live, I'll never forget the look that old man gave me."

"The printer?" I asked.

He nodded and said, "Yes, the printer. Of course, he's dead now. So's Bert Gordon. Bert died in that very Hudson about three or four years after that. He crashed it into a telephone pole one night, out near Sunbury, on the Sunbury Pike, and I heard that the speedometer was jammed at eighty. He was drunk, of course. Already, all those books had been scattered to the four winds and were in places I'll never hear about, never know about."

"I'd guess most of them have been destroyed by now," I said. "It seems to me you could relax about the whole thing. Hell, the way the world's gotten since then, what you did doesn't seem any crummier than a lot of things. Haven't you ever seen an X-rated movie?"

He just looked at me then, as if he hadn't understood what I was saying, but didn't want to bother asking about it.

"No," he said, nodding, "I wasn't alone. But that doesn't make any difference. The idea of some of those books still lying around and being read and looked at . . . I don't know, I just can't hardly stand the thought of it, sometimes."

"Yes, I can see that," I said. "But that was so long ago, nobody'd recognize you now."

"If there's an afterlife," he said, "that's the age I'll be, not what I am now, old and sick."

"I've never heard it expressed quite like that," I said.

"That's why I don't tell people."

"I understand."

"I often wish that Bert had crashed that Hudson earlier, even if I'd been in it. Maybe it would have been better if the two prostitutes and Bert and I had all hit that telephone pole near Sunbury that night before they took those pictures. Wiped off the face of the earth!"

"Well," I said, "I guess we can all improve on the past in one way or another."

He smiled then, and said, "Do you think *you'll* have anything like this to improve on?"

"What do you mean by that?" I said.

His smile drifted off a little, and his voice got lower, as if he was now talking to himself. "Yes, when I first came in here, I imagined I could see it."

"See what?" I asked.

"That you . . . well, this is going to sound strange, but it was the way you sort of remind me of how I was back then. I don't know; something about the way you talk. The way you kind of grinned at me after I got the book. There were several little things like that. Not very important, I guess."

"I don't know why I'd have been grinning," I said. "You must have imagined it. It doesn't make any difference to me what kind of books people buy."

"Well, maybe it should," he said. Then before I could answer him, he got to his feet and moved to the door, still clutching *Lucy Lets Her Hair Down*.

He staggered a little at the door, but when I said he'd better come back in and rest a little longer, he just shook his head no and started down the steps.

I watched him go out the cement block walk to his car. This time he didn't drop to his knees to give a prayer of thanks. In fact, he didn't even turn to look back, but just got in the car and drove away, very slowly, as if the road were covered with ice, and driving on it was difficult and treacherous.

What I've just written is the substance of this account. That was the first and last time I ever saw the old man. And that was three or four years ago.

The only additional information came with what I got yesterday, when I went through a dozen boxes of books I had bid successfully on at a farm auction out off Route 56. Most of the books were pretty drab: an old Arlington edition of Washington Irving, a few novels by E. P. Roe, Mary Roberts Rinehart, and some Grosset and Dunlap reprints of Zane Grey. Of course, I'd known pretty well what I was bidding on, and I wasn't prepared for anything in the way of a surprise when I got back to my trailer and shuffled through the boxes.

But pressed down at the bottom of one box was a drab book bound in cardboard, and the instant I saw it I felt this little nudge of familiarity, the way it comes now and then. So I picked it up, and for the second time in my life held a copy of *Lucy Lets Her Hair Down* in my hand. Who would have thought it?

I got on the phone after five o'clock (it's a toll call, but it costs only fifty cents after five) and rang Fred Davidson and asked if he knew where I could get in touch with the man he'd sent to see me one time.

"Yes, I know who you mean," Davidson said, "but he died a year or two back. They found him dead in his room. He was renting a room from Mrs. Renner, back on the Owl Creek Road, right outside of town."

I remembered the house he was talking about, and for a couple of seconds I tried to imagine the old man sitting at one of the second-story windows, holding a Bible in his lap and watching the cars go past the house, heading for the freeway.

I thanked Davidson and hung up.

Then I went to the chair where he had sat and picked up the book I had laid there. I opened it and looked at the drab old pictures. There was only one man featured, so it had to be the one who'd told me his story . . . but it would have been hard to connect the two, otherwise. He had been a heavy, muscular young man, with what was supposed to be an example of the patent-leather good looks of a 1930s film star. He was entirely naked in two of the pictures, with the exception of dark shoes and socks and garters.

The sight of these, and the sight of the two whores (one skinny and the other old), gave me an uneasy feeling. In fact, I was sorry I had looked. The sordidness of the cheap dark photographs was too much. The change in the old man's face and body, the terrible urgency of his only visit, the crummy print on cheap browned paper, the tired and hopeless evil of the two whores . . . all of it was too much for me; it was almost as if I could feel a coldness coming out of that drab little book, so I suppose it wasn't surprising that I did the obvious thing and took it out in back of my trailer, where I burned it, along with the Sunday newspaper, in the rusty ventilated drum I use for an incinerator.

IRMA, THE GOOD SPORT

"I have two vices," Irma would tell her friends and beauty shop customers: "coffee and cigarettes."

In fact, she'd tell them this with a cigarette actually hanging out of her mouth.

Irma was the best hairdresser in the shop. She was a widow in her early forties—a wacky sort of girl who liked to clown around and slap her muscular thigh with her open palm when she laughed. Irma just couldn't help having a warm interest in people, and the women found her sympathetic and tough, in a feminine way they liked, and she was good to talk to when they didn't feel like reading magazines.

In spite of the fact that Irma advertised her vices of coffee and cigarettes in a loud voice, she had secret dimensions she didn't talk about. One in particular, which was surely not a vice (but perhaps even worse: foolish), she had not mentioned to a living soul. This was her recent enrollment in a lonely hearts club. It was called something quite different, of course, but that's exactly what it was, and Irma knew it. She also knew all of the arguments against such an organization, and what's more she believed in these arguments. Nevertheless, she had joined the club anyway. Because how in the world could a woman like Irma ever meet a man when she spent her days exclusively with women, and had no other contacts? Once, years before, she had read in Dr. Crane's column that church was a good place to meet a man; so she attended church three Sundays in a row, but for some reason the minister's grave cheer and the sad music that spoke of holy joy and the respectable faces of the people depressed her terribly. She liked to laugh out loud and smoke cigarettes and drink coffee.

As a matter of fact, she also enjoyed lively music and movies. She went to the movies almost every night, and one of her favorite arguments in the beauty shop had to do with the superiority of movies over television. It was a good controversy, because almost any woman you could name would come to the defense of television, since most of them were mothers of young children and couldn't see enough movies, anyway, to make a good judgment.

Irma was certainly full of life, and her friends and customers sometimes said it was a shame she didn't have a good man to share it with!

Eventually through her membership, Irma started corresponding with a man named Harry King. He was a disc jockey on a radio station in San Francisco, and this fact alone excited Irma. She pictured him spending his nights in a semidarkened studio, playing lively music, smoking cigarettes and drinking coffee. There was a vague suggestion of night life and wickedness in her feelings about Harry. And for the first time in years, she began to forego seeing new movies occasionally, so that she could spend her time at home listening to the local disc jockeys and trying to imagine that they were all different versions of Harry speaking to her from clear across the continent in San Francisco.

Irma's best friend, if you could really call her that, was another hairdresser in the shop named Grace. Irma liked Grace pretty well; but she didn't like her hair, which was dyed a crayon yellow, and she didn't like Grace's way of always making little slanting remarks about her large size. Grace was small and angry looking.

Eventually, however, Irma broke down and brought some of Harry's neat, gentlemanly, typewritten letters for Grace to see, and told her all about the correspondence.

The first thing Grace said was: "How tall is he, Irma? You know you have to have a tall man, with your size."

"He's six feet two," Irma said.

"Well, that's good. Just right for a woman who's five ten."

Irma slammed a comb down on the table in front of her. "Grace, I certainly do wish you would quit saying that I'm five feet ten. I'm only five eight and three-quarters, and I've told you that a hundred times!"

"I only say it's a good thing he's plenty tall," Grace said, sighing—as if Irma's size were also a burden for *her* to bear.

"Here's his picture," Irma said, showing a newspaper clipping to Grace. "And that's a write-up on him. He's a disc jockey."

"I know; you told me that," Grace said, taking the clipping.

She stared at the clipping a minute, and then said: "Why he has a teeny little mustache. Men don't wear teeny little mustaches any more."

"Well, *Harry* does," Irma said, as if that was simply indicative of his superiority over other men.

"He *looks* tall," Grace said, grudgingly. "I mean, he has a long face, like a tall man."

"The clipping says that he has an old-fashioned motion-picture handsomeness. That's what it says right there: 'an old-fashioned motion-picture handsomeness.'"

"I see it," Grace said. Then she frowned. "What's this word here?" she asked. "It's crossed out."

"I couldn't make it out either," Irma said. "It's the word before 'and dapper.'"

"Yes. It looks like ink spilled on it, or something."

Grace was silent again, staring at Harry's picture.

"Don't you think he's dapper?" Irma asked.

"Oh, he's dapper all right," Grace said. "What I can't understand is why somebody like this, who's a radio disc jockey and all, and is tall and dapper like you say . . . why would he be writing to a forty-five-year-old widow who lives clear across the country? I mean, I'll bet he has women just chasing after him."

"Grace," Irma said, suddenly breathing heavily, as if she'd just run up a long flight of steps . . . "Grace, you have a vicious and cruel tongue. You *know* I'm only forty-three. And I never *did* like your hair that way!"

With that, Irma sobbed and ran back to the wash room. The women sitting under the hair-drying machines all stuck their heads out, like so many milk cows pulling out of their stanchions, to watch her run by; then they turned and stared at Grace, who shrugged her shoulders and said: "Can you imagine *her* saying anything about somebody *else's* hair? I only wish she'd do something with that stringy mop of hers. Can you imagine somebody being a hairdresser and keeping her hair like that?"

Irma had been caught by surprise . . . defenseless in her love for Harry (there was no disguising the fact by now that she loved him). But she was every bit as strong as Grace—stronger, in fact, because Irma had a sense of humor, and Grace didn't.

So for the next week or so, Irma was in control. She'd make stinging little digs at Grace, until Grace tried to defend herself, then Irma would cap it all with a funny word or two, slap her thigh and give her hearty laugh. The women were mostly on her side, because they all considered Grace mean and sneaky.

"Well, the sun's coming up," Irma would say, when Grace came near.

Grace would glare up at her from her skinny five feet two.

"Does that butter on top of your head ever melt and run down into your eyes, Grace?"

Silence. Glaring from Grace, then a twisting of the comb in a customer's hair, until the woman would yell: "Ouch. Don't take it out on me, Grace. Take it out on Irma. I want some hair left."

"Aren't you putting on still more weight, Irma?" Grace would ask.

And Irma would laugh and say that he-men liked a full and abundant woman. She'd never heard of a he-man who wanted a blonde spider.

By now, it was clear that Irma and Grace were deadly enemies. They had broken up over a man who lived three thousand miles away, whom neither had ever seen.

"There's something fishy about all this," Grace said to her customer, in a voice loud enough for Irma to hear. "No man who's a disc jockey, and six feet two and dapper has to write to a forty-five-year-old widow for companionship. There's something fishy."

Irma snapped a hair off with her comb, and her customer grunted and turned watery eyes up to glare at her. But Irma wasn't looking at her; she was looking at Grace.

"I've told you a thousand times, Grace, that I'm *not* forty-five, I'm only forty-three. And I'm *not* five-feet ten inches tall, I'm only five feet eight and three-quarters. And I *don't* weigh a hundred and seventy pounds. I weigh a lot less. And if you don't stop telling those lies about me, so help me, Grace, one of these days I'm going to pull out all of that crinkly Halloween hair of yours."

"Huh!" Grace said, dunking her customer's head abruptly into a wash basin filled with soapy water. "There's still something fishy, when you have to go that far to get a man."

Irma slammed her comb against the floor, so that it broke . . . one broken piece sliding clear through the door into the waiting room.

"You *bitch!*" she screamed. And was on top of poor little Grace in an instant, grabbing her much-discussed hair with both hands and twisting the little woman's head down until her knees went bowlegged and she could only squat there, like a baseball catcher, with her arms outstretched and her fingers splayed open in pain. Irma was terribly strong; there was no doubt of that, and scrawny little Grace didn't stand a chance.

With another violent twist Irma threw her to the floor, where Grace's body thumped loudly. The women under the hair dryers were all staring wide-eyed at the fight, while Grace's customer was standing up watching, with her wet hair streaked darkly down the side of her face like seaweed pasted to a smooth stone.

By now, Grace was screaming holy murder, and Irma was still clutching her hair with both hands . . . puzzled as to what she should do next, but not relaxing her hold in the least.

Mr. Jene, the owner of the shop, walked rapidly into the room, shouting: "Girls, girls, what *is* it?" He snapped his fingers in confusion, turned around once in a pirouette of sheer bewilderment, then stamped his foot. "Oh, you *bitches!*" he screamed. "You're fired! Do you *hear?* Leave this place this very *instant!*"

Then he stood there holding his hand over his brow, keeping his eyes closed before he could pour his heart out to his alarmed customers.

"Why not?" Irma asked herself. Didn't they have hairdressers in California, as well as here? Couldn't she find a job there, just as well?

So she bought a Greyhound bus ticket for California, and by the end of the second day, everyone on the bus knew Irma . . . knew her jolly laugh, the sound of her big palm slapping her meaty thigh, the wide sympathy in her eyes as she listened to whatever they might say to her. She could accept anything but open cruelty from people. She was large-breasted, warm, gentle . . . if you just *let* her—which Grace surely had not. She was proud of her copious breasts, and wore uplift bras that made her look like a May Day float, when she wore a frilly blouse over it and walked slowly, in what she felt was a dignified and ladylike manner. They knew the smell of her cigarettes and the sound of her voice as she asked for a cup of hot coffee at every stop.

In San Francisco, she found an apartment and a job within three days, and then she found out where Harry King lived, and—with heart pounding—went up to his apartment early one afternoon, when she thought he should be awake, even if he had slept nine hours straight.

The apartment was well-kept and solidly respectable, although it fell considerably short of the sophistication suggested by the young, naked—almost breastless—statues of girls placed in the corners of the carpeted halls. Otherwise, the building was content to be simply clean and well-worn.

Never in her life had she been so nervous as when she rang the buzzer on Harry King's door. Her heart drummed a confused and ecstatic obbligato to the footsteps she heard approaching, as she looked up to meet the man she loved . . . saw the door swing open, and was faced by a virtual midget, with the old-fashioned, mustached, moving-picture handsome face of Harry King.

Irma gasped.

"Who are you?" Harry King asked in a vibrant, radio announcer's tone.

She swallowed once, and then said, "I'm Irma. Don't you recognize me from the picture I sent you?"

"Irma. The one who lives in Ohio?"

"Yes. That one," she said fatuously.

"Well, I'll be damned," Harry King said. Then he glanced back into the apartment, without opening the door any wider for her to come in. Irma wondered if he might have a woman in there. For the first time in her life she actually felt like fainting.

"You mean you came here all the way from Ohio to . . . to see *me?*" Harry asked, still not opening the door any wider.

"Not exactly," Irma said. "I live here now. I have a job, as a matter of fact. I'm a hairdresser, you know."

Harry King bit his lip and nodded. "Yeah," he said. "I remember you mentioned that in one of your letters."

Tears came to Irma's eyes. She just couldn't help it.

"You sick or something?" Harry asked suspiciously. "Want a drink of water, maybe?"

"Do you have any coffee made?" Irma asked. "I could use a cup of hot coffee and light up a cigarette."

"Well, sure," Harry King said. "I mean, Jesus Christ . . . Ohio. That's a hell of a distance."

As she walked in to sit down on the sofa, Irma remembered that he had never said a word in his letters about using profanity; and she was so disappointed that she just sat there trying to swallow, but she couldn't do it, and she wondered how on earth she would ever be able to drink her coffee.

While Harry was out in the kitchen, fumbling around, she decided to calm her nerves with a cigarette. So she lighted one, and sat there smoking with a worried look on her face. Two and a half thousand miles, she was thinking. Two and a half thousand miles.

Having finished her first cigarette, she lighted another. And when she had smoked that one down, she stood up . . . suddenly aware of how silent the kitchen was. Maybe Harry King had climbed out of a window and was now running for his life down the streets of San Francisco.

She walked to the kitchen door and peered in. There was the little man standing with his legs spread and holding a bottle of liquor up to his mouth. She saw his Adam's apple jump twice in big gulps, before he became aware of her and lowered the bottle to glare out upon the landscape of herself through two soapy-looking eyes.

"Goddamit," he said.

"You're not even *trying* to make coffee," Irma said.

Harry paused and looked at the stove. Then he nodded. "I guess you're right. Irma. I guess you're right."

They were both silent a moment.

"Would *you* mind making it?" Harry asked politely.

"I guess not," Irma said, stepping over to the stove and picking up the pot.

When she had it on the burner, she turned to Harry who was standing there stargazing into the ceiling, and said: "Mr. King, you *distinctly* said in your letter that you were *six-feet two inches tall.*"

"Yeah," he said. "I guess my finger hit the wrong key on the typewriter."

Irma was silent.

"Easy to do, you know," Harry King said. "I'm not much at typing."

Irma didn't answer.

When the coffee was made, Irma filled two cups and took them into the living room. But Harry didn't touch his. Instead, he jumped up and walked erratically into the kitchen. Irma sipped her coffee for a minute, and then followed him . . . and found him holding the bottle up in one hand and walking around in little circles.

She went up to him, took his hand and led him into the living room. She put him down on the sofa beside her, and finished her cup of coffee, while he stared off into space, mumbling incoherently.

Suddenly, as Irma was pouring her second cup of coffee, she noticed that Harry was quiet. She looked at him and saw that he was sound asleep with his head thrown back . . . his Adam's apple—the home of that deep, manly voice—jutting up like a chicken breast.

"Well, he can't sleep comfortably there," Irma whispered, as if arguing with herself.

So she stood up and picked Harry King up in her arms. Then she walked with him into the bedroom, thinking: "The bride carried the groom across the threshold, and they lived happily ever after."

She put him in his bed and returned to the living room, where she drank the whole pot of coffee. When she finished, she took the cups out to the kitchen and stood there washing up the pot and dishes, with a lighted cigarette in her mouth.

Once, she heard Harry snort in his sleep . . . it was like the start of a gigantic snore that suddenly changed its mind.

Hearing it, Irma started to laugh out loud. She slapped her thigh with her open palm, and just kept on laughing. What if the women in the beauty shop could have seen her carry him into the bedroom? What if Grace could have seen it?

She wiped the tears out of her eyes with a Kleenex, and then left a note for Harry, saying that she was working in The Albitore Beauty Shop, on W. Ferris St. If he wanted to call her up, that was all right with her. Because no matter what you said about Irma, she was one hell of a good sport.

THE KITTEN

Roger opened the back door on weather that the morning news on TV had designated a "Polar air pocket," and the term seemed precisely right. The sky was a clear inhuman blue, and from her place at the stove, Linda could feel the frigid draft on her bare ankles. She shuddered all over and cried out, "Don't leave the door open, please!"

"The milkman hasn't come yet," he said.

He stood for an instant, staring at a dirty gray canvas newspaper sack next to the garage. It was crumpled and frozen, covered with tiny ice crystals, so that he could no longer read the name of the newspaper.

Then he first saw the kitten. It was very young—no bigger than a guinea pig—and he watched it as it struggled up the back steps toward him. He started to say something to Linda when it reached the top, but before he spoke, the kitten had trotted past his foot into the warm kitchen.

"Will you please close the door?" she said. "I'm freezing."

Roger pulled the door shut and said, "We have a visitor."

"What is it?" she asked, not turning around from the stove, where she was studiously nudging at an egg in the skillet.

"It's a kitten," he said. He watched it walk under the breakfast table, and then heard it start to purr loudly.

She turned around from the stove, leaned over with her hands on her knees and said, "What's it doing *here?*"

"Who knows? Someone left it, I guess."

"I'm not sure I like cats," Linda said. She laid the spatula down on the counter and frowned. She was chronically intense upon defining her precise feelings toward things. It was a moral concern with her.

"Well, let it stay here this morning, and maybe you'll find out."

She glanced at him to see if he was being sarcastic, but he was looking crosseyed at his coffee as he blew on it, and she couldn't tell. Often she analyzed what seemed to her to be strange little acts of evasion in him lately, and she tried to understand exactly how much she resented them . . . if, indeed, she resented them at all. It was hard to tell.

"Ouch," he said.

"What's the matter?"

She turned around and saw him pluck the kitten from his pant leg. Its front legs and claws were distended, and briefly the little creature reminded her of a picture she'd once seen of a hawk about to land on a limb—its legs rigid before it, and the talons curved and glistening, like machined steel. Even the kitten's eyes had something of that mad, wide-eyed expression she'd seen on the hawk.

"Don't be late for class," she said.

"I won't."

She sat down opposite him, and studied him as she blew on her own coffee. It occurred to her, with her compulsive sense of the theatrical, that now she was doing exactly what he had been doing a minute ago. Only reversed, on the other side of the table. They were mirror images. Male and female.

"Son of a bitch," he said, reaching under the table.

"Is he scratching you again?" she asked.

"Yes," he said. He pushed the kitten away with his shoe, making it skid on the linoleum. Its head hung heavily as it was moved. She could sense exactly how it must feel: stupid and confused and maybe a little sleepy from the heat of the kitchen. Why on earth would it want to climb his pant leg?

"Don't be late for class," she said.

"I know, I know," he grumbled.

He got up from the table, picked up his books, kissed her quickly and left.

After he had gone, she sat drinking her coffee, wondering how many times she had reminded him about class, and wondering if it was conceivable that someday she would sound like her mother talking to her father. How would she feel if she discovered this quality in herself?

Then she felt the needle claws in her right ankle. She sucked in her breath; she hadn't realized they were so sharp. She plucked the kitten off and put it several feet away on the floor. It stared up at her. Its face was like a crooked little star of hair, or the drawing of a demented child.

She shuddered at the thought, wondering why such bizarre ideas came into her head. Maybe it was a secret fascination with the abnormal. She thought about this for awhile, and then the telephone rang.

When she answered, she heard the milk truck stop in front. It was Sandy on the phone. She asked Linda if she had finished her coffee and wanted to talk, and Linda said yes. Sandy started talking about some new materials she had gotten for a dress.

Linda sat down and chatted a few minutes, and then she once more felt the needles in her ankle. The same ankle.

"Oh this stupid kitten," she thought. But she didn't mention it to Sandy. It was as if the kitten's world and Sandy's world didn't come together anywhere. Weren't even in touch. When this thought flicked through her mind, she recognized it for what it was—the source of more questioning and brooding; but the idea didn't alarm her.

In fact, fewer and fewer things alarmed her as time went by. She was standing farther away from herself, and watching what she did as if she were a dull or inexperienced actress challenged by an inscrutable and vaguely unimportant role. Was she too stupid to play herself?

Then she thought of something her philosophy professor had quoted in class: the remark of an intense young student, parodying Socrates: "The overexamined life isn't worth living."

The thought made her laugh briefly, and Sandy asked what she was laughing about.

"Nothing," Linda said. "I'm sorry. I was trying to catch a sneeze, and it stopped my ears up."

The lie surprised her a little, it seemed so senselessly inventive.

Once again, the kitten climbed up on her shoe. It was hardly bigger than a man's hand, but fluffy and soft and sort of helpless.

She pushed it aside with her foot, and then placed her foot on its back, realizing that she could crush it by just shifting her weight. The thought was only momentary, of course; then the kitten turned over on its back and hugged the shoe. It was playing with her; and yet it was probably hungry.

Linda heard it start to purr with startling noise. It was an amazing little thing—complicated and resourceful, in its own way.

She decided to give it a saucer of milk, now that the milkman had come. Although she still wasn't sure she liked the kitten; it was possible, in fact, that she disliked it a little, and was maybe even a little bit afraid of it, for reasons she could not understand, but would undoubtedly begin considering.

That night the kitten chewed two holes in her best wool sweater, and Roger was furious when he went to class. He told her to put the damn thing outside, or get rid of it in any way she could.

But she was reluctant. She wasn't sure about it; certainly, she wasn't attracted to it. In fact, there was something about it that made her uneasy. Especially when it rubbed against her ankles; this was almost worse than when it scratched her, trying to climb her leg . . . just as a fear is more powerful than a fact, for whenever the little thing rubbed its warm fur against her skin, she thought of the claws, and wondered what sort of satisfaction it could get out of rubbing against a human. It was incapable of real attachment or affection; she was sure of this. And she was determined not to name or personify it in any way. She didn't even want to know what gender it had. It would have to remain a thing.

When Roger came home from class, he got a beer out of the refrigerator and sat in the kitchen drinking it.

"Do you want a sandwich or something?" she said.

"No, but if you want to do something useful, you could take this goddam kitten away and strangle it."

"Is it on your leg again?"

"What do you think?"

"Well it isn't my kitten," she said. He turned aside and stared at it for a second, clinging to his pant leg and staring back at him. Slowly, he pushed if off with his other foot, as if it were a clot of mud on a boot. As soon as it touched the linoleum, it started purring again and moved once more towards his leg.

"Roger," she said.

"What is it?"

"What's wrong? What happened in class?"

"I'm sick of class," he said. "I'm sick of the whole business."

She went into the bedroom and picked up one of his socks which she'd been darning, wondering if she might be included in "the whole business."

She heard him yell out again, and start cursing, and she knew the kitten had attacked him again. It was so funny, she started laughing, and then suddenly she was crying. She threw herself on the bed and muffled her sobs in the pillow.

"What in the hell's so goddam funny?" Roger asked, coming into the bedroom. She turned her warm wet face toward him, and cried, "I'm not laughing, can't you even see that?"

"Go on and cry then," he shouted. "You're so fucking neurotic I should never have married you. Go on and cry. Get it out of your system."

A soldier who is shot through the heart might experience such a sudden discovery as this, she thought. The pain was right there in her chest and the fear and hurt were so sudden and so sharply focused that she was almost grateful for the discovery.

"Every divorce must start exactly like this," she thought.

Then she wondered how she felt about it, and as she did so, she heard the refrigerator door slam again. How he could drink cold beer in this frigid weather was something she could not begin to understand.

When she sat up in bed and put her feet on the floor, she felt one of her feet nudged, and then the pricking of her ankles. She screamed, and shouted, "Roger, get this goddam kitten out of here, please!"

"What?" he called from the kitchen.

She kicked the cat away, and at the same instant realized she had been hysterical and hadn't spoken clearly. She felt the floor move a little, and heard Roger step into the bedroom.

"What did you say?" he asked. His hair was mussed-up and he looked bewildered as well as angry.

"That kitten's like a devil," she said.

"That wasn't what you said."

"Well, it's what I'm saying now."

The two of them looked at the kitten for an instant, their two hearts beating together as they watched it start to move toward Roger's foot.

"If he touches you, I'll scream," she said. Her voice was almost tentative.

Roger took a drink of his beer and watched as the kitten came up to his pants leg and began methodically to climb his leg, swinging back and forth each time it reached higher.

Both of them were silent, and then Roger reached over and plucked it loose.

"There's something wrong with it," Linda said, after a second. "Get rid of it, why don't you."

"Yes, I guess I'd better," he said.

He drank another beer, and then went out in the back yard. The frozen newspaper bag lay glistening in the afternoon sunshine, and he went over to it and kicked at it until it was shaken loose.

He picked it up and went back up on the back porch, where Linda was waiting—hugging her arms and staring wide-eyed at him.

"What are you going to do?" she asked.

"I'm going to drown it," he said. "I've been wanting to get rid of this damn thing anyway. I never could figure out who left it there."

"You're going to drown it?" she asked.

"That's right. Two birds with one stone."

"I wish you hadn't told me, somehow."

"I don't want it to grow up and kill birds," he said.

"Yes, but I just wish you hadn't told me about it."

They both went back in the house, and Roger started calling, "Here, kitty, kitty. Here, kitty."

But the kitten suddenly wasn't there.

"Maybe you're frightening it with that bag you're carrying," Linda said.

"If I sit down and drink another beer, it'll come," Roger said. He got another beer out of the refrigerator and sat down at the table, snapping the cap off.

"It's just a matter of time," he said.

When he was halfway through the beer, the kitten appeared in the hallway, and Linda felt her stomach tense up. She wondered if she was pregnant, the way she'd been feeling lately . . . like it was her period due. Although, aside from morning sickness, you were supposed to feel good when you were pregnant. She went into the bedroom and sat down on the bed, wondering how she would feel about it, if it turned out to be true.

The back door slammed, and she knew Roger had left with it. The thing was probably wrapped up in that heavy canvas newspaper bag.

When he came to the pond, he looked out and saw that the ice ended about forty yards away. No one was about.

He felt the soft little bulge in the newspaper bag, and then took hold of the straps and began to swing it back and forth. It was like a giant sling, and he realized that with a reasonably good throw he could hit the ice near enough the open water so that the newspaper bag, helped by the weight of the kitten, would probably slide into the water.

He slipped a little, and realized that he was half drunk. Then he laughed and began to swing the bag around and around, until it felt good, and he let it sail out over the ice.

It hit almost where he'd hoped, and slid swiftly towards the open water, and finally in. It floated briefly, like a huge, crumpled bird; and shortly before it eased under the water, Roger saw the kitten's head appear next to the ice. Then its front legs were up on the ice, and it appeared to remain there, poised and patient, as if waiting for him to come out.

"Nothing doing, little pussy," he said. "Nothing doing."

Then he turned and walked away.

"You should have made sure," she said.

"Shut up."

"Or at least you shouldn't have told me about it. You know how things like that eat at me."

"Everything eats at you," he said.

"That isn't true. But things like that do."

"You said get rid of it."

"I know, but I meant give it to somebody or something."

"You did not."

"I did too. How can you say what I meant?"

"I just can, that's all."

She had dropped the magazine she was reading on the floor. Now she sat there thinking of the kitten, and trying to picture it in the freezing water, poised, with its front legs on the lip of ice. She could see its eyes opened brightly, and its cold wet hair plastered against its small head.

Now would be the time to tell him. She tried to assess all that would happen if she told him now.

"Roger," she said.

"Yes?"

"You know something? I think maybe I'm pregnant."

"What?"

"I said, I think I'm pregnant."

"Are you sure?"

"I don't know. I feel that way."

"How do you know? You've never had a baby."

"No, but I feel differently, somehow."

"Well," he said. "Well."

"I knew you'd be delighted," she said. But, as always, her sarcasm didn't come off.

That night, she heard a cat meowing somewhere out in the darkness, and she asked Roger to go down and see what it was.

"Go yourself," he mumbled, burying his face in the pillow.

"I'm afraid," she said. "Please go. *Please!*"

"Not a chance," he said.

"Could it have found its way back here?"

"No," he said. "I don't think so."

"It'll drive me crazy," she said. "I can't stand to hear it crying."

"Look," Roger said, "It lives in *its* world, you live in *yours*. So why don't you just lie there and shut up and grow your baby like a good girl."

She was silent for a few minutes, and then she said, "It's *our* baby, Roger."

He surprised her by answering, "I should hope so."

Then the cat stopped crying, and she lay there wondering what sense she could make out of these two events: the kitten dead—drowned or frozen in the pond (or was it?)—and the baby growing in her stomach.

She was going to wake Roger up and tell him that their baby might, at this moment, be the size of a kitten. And it would be snug and warm, and not even remotely aware of the terror and confusion and simple meaninglessness of the world outside her belly.

But he was probably asleep again. And still cross, and worried about money, and disgusted with his classes . . . and she didn't know what all.

She wondered what would happen to them, and what their baby would be like. And how, beyond all the obvious maternal compulsions, she would *really* feel about the baby.

Almost as if he heard her thoughts, Roger mumbled something like, "It's all right now."

"What is?" she asked him.

He lifted his head from the pillow and said in a voice that was muddy with sleep and resentfulness, "The kitten. One way or the other. Look, there are some things you never really know about, and I wish for God's sake you would learn to accept that."

She settled down once more in her covers, and half-brooded and half-dreamed about his words.

The shadow of something big and incomprehensible had passed over them, but she wasn't sure what it was. The kitten was gone, whatever had happened to it. And the baby was growing deep in her belly.

Things come and things are taken away.

Beside her, Roger began to snore—angrily and tensely, as if he were about to bite the pillow and tear it with his teeth.

The kitten clambered up to the edge of her dream, and clung there, poised and helpless. Its face like a Rorschach, its eyes like those of a hawk . . . its needle-sharp claws gripping the ice as if it had been a pant leg, or human flesh.

THE PILGRIMAGE

Even though it was only ten o'clock in the morning, the temperature had climbed above ninety. The glare was so bad at the Texaco station that the attendants were wearing sunglasses and moving about with their heads held high and stiff, like men trying to resist fatigue.

A pale and tired-looking old man and his wife sat in the front seat of a Buick sedan, with the windows rolled up, and the air conditioner on. The man was smoking a cigarette as he watched the attendants at the Texaco station.

"This is the last cigarette I'll smoke here," he said, stubbing it out in the ashtray.

"I think that's a good idea," his wife said. She hardly opened her mouth as she spoke and she didn't turn her head. She wasn't watching the filling station attendants. She was looking past the filling station at nothing. One of her hands played with a button on her skirt, twisting it first in one direction and then in another.

"Isn't he supposed to be here by now?" she asked.

"In a few minutes."

"Are you sure you don't want me to come with you?"

"Positive, Elsie. Now don't start fussing."

"Well, I'm sorry. Only. . . ."

"You just don't understand," her husband said, reaching for another cigarette and then stopping the movement as he remembered his resolution. But his wife didn't notice anything.

"No, I don't understand," she said. Then she sighed deeply. She was suddenly aware that she was sitting with one shoulder higher than the other, the way old people do. And she didn't care . . . didn't bother to move, and she guessed that was still another sign of old age. Sometimes she sat like something thrown down, and she just didn't have the energy or the volition to adjust the weight of her body more comfortably.

"All right," her husband said. She saw his hands tense at the top of the steering wheel, where he had been holding them together. "Just say I'm crazy, then. But it's what I'm going to do."

"I'm not trying to stop you, Bill," she said. "I haven't said one word against it. Now have I?"

"No. Not exactly."

"Not in any way," she said, shaking her head back and forth as if to convince the distance. "At least, I'm glad nobody has recognized you."

"After what . . . fifty-eight years? Who would recognize me?"

"Why, you've been here more recently than that," she said, turning her head to look at his profile.

"Only on quick visits. An afternoon, or maybe overnight. But it's not the same, Elsie."

"Nothing's the same," she said.

Her husband was going to ask her what she meant by that, but he decided not to. For one thing, he was too tired and weak. Maybe from having to overcome the spirit of his wife's skepticism and incomprehension.

"Promise you'll let him drive," she said a few minutes later.

"I've already promised that," he said. "I don't want to drive."

"I just hope it's worth it."

"It can't hurt anything. The doctors haven't done much good, have they?"

"Do you suppose he's a careful driver?" she asked, starting to twist the button on her skirt even harder.

Her husband took a deep breath and stared at her, trying to control a feeling of irritation. "Don't worry about me," he said. "Will you be all right in the motel?"

"Of course I will. But do you suppose he's a good driver? Some of those roads in the hills just scare me to death."

"Forget it," her husband said. "Here he comes now."

The two of them watched a man dressed in a green work shirt and trousers approach the car. He was about fifty years old. He had a sun-burned face and bulging eyes.

Mr. Fisher pressed the window button and held his hand out. "Are you Clyde Washburn?" he asked.

"Right," the man said. "You're Mr. Fisher?"

Bill Fisher nodded and said, "And this is my wife. Come on and get in. You can drive past the Twenty Winks Motel and let Mrs. Fisher out. She isn't going with us."

"Sure," Clyde Washburn said. He edged behind the steering wheel and Mr. Fisher pulled himself slowly over toward his wife. He heard her say, "Oh, dear, I pulled this button off my skirt; I knew that would happen."

But he didn't pay much attention to her fussing because he was thinking ahead.

After they let her off at the motel, the two men drove silently along the highway and then turned off on a bumpy gravel road that crossed a flat field and then disappeared in the trees that flanked the first hill.

"Does this all look familiar to you, Mr. Fisher?" Clyde asked.

"In some ways," the older man said. He crossed his legs and folded his hands in his lap and he watched the trees and weed-smothered fences rock silently by. The whirr of the air-conditioner felt a little chilly on him, but he didn't adjust it. There was something else, something beyond and behind that needed all his attention.

Whatever it was, it wouldn't be possible with talk. In the way he had just now answered the man he had hired to drive, he had made it clear that he wanted silence. And poor Elsie . . . her bewilderment had been as apparent as a sound or an odor. Even now she was probably sitting in the motel room with the television going, filing her nails and worrying about him . . . and about this "pilgrimage," as he had once referred to it with gentle, self-directed irony.

Coming abruptly over a hill, Clyde Washburn pressed the brakes and Mr. Fisher put his hand against the dash board as his body eased forward. There was a big, rangy Holstein cow standing with her hind quarters on the road. Down in the gully below was her calf, mostly black, standing shoulder deep in thistles.

Clyde tapped his horn lightly as the car moved past, and then they started rising on the next hill. The road was almost choked off, here and there, by the thick undergrowth, but Clyde knew every dangerous turn and bend, and they progressed steadily until the woods began to thin out near the summit of the hill. Mr. Fisher felt the strangeness of it—the deep muted sense of both recognition and discovery that lies at the heart of time. His mouth eased open and he took a deep breath.

"Your ears pop?" Clyde asked.

"No. That usually happens only when I go down a hill fast."

"That's the way with me. If I go down fast, they pop like firecrackers."

"It should be right along here someplace."

"Right, if it was the next place beyond the old Hardaker farm. In fact. . . ." Clyde leaned forward over the steering wheel and narrowed his eyes. "In fact, there's the fence line right up there. You can still see it. And that field beyond has been state land for twenty years or more."

"But at one time, it was ours," Mr. Fisher said, reaching for a cigarette, remembering, and then just patting his pocket.

Clyde pulled the car well off the road, up into what had once been a wagon track leading into the field. Mr. Fisher eased the door open and felt the hot air, insect noises and sour grass smells slap against his face . . . indistinguishably one, as if all sensations had melted into a single, palpable substance.

Clyde handed him his cane, and then held his arm as Mr. Fisher paced slowly up through the old gate area, into a field of thick weeds and saplings.

"It looks like something's been grazing here," Mr. Fisher said a few minutes later, when they stopped.

"Goats," Clyde said. "There was an old Swiss who raised goats here years ago, and some of them went wild. They're as wild as deer, now. You can't even get close enough to shoot. *Wilder* than deer, as a matter of fact."

"Strange," Mr. Fisher said. He was standing now with both hands on the cane, his head thrust forward as if he were trying to hear distant footsteps in the grass.

"Is this far enough, Mr. Fisher?"

The sick man swallowed and seemed to listen to the silence for the duration of two heart beats, and then he nodded. "Yes. This is far enough, thanks. I can make it from here. Why don't you go back to the car and wait. I don't know how long I'll be. I might be a long time."

"All right. If you need any help, just call out. I'll hear you."

"No. You close the window and keep the air conditioning going. I don't want to think of you sitting there listening for me. I'll be all right."

"Whatever you say," Clyde Washburn said. He stepped back and wiped a gray wet handkerchief across his forehead. Then he started walking toward the car.

Eventually, the sound of his footsteps ceased, and a few seconds later Mr. Fisher heard the heavy, solid sound of the door closing. He just stood there for a while, looking around and listening. Somewhere up on the hickory ridge, a blue jay was squalling. But his racket merely seemed to italicize the deep, warm silence of the land.

Mr. Fisher started to walk forward, leaning heavily on his cane and turning his head this way and that. These trees and shrubs that surrounded him now were younger than he—had not even existed in that time long ago when, as a boy, he had made hay on this crooked, steeply-gabled hill, driving the mules to each hay row, and then getting off to pitch the hay onto the wagon.

After several minutes of walking, Mr. Fisher stopped to catch his breath and get his bearings. By now, he should be able to turn to the left and see the huge old beech tree that stood by the spring. Maybe it was still there.

And indeed, after he had walked a few steps, he could see the top of the old tree jutting far above the tops of the scrub elm and honey locusts that had sprung up all over the meadow. There was a strange and sudden sadness in seeing that old tree. Perhaps it was because he had prepared himself to believe that it had died years ago, and now that it still stood it was as old for a tree as he was for a man . . . and death waited for both of them, alike. As if the tree had been waiting, too, for some such moment of ceremonial recognition as this.

But of course this was silly, fanciful. And at any rate, it wasn't the tree itself, but rather the spring from whose depths the roots of the tree had drawn life over this half-century of waiting and survival.

Mr. Fisher stepped carefully over some thistles, tangled like green starfish in the sod, searching warily for copperheads. When he looked up once more, he saw the glossy dark ferns that bordered the spring. And when he took one more step, he heard a deep gulp of water as a frog dropped into the spring and plummeted toward the cold leaves at the bottom. Still, there was the little rill of water that curled smoothly and subtly down over the rocks, past the massive roots of the beech tree, and then slipped underground. Seeing such a rivulet as this, he understood how ancient men could attribute femininity to streams and rivers . . . as well as sweetness and guile, mystery and the forgotten melodies of a dream.

Slowly, Mr. Fisher knelt to the ground, smelling the cool mint leaves that flourished about the pool of water before him. With one hand, he dusted aside some cobwebs that lay in a delicate, transparent canopy a foot above the water. A gnat fell upon the surface of the spring, scarcely trembling the water's soft skin. And as he leaned forward to drink, Mr. Fisher saw his mirrored image turning toward him . . . as if in acceptance and recognition. He looked, he thought afterwards, like a man leaning over to pray, not to drink water from a spring.

"And was that all?" she asked, a look of concern on her face. "You just drank from that spring you've remembered all these years, and nothing else?"

"Practically nothing," Mr. Fisher said. The two of them were sitting by the window of their room in the Twenty Winks Motel. Mr. Fisher reached up and pulled the cord to open the venetian blinds.

"I can't understand," his wife said. "Can't you tell me what you thought about?"

"It was something I've been thinking of for a long time . . . going up to that spring. It had been so long since I had worked in that field, and so long since I had drunk from the spring, that I wasn't even sure they were there at all. I mean, it seemed unreal, like a dream instead of a memory."

"But coming down here in your condition, all these miles, and spending money for a motel and restaurants . . ."

"Please," Mr. Fisher said. "Don't talk like that. You don't understand. What is there that's more important than that spring—so cold and clear and . . . well, part of what I remember from fifty-eight years ago?"

"I can understand that it is a lovely spring and that it reminds you of your boyhood. I can understand that the water is cold and pure, and that anyone would enjoy drinking from it. But there's something else. And that's what I don't understand."

"Well, maybe I can't explain it."

"Maybe not. I don't want to worry you. I know there are things that can't be explained. I suppose I should leave you alone." She got up and walked into the bedroom. Mr. Fisher heard her opening the drawer of the vanity, and then he heard the clatter of combs and brushes as she made preparations for fixing her hair.

She would find comfort in such a ritual. In another twenty minutes they would be getting in the car, turning on the air conditioning and driving downtown to the Maple Inn. And no one would recognize him, because they were all dead, or had moved away . . . or had quite simply forgotten.

Mr. Fisher breathed deeply and sat absolutely still in his chair as he thought of the afternoon. He remembered the way in which Clyde Washburn had kept his silence, refraining from making any comment about a sick old man's pilgrimage to a spring he had drunk from half a century before. After all, he was being paid for his day's work, and it shouldn't have mattered to him what crazy things the old man did. But of course he couldn't help wondering. And on the drive back to the motel, he had said, "Sometimes these old springs have good water. I mean, a lot of minerals in them that are good for the body."

Mr. Fisher was willing to have him understand it in that way, so he nodded his head and said, "Yes, they're good for the system."

Clyde Washburn nodded vigorously. He was happy that there was a reason for the trip. The twenty dollar fee he'd earned for the day was now rendered clear and comprehensible as profit, as money earned for time and work whose value was apparent and real.

It made Mr. Fisher feel better to see Clyde satisfied, and he said, "Yes, that water is better than anything you'll find in the big city."

"I never did like city water," Clyde said.

Then they had come to the highway, and a few minutes later Mr. Fisher had let the other man off at the Texaco station and started back toward the Twenty Winks Motel.

Even she had wanted to understand, but with all her old prejudices and reasons had come at the thing parabolically, much as Clyde Washburn had done. And not being able to understand what it was he could never have expressed, she had felt alienated, shut out.

But there it was. There were no explanations beyond the primal truth of his need, and the potency of this thirst and hunger that carried him through all the social difficulties of the approach, and saddened him to shut so many out of what was surely part of their own truth, too, if they could only have known.

Perhaps there was only one who could have understood. And that was the boy he had once been, fifty-eight years before, and to whom he had wanted so much to return on at least one day before the ultimate, deeper and uncompromising return. That boy needed and deserved this pilgrimage, this turning back to greet a truth that was once and for all rendered mute and ineffective.

Somewhere in the dark woods near the spring, he and that innocent lost child he had once been had passed each other. How could he have explained this to anyone?

WHO IS WHO, AND WHEN WILL WE BE REAL?

Like Lear, I am old and have three ripe daughters. I am a widower, also, and king of my domain. This domain happens to be a little over two acres of choice wooded land, four miles from a freeway, and thereby (oh bless us, Lord, in our confusion) only fifteen miles from a shopping center.

My daughters, my *girls*, are all married, and fixed with fat annuity programs from daddy, leaving my income and holdings adequate, comfortable, and—as much as one can say it of anything in this world—invulnerable. (Exit Lear.) Our once-modern redwood home hangs seemingly precariously on a semicliff, cantilevered against gravity and the faint epidermal twitching of a conservative old land fault. Eleven spacious rooms, and a pool I haven't bothered having filled since my wife died last year. She liked to doze in it, swaddled in a cozy pink and womblike waterseat. Off our rear deck, there is a long, intricate network of descending steps, also redwood, safely and solidly constructed with railings on both sides. These lead to a little dammed-up goldfish pond at the floor of our little valley, where our property terminates against the property of a man named Robert Childs Ridgeley.

My wife, Beanie, knew she was going to die and insisted upon recording her voice for me on tape. She claimed there was a lot she had always wanted to say to me (nobody else should know about it); she had *so much* to tell me; the tragedy would be in not getting everything said . . . all the secret, private things. And since I had just bought an excellent tape recorder, without knowing quite why, it now appeared I had a reason. *Had* had one, all along, without knowing.

When we both had to face up to the fact of her imminent death, I was too fogged with grief and crisis to think much of anything. I do, however, remember quite distinctly thinking that this suggestion of hers about *recording her voice*, for God's sake, was simply too much. This was going too far. It was lugubrious, horrible, maybe even sick. Beanie had always had this thing about coming up with offbeat ideas, but . . . I mean, she was absolutely, all her life long, irreverent and kind of brassy gutsy (in a purely feminine way, I assure you—that is what gave her bite); but I mean, what the hell.

She talked to me about it, the whole business (that's what she started calling it). She had once read a book about death, which claimed that death can be beautiful, because it was an essential part of life . . . which was beautiful. It was the *completion* of life, and Beanie had always had this almost neurotic passion to *finish* things, and thereby leave nothing undone.

"That's the way I want *you* to look at it," she said, patting my hand one evening. She had been speaking of the idea of completion. All I could do, if I remember right, was swallow and try to look understanding, casual, and wise—all at once.

No, that's not exactly true. I could also do something else—humor her. Or at least, do anything that was possible to help her get through this thing (that is, *get out of it* . . . but I couldn't think of it that way, then). So Beanie began "this business of" recording her voice.

I came down the stairs one morning, and she said, "Hi, there, Honey! Feeling chipper today?"

I said, sure, about as chipper as a mud turtle in a washing machine (that was an old folksy joke we had between us), and then I rounded the corner of the kitchen (you can hear all over the damned house, because the walls don't go all the way to the ceiling, and there's this one place when you come downstairs that anyone sitting at the breakfast table can speak in a normal voice, and you hear perfectly). Anyway, I rounded the corner, and there was Beanie, sitting at the kitchen table, a mug of hot coffee beside her, and the mike to the tape recorder in her hand.

Yes, this is the way it happened. She was sassy and smiling, awaiting my answer as if "this business" were no more than a silly little joke between us.

"How're the batteries?" I asked, feeling I had to think of something sensible to say, and she said, "Fine. I tested them first thing. I'm coming through loud and clear."

"That's swell," I said, pouring myself a mug of coffee. My voice was not picked up, I found out later. I was too far away.

Well, she recorded her views on current events and an occasional bit of gossip (yes, this was part of her; this too must be preserved). She read from a number of things that she claimed she had always loved. Some of them I hadn't even heard of: syrupy passages from Tony Won's *Scrapbook,* some of Edna St. Vincent Millay's poetry, and a couple of lyrics from Bob Dylan that our daughters had infected her with. Also, she recorded better poems, and some of these surprised me a little, they were so dark and troubling; you could hardly believe that Beanie would want to *read* them even, let alone *leave* them. (I realized then that the very act of recording evokes things that years of conversation and loving sympathy may not evoke; it was very strange.) She also recorded some recipes. After finishing one such session, she switched off the mike, laughed, and said in a pretty good imitation of me: "Now isn't this a bitch?"

I would have given anything if she'd had the mike turned on then. I mean, that was part of the "real Beanie"—the Beanie everyone knew and sort of marveled at. It was part of the sassiness, the irrepressible spirit.

But the irrepressible spirit was not enough. And after her tape collection got fat, and everything just sort of came to a pause—as if inscrutable elements were conspiring toward this moment—there came that chilly December morning when Beanie found out she couldn't get out of bed. She asked me to get the tape recorder and call the doctor. In that order.

And by God, I did.

Right after she left me the last time, I wasn't worth a damn. There must have been a hundred people—business associates, friends, relatives (no neighbors, because we're too insulated from one another in our two-acre lots)—who came by to pay their last respects. A lot of people wanted to take care of me—mother me, brother me, daughter me. One of life's little miracles, life being what it is today, is that every one of my own three daughters wanted to daughter me. And that, I think, is a rarity that is *so* rare, I don't even want to talk about it. (Exit daughters; banish all and any remaining thoughts of Lear.)

The fact is, after I had shooed them all out, letting them know I was by God a man and could still tie my shoelaces and get a glass of water for myself if I woke up at night . . . after they all left me in that fine big house I've been bragging about, I collapsed like an empty suit of clothes.

I don't mean I wanted company; just the opposite, because there's not a single person I would have called back to share with me what it was I knew I had to go through. Beanie had had her way (crazy as it was, with cheery smiles and dumb comments and tape recorder); and now, I had mine. There wasn't any other way for me to go through my place except *in my own way*.

I have only vague memories of what it was like, because it was all so gray and dimensionless and god-awful, for awhile. It was like some terrible cosmic drunk among strangers. Only, there weren't any strangers at all; even they would have been something, and would have afforded a comfort those closer to me could not have given. There was nobody. Mr. Nobody. Colonel Nobody. General Nobody. President Nobody. Uncle Nobody. Daddy Nobody. *That's* who it was. All of that *Him,* all of that *Nobody.*

The two of us would sit without speaking out there on my fine redwood deck early in the morning—sitting in our bathrobes, our naked ankles freezing from the cold dew, while the birds chirped and sang in all our flowering trees. And we'd look down in the valley behind and wonder by what roads we had traveled here. How had we found this place?

(I will tell you something: I was a child, once; a little boy.)

The powerful sweep of sad and majestic thoughts disarmed my realities. There would be times when I couldn't believe that there was a road some 140 feet in front of the house that would lead me—whenever I chose—to a highway, that would lead me to a shopping center, where . . . .

No. I stumbled around, dazed and mercifully anesthetized by her death. I awoke, made coffee, turned on the television, and—if the weather permitted—went out in back to stare at the trees, and the strange marbled configurations of clouds in the patient sky. Sometimes I would hold a book (*any* book) in my hand for comfort; but it seems that I seldom had the strength to open it and read.

Then one day I put her first tape on and listened guardedly as she said, "Hi there, Honey! Feeling chipper this morning?"

You might think I would start weeping or cry out at the sound of her voice (yes *I* might have thought so only months before), but this wasn't the case. Instead, I listened all the way through the tape. The fidelity was uncanny. Perfect. *This was Beanie's voice!* I mean, that voice was there as surely as I was sitting in a half-darkened room listening to it. A fact. Nothing but a single, solitary, God-blessed fact. Her voice. More alive than any image, any photograph, any movie film could have suggested. There. Total. Disembodied, and real. Liberated.

Her voice.

Now wasn't, I whispered to myself, *that a bitch!*

Well, of course, occasionally I drank too much. But what difference could it possibly make now? Most of my life had been lived with Beanie. What I was before, I can scarcely remember or imagine—a shadowy and ignorant boy, groping toward something, some forgotten ideal, that I could not possibly understand now.

And Beanie, perhaps with prophetic compassion, had not recorded any of her customary nagging against my drinking habits. So I would sit out there in back, high above those steps that dangled precariously down the hill (or cliff), breathing the cool fresh air. I would sit with a bourbon and ginger ale (a vulgarism I had cultivated years before), and puff on my pipe.

By now, I was hooked on Beanie's voice, so I would turn the tape recorder up loud and leave the sliding doors open. Then, out of the dark interior behind me, her voice would go on and on, speaking clearly and distinctly and naturally (for she learned this final art in her final days), while I would sit and think my thoughts. After a while, it pains me to admit, my thoughts were more-or-less detached from the sound of Beanie's voice. I realized that I had soon heard everything she had to say over and over, and the carefully worded phrases dropped out of the darkness into the air, as meaningless as snowflakes falling into an unfrozen lake.

Occasionally, the phone would ring, and I would go back into the house and answer it. It would prove to be an acquaintance or an insurance man or maybe my broker. I would listen to them all (voices chirping at me from something no bigger than a revolver) with a fading sense of reality. Sometimes during the conversation I would glance at the tape recorder just visible on the marble-topped cherry stand in the alcove, and consider that turned-off silence in relation to the present voice sawing at my ear. Which was real? What if I had been stricken with madness, and consigned to a world of comfortably disembodied voices coming out of small machines?

But this fantasy was always a brief one. I could look out my front door and watch cars moving past on the road, each one inhabited very tangibly by someone with problems and dreams and his own private illusions. And on Mondays and Thursdays, Whittaca Bass would visit and clean up the accumulated mess of my living.

I did not tell Whittaca Bass about my little secret; it was, after all, too personal. And there was something unnatural in the silence that prevailed on her cleaning days, and this something did not seem to me to be quite explainable by Beanie's death alone.

Whittaca herself was something of a mystery. She was a divorced black woman (by which I mean a woman with a rich brown complexion, several shades lighter than the cherry finish of that marble-top stand in the alcove). Her features were subtly blurred by a faint softness that seemed almost oriental, and gave to her face a masklike quality. This effect was intensified by my vague knowledge that Whittaca Bass had a dark history of serious mental illness, violence (she had intentionally set fire to her own house years before), superstition, and a brief fling at whoring when she'd been only fifteen years old.

This was information that trickled down to me through Beanie, of course; and had come bit by bit, precisely as we were learning to trust Whittaca. Now, I was even more curious about the woman who faithfully came to clean our house twice a week, and had always found a reason to leave any room I might enter, on the pretext that some other, more urgent chore awaited her somewhere else.

This might have been simple unobtrusiveness, however, or a feeling for privacy. I can see no particular reason why Whittaca Bass might have disliked me; she was always polite and reserved in our relations with one another; no, there had to be something else occupying her in that protective silence and industry she always displayed in my presence.

She had been much closer to Beanie, of course. Often, I had heard the two of them in another room, speaking in a soft and lazy duet on topics unknown. I think this fact gave me the impression that Whittaca and Beanie (in spite of their employer-employee relationship) had grown into some kind of elemental female intimacy that would forever be alien to the world of men I knew and understood. And as insignificant as it might appear, this fact gave me a secondary wry and wistful comfort, an insulating warmth around the little world we inhabited. Their friendship had been part of the grace of our life "back then."

After the death of Beanie, Whittaca returned dutifully to the house, slightly altered. It was as if she was now constrained to look at me as someone she had never really had to consider before. She was now working for someone else, and there was a polite but unmistakable silence between us, and that silence was not precisely the shape of Beanie's absence, but the shape of something that had never had to be formed until this time.

Whittaca's duties had never been rigidly prescribed. Always she came, did light housework (once a month a professional cleaning service sent three men to clean the house thoroughly, inside and out), and prepared lunch and cocktails before leaving. Sometimes she would come with a nephew to help in the catering, if we had a party. But all of this was now past. Or seemed to be. And for several weeks, twice a week, the two of us moved past each other and adjusted subtly to the new relationship.

Of course, I did not let Whittaca hear the tapes. Sometimes, however, I would play them quietly in my room, while Whittaca was working in another part of the house. At such moments, my pathetic comforts were compounded, almost as if these fragments added up to a simulacrum of my life before: Beanie's voice turned low, reciting all the old and by-now familiar passages; and the realization that in some distant room, Whittaca was dusting or sweeping or waxing the floor. I imagined I could feel the heat of her body in the house, along with faint reverberations from her casual but focused movements.

The notion came to me that in a way Whittaca might have been closer to Beanie than anyone else. Beanie's friends might have all been in some tacit female competition, and of course our daughters were from a different generation. But Whittaca and Beanie had spent all those lazy-sounding hours together in those other rooms, comfortably saying anything that came into their minds, and thereby—without knowing—expressing and revealing themselves more profoundly than they had ever intended or thought necessary.

Yes, this is the way I began to think of it. Undoubtedly, I was risking a sentimental and foolish—if harmless—error in my assumption. I knew very well, almost from the start, that I might be idealizing what were in reality bored and meandering conversations that did nothing more than help two indifferent women pass through hours of potentially greater boredom. And yet, nothing had ever required Beanie to stay in a room with Whittaca and help her, or work alongside her, or simply move about, talking. In fact, her presence undoubtedly slowed the black woman down in her work.

No, there was something here, something deep and possibly, in some obscure way, beautifully friendly. Beanie had never been all *that* much a talker; but with Whittaca, she changed. And in spite of our walls that stopped short of the ceilings, I had gotten sufficiently deaf in my cranky, incipient old age that I had never found out what it was, exactly, the two of them had talked about. Possibly, I had never really wondered until now, when it was obviously too late.

My curiosity about Whittaca Bass ripened. I decided to seek her out and talk with her about Beanie, and maybe find out something of how she felt, and what she knew. By now, I was convinced that she knew something I did not know.

I made my decision on a Monday evening, just after Whittaca left. I was sitting on the patio in back, halfway through my second bourbon and ginger ale, and already feeling a little tipsy. I could hear Robert Childs Ridgeley on the other side of the gulley that separated our lots, shooting his high-powered air rifle at tin cans he had tied from tree limbs down below. (Why did I remember his sonorous name? Because years before, Beanie and I had seen it in full splendor on his mailbox as we drove by, and ever since, Robert Childs Ridgeley had occupied a whimsical place of honor in our thoughts.)

Yes, I would talk with Whittaca on Thursday, when she came. Definitely. I finished my drink precisely as Robert Childs Ridgeley's air rifle thwumped, evoking a flat ring from an invisible can.

It was odd that I had never once seen him, for his patio deck was hidden behind some evergreens.

Ah, but I knew he was there. I had heard him often.

Somehow, I conceived of him as a widower like myself (*but one who had gone before,* in that his wife had died earlier). I had the impression that he never thought of people at all, and never felt sorry for himself.

But Whittaca didn't come on Thursday.

I was surprised, for she very seldom missed work. At nine-thirty, when I finally realized that she really wasn't coming, I felt terribly frustrated, indignant. In fact, I had to fight what I told myself was surely a tendency to exaggerate the importance of my talking with her. And yet, the more I tried to resist, the more I realized how much I had looked forward to some sort of clarification that Whittaca Bass alone could afford.

At eleven o'clock, when I still hadn't heard from her, I looked up her number in the phone book. The young man who answered was obviously Claude, her nephew. I clearly recognized his voice from the times he'd helped in catering our parties. I told him who I was, but he didn't identify himself.

"I wondered if Whittaca's ill," I said. "She didn't come to work today."

"Yes," he said.

"What?"

"She's ill."

"She's ill?"

"Yes."

I paused, and then said, "Well, I certainly hope it's nothing serious."

No comment; at least, nothing audible to me in my growing deafness.

"I mean, do you suppose she'll come on Monday?"

"I couldn't say," Claude answered.

When I hung up, I decided to go out and do some shopping. Maybe drive around. I suddenly couldn't bear the thought of staying in the house alone.

She did not show up next Monday, either. Nor Thursday. Nor the Monday after that.

On each day missed, I phoned her house, and my call was answered every time by her taciturn nephew. He always picked up the receiver after the second or third ring, and I got the crazy impression that he had been sitting there waiting for my call . . . and that each time Whittaca was sitting there with him. I could visualize both of them in a dark, cluttered room, facing a telephone, knowing that I was about to call.

Of course, I tried to find out what was wrong, but I got only the vaguest answers. "Ill" was replaced with "not feeling well."

"Why?" I wanted to shout. *"What's wrong?"*

But of course, that was impossible.

On my second or third call, I had asked, "Is this her nephew? Is this you, Claude?"

There was a pause, and then Claude very distinctly said, "No."

Since they were obviously anticipating my call at precisely this time of day, I decided to phone at other times. And I did. Twice, the same voice answered; and another time, there was no answer at all.

When Whittaca didn't show up on the fourth Thursday, I realized that she had no intention of returning to work for me. Perhaps she really was ill. Perhaps she had suffered a recurrence of the old "mental trouble" she'd once been hospitalized for.

It was in response to such thoughts that I decided to go to her house and find out for myself what was wrong.

I had had enough. I couldn't wait any longer. I deserved an explanation of some kind.

This was on Friday morning.

I looked up her address on a city map, and saw that she lived in a large subdivision almost twenty miles away. I knew she had long ago left the house she had set fire to, and even the neighborhood. I was vaguely aware of this new section: remembered long low ranch houses that were cropping up everywhere ten years ago. And remembered that this section was pointed to proudly by the city administration that had in effect promoted it, as an example of enlightened racial integration.

In fact, it had been almost ten years since I had been in the area (Beanie had been with me), at which time I'd felt a certain depression from the sight of so much naked clay, weeds, and burnt-out sod around the new houses.

But on this Friday, I was pleased to see that the area had improved. There were some trees, and the yards were better tended, and most of the houses were well-painted and otherwise in good repair.

Whittaca deserves this, I remember thinking. She has pride.

And my sudden momentary pride in *her* pride gave me a lump in my throat. Which is maybe not so unexpected, when it is considered that this feeling of shared pride was somehow, mysteriously, connected with a deep sense that after all, Whittaca and I had something in common. We shared Beanie, and maybe even something that was larger than Beanie, even though she was at the center of whatever this might be. Also, Beanie and I had kept Whittaca on during all these years, even after the revelation of her mental troubles. We had *trusted* her.

I found Whittaca's address, and was confirmed in my sense of her. The house had been recently painted a liverish gray, with stylish white shutters. The yard was well-combed, neatly trimmed, and bordered along the driveway with petunias.

It was while walking up this driveway that I realized something: the amount we paid Whittaca, while substantial (and even rather handsome, if you thought of her as just "help"), could not really explain this residence. There was more here than I had a right to expect in terms of what I knew about her. This represented more pride than I could reasonably take pride in.

Never mind. My mission had nothing to do with sociology. It was personal. I reminded myself of this fact and pressed the doorbell almost defiantly.

I turned and gazed out upon the street as I waited. And suddenly I felt this sense of indelicacy, of imprudence, of arrogance in my being there. It was so strong, and I was so defenseless against it, that I would have left that instant if I hadn't already rung the doorbell.

As it was, however, I both felt and heard the door behind me open; and when I turned around, there was Claude staring at me out of an absolutely expressionless face.

Nor did he relent in any way when I stated my reason for coming. He did, however, tell me that Whittaca was "back in the hospital."

"Back?" I asked.

He looked ostentatiously past me and said, "It's something I can't talk about. Not at all."

"But surely . . ." I began. And then stopped and shrugged my shoulders.

Which gesture was apparently lost to Claude, for he was at that very instant slowly but firmly closing the door in my face.

Perhaps, I thought, both abandonments—Beanie's and now Whittaca's— were inexplicable. But this was too Jovian a view to contemplate seriously for long. Given the elemental importance, the tragedy, of Beanie's death . . . it was nevertheless in the nature of things. After all, isn't most of what we consider understanding simply a matter of expectability, and therefore conventional?

But why would Whittaca refuse to come back? Now, of all times. And if she was *truly* ill, if she had indeed suffered a relapse of mental illness, why had she avoided any communication with me during those first days, when Claude had clearly suggested, at least, that she was home?

No, it was not important to me. It could not be.

On Tuesday of the week after I had seen Claude shut the door in my face, I slept late, and then made a small pitcher of Bloody Mary's to drink with my breakfast, and ate slowly and with great leisure on the back deck.

Robert Childs Ridgeley was already thwumping away with his air rifle, and I found a strange and wistful comfort in the sound. At this moment I understood with perfect clarity that Robert Childs Ridgeley *was* a widower, as I was; but in this lucid moment I also knew (or *felt* I knew—but what difference could *this* make?) exactly what Robert Childs Ridgeley looked like, and how old he was. He looked a little like Robert Young, only heavier and grayer and not as handsome; he held one shoulder higher than the other when he walked (and of course when he sat on his deck, pumping his air rifle up); and he weighed exactly 187 pounds. He had a bald spot in the back of his head, of course; and suffered from slight but chronic indigestion, and mild nightmares. Oh, yes: at that moment I understood all of this perfectly well; it is only now, in retrospect, that I entertain a slight doubt in honor of my sophistication and sanity.

After my late breakfast, I filled my pipe and sat and smoked. It was a fine day, I think. The angle of the sun was such that only the toes of my white sneakers reached comfortably into the hot band of sunlight that lay burning on the deck.

A fine day, surely, with busy and silent hummingbirds feasting on the flower borders beside the deck. (By now, all birds are silent; their songs have been the first to go.) Idly, after several minutes of smoking and contemplation, I decided to turn Beanie's voice on, so I fetched a cassette from the house. This was the one that had upon it a poem that Beanie had written in college, almost two generations before. Of course, I knew it by heart, and by now almost felt, rather than heard, the opening words:

> What do we see when we see each other?
> Is it always rehearsal time in the heart?
> I see my father, you see your mother,
> Still trying out for the same old part.
> Who is who, and when will we be real,
> And know our loved ones like a coin

The hand has learned to know by feel,
Instead of the same old lying human sign?

It was while I listened to Beanie's voice repeating this verse that I had my revelation. It was suddenly all perfectly clear to me: on those days when Whittaca had come to clean and I had retired to my room to listen in private to Beanie's voice, *Whittaca had heard!*

Of course! I should have realized it before this. At some time Whittaca must have come close enough to my room to hear that voice speaking to me behind the closed door. Because that voice would have to be audible to someone of normal hearing—even beyond a closed door—for me to hear it at all inside my thickening cocoon of deafness.

And this discovery brought with it the suspicion that Whittaca's relapse might well have been caused by her hearing the dead woman's voice. For not only would it have been a voice from the past in the obvious sense, but in that darker sense that once more the old madness and superstition had visited her . . . this time, insidiously, in a voice that she had learned to trust and perhaps even love.

During the next two days, my phone calls to Whittaca's house received no answer. Perhaps Claude had moved. I enquired of the phone company. They knew nothing. I phoned all the psychiatric hospitals in the area, but none of them admitted to having a patient named Whittaca Bass. Several would not divulge the names of their patients, however. Eventually, I was so exasperated by one such answer that I candidly told the woman on the other end of the line that I had information that might well cure the patient I was seeking.

Perhaps you can imagine the silence that followed this statement. The woman quite obviously (and understandably) concluded that I myself had psychiatric problems. And our conversation ended in wariness and confusion.

Exasperated, I gave up for the moment; but I was determined to try again. There were several errands I had to attend to in the city that day, and after I finished them, I made a detour on my return, and passed the house where Whittaca and Claude lived. But the house seemed to be shut up; and the lawn was overgrown, and in fact the whole neighborhood seemed dispirited, shabby, decadent, and full of high weeds . . . reminding me somewhat of the neighborhood when Beanie and I had first visited it, years before.

The next morning, I was not feeling well. For possibly the third or fourth time since Beanie's death, I made a small pitcher of Bloody Mary's and drank it with my breakfast. A thin haze filled the sky, and there was a mild chill in the air as I sat comfortable, but half-drunk, on the back deck, and thought distantly of aphids and Whittaca and Life and Beanie and Death . . . and, yes, all the Four Last Things.

The sound of the mail truck passing in front interrupted my Jovian contemplations, so I gathered up the necessary energy, stuck the cold pipe in my mouth, and ambled around the house to make my way to the mailbox, stopping several times to look at the roses. (They had failed sadly, without Beanie's touch.)

In the mailbox I found several circulars, along with a small package, slightly larger than a five-pack of coronas.

"What in the hell's this?" I asked aloud, shaking it.

Then I shoved my still unlit pipe in my pocket and ambled back round the house, to my chair on the deck. I sat down and listened momentarily for the sound of Robert Childs Ridgeley. Silence.

Very well. To the package. I tore it open, and found what it now seems I might almost have guessed or half surmised I would find: a cassette. The same kind that Beanie had used. Also, there was the following note, printed with ball point, and unsigned, but obviously from Whittaca Bass:

> I hesitate over sending this because she asked me not to and even made me swear I would not do it. But after I heard you playing her voice in your room and trying to *spook* me in to thinking she had come back and that it was her own ghost talking I figure there is no reason under God I should not give you the same cruel treatment so here it is. What comfort I ask you could it give you playing that thing and trying to make me think it was her? Don't you know about the troubles I have had? Were you trying to make me kill myself? Or have them send me back here? If so *why?* Did you think she give me money or something? I admit for a while there it was spooky all right but then I knew what it was because I had one of my own which is the one I am sending to you. You will not like what you hear on it but it serves you right. And as for you having any part in my flipping out again I am going to tell you something you didn't have a God dam thing to do with it. I got other troubles you would not know *nothing* about in my life.

After reading the note, I sat there a long time, without moving. The neighborhood, it seemed to me, had gotten unnaturally quiet. Had I gone totally deaf, so that I couldn't ever hear Robert Childs Ridgeley's air rifle? Or had he died in his sleep? Or perhaps gone mad, and wandered away like a lost boy?

These are some of the things I thought about as I sat there; but all the time, the cassette was lying on the railing of the deck, waiting. On it, there was Beanie's voice, saying things I had never heard, things she had never wanted me to hear.

By the time I played it, I admit I was pretty drunk. I can remember only parts of what it said (of what *she* said), and it seems to me that it was probably every bit as bad as Whittaca had intimated.

The thing I have to make clear to myself, now, is that it is not true in any way that Beanie "hated" me. Not even that little bit that some people claim is the dark rim of love. Or at least, no *more* than that. Did she feel *confined* by me? Limited? Even trapped? Why, of course she did. How could this not be so? Always, I think, we know that there is this silent, inevitable little nay-saying deep down in even our most ardent, most committed, most living moments. The pity is, the tragedy is, that for Beanie this was apparently too much to stay down, to keep down, even during those last, swiftly diminishing days, and it had to be expressed.

What was the burden of her resentment, even "this little bit"? Oh, God bless us, it was of almost everything she herself had loved, doted on, perpetuated with all her spirit, *conspired in.* She had even, it seems, tired of that sweet dopey nickname toward the end of her life. She felt defined by it, as by all she had become. How could this be, when she ostentatiously reveled in it? She would phone a woman friend and say, "Hello, Marsha? This is Beanie. Listen, have you gotten those invitations out yet?"

Her Christian name was old-fashioned, comfortable, very feminine: Clarissa. On a dare, over forty years ago (for God's sake!), she wore a freshman beanie to the Golddigger's Prom in college. And from this spectacular rebellion in that time and place of rigid proprieties, she had gained her affectionate nickname, which had always signified to everyone, through all those subsequent years, her slam-bang courage and irrepressible spirit. But was it *my* fault she had lived so long with the label of that act?

The following words—almost verbatim, I think—stand out from that sleep-talking strangeness of her voice: "Whittaca, if you think of me now and then, I want you to think of me as a woman whose first name was 'Clarissa.' I don't for a minute suppose that anyone will waste much time thinking of me, because I am not important in any way . . . and *nobody* is really remembered for very long. But for a little bit, even if it's only a second or two once a year . . . you'll see my face or maybe hear my voice in your mind or maybe even on this cassette . . . you might think of me as someone nobody ever really bothered to understand, or *could* understand; and even her name was sort of a joke, most of her life. I'm sure it's this way with everybody, in some dimension of their lives; but then, I guess it doesn't hurt if one of us cries out against it for once, even if it doesn't make any difference, or even much sense."

There was much more. Beginning and ending each revelation, there was Beanie's insistence that she really did love me (her husband, *me*) . . . passionately; that she always had, and that I was the only one conceivable for her, but. . . . But that wasn't really the point . . . or perhaps, in another way, it precisely *was,* for she was imprisoned by all the right and happy things, as well as by the other.

And she spoke of those dark and insidious little resentments—some of which I had heard in our various (what we'd later refer to as "healthy") arguments and spats; but others which (like the business with her name) were astonishingly unexpected. Even my success, even my ostensible virtues, had their dimension of pain and frustration and distrust for this woman in the dark privacies of her mind. She had for years entertained furious dreams of secrets *I* kept from *her* (!) . . . of devious business dealings, of love trysts and more casual infidelities . . . all part of the familiar litany of hysterical wives, *but here saved for this last unanswerable secret revelation.*

The details blur impossibly. If there are things, notions, uglinesses, dishonorable inclinations that I cannot face in myself . . . and if this unwillingness to face them is, not cowardice, but is rather its near opposite, character . . . *if* these things are true, then it is true that I am now unwilling for Beanie to have betrayed herself so pathetically in her last defiant act.

Yes, she explained partially why she was compelled to make this private cassette for Whittaca (her shadow, her dream, her other, unrealized, unlived, trapped self): it was her typical old fear of *not finishing,* of leaving something incomplete, of not getting it all said. I imagine it possible that her final moments were filled with a strange sickly peace of composition, in which a great surge precedes and then finally reaches the tonic chord, saying This is Death. You've gotten it all said, all recorded. Finis.

But of course, *her* finished business is precisely that which for me can never be finished. We truly are strangers to each other, oh Lord! If we were not, what need would there be of Thee?

For example: did Beanie ever think that Whittaca was a safe repository for her secret? *Could* she have?

If not, then she was more or less knowingly speaking to me, too . . . which of course would itself have been necessary for any *real* completion. The Last Word, you might say . . . against which there is no rebuttal, no explanation, no riposte, no defense. And yet, it transpires by this alone, that such is not the case.

Once was enough. I burned the cassette, in a roar of redwood scraps, doused with drunken liberality in gasoline. The cassette is rightly advertised as nonflammable, but such claims are always relative.

And in this conflagration, I myself achieved something in the way of completion. I'm sure Robert Childs Ridgeley has gone through an experience similar to this. Whittaca is probably still working on it, without quite knowing who the antagonists really are, and what the rules and issues will prove to be. I wish them both well, but over a great distance.

As it is even with Beanie: she would have understood, and even respected me for it. As for Clarissa . . . well, that is part of the point in this testimony, and must ever remain (as they say) a mystery.

NO MORE BABIES

The afternoon sunlight lay heavily on the green blind, saturating it with its fire, rimming it with silver. Randa stood in the doorway, feeling the heat like something palpable in the room and wondering without pity how Claude could sleep on such a hot afternoon.

He tired from all that PROducin' and WHISkey, she told herself.

She walked slowly toward his bed, looking at his rigidly open mouth, the eyes nailed shut. He was in his tattered undershirt and drawers, his arms raised, showing the kinky hairs in a patch the size of a half dollar under his arms. The skin on his face and hands was the color of cocoa but on the rest of his body it was the color of creamed coffee. On his cheek was the perfect scar left by the removal of a mole, which had once stuck out from his face a quarter of an inch. The scar looked like a small flower . . . or the fossil left by a tiny sea animal in the shadowed fold of a stone.

He sleep like some men die, Randa said with satisfaction. All the way and with no nonsense like snorin' and tossin' about in the sheets.

Randa gathered up her skirt in her fist and knelt down. Her knees cracked loudly and she groaned, but Claude kept on sleeping without the least sign of agitation on his features.

When she was on her hands and knees, she reached into the pocket of her dress and withdrew a small piece of salt pork. She wiped the sweat off her forehead with the back of her hand and wet her lips with her tongue.

Then she recited:

> No more babies, no more care
> Don't want none from ANYwhere!

She put the piece of salt pork under the bed, trying to judge as near as possible the location of his head. She shuddered as she thought what would happen if she put it under the place where HER head would lie.

Don't want that pork a spoilin' and my brains a rottin' away with it! she murmured, closing one eye and adjusting the pork.

Lord knows what I'd do if it was ME lost her brains!

She got up and stood watching her husband for a moment, thinking that it was a blessing to her he didn't notice things.

His brains'll be gone before he can notice that there piece of salt pork rottin' underneath his damn old head, she said half-aloud.

She went down into the kitchen trying to remember all the other things old Auntie Kye had once told her about spells and other black magic.

What I do if that there piece of salt pork slides over under me? she wondered.

She closed her eyes and crossed her fingers, saying, Oh Lord! several times. She wet both of her index fingers with saliva and rubbed them on the back of her neck. She turned around three times in the kitchen.

And I'll look every night, before I get into bed, she said half-aloud. Pork cain't rot away in just one little old night!

She cooked a chicken stew for that evening. She saw two of her boys, Ransom and Jacob, walking slowly up the alley along about four o'clock, but she didn't call out to them for fear she might wake up Claude, who was sleeping his brains away if everything was going according to plan.

They'll put him in one of them backward shirts made out of canvas and take him away, she whispered as she plucked the chicken. She pictured two white men with military caps, looking like President Eisenhower, dragging Calude across the bare floor of her front room (she would re- move the torn braided rug before they came). Claude would be screaming and biting his tongue until the blood seeped out of the corners of his mouth and his eyes would be clamped shut and spitting tears.

After he left, Randa promised herself things. She'd right away sit down in the chair with her knees apart and smoke a cigarette. She'd sit there and dream for a half-hour. If any of her boys came in, they'd think she'd gone off into a kind of trance, because she wouldn't do anything but just sit and smoke and dream.

Maybe she'd recite the names of the babies she would now have if the last six pregnancies hadn't ended up in miscarriages.

Somethin' down in me don't WANT no more babies, she had told Claude. And Claude had thrown back his head and laughed like an alli- gator.

After the sixth miscarriage, Randa had thought about killing him some night with a knife. Or maybe just poisoning him. Only thing wrong with that was that the POLice would come and electrocute her in that big chair.

Can't you hold a baby 'til it's ready, woman? Claude had asked her once, his lips around a cold cigar.

She hadn't answered right away because something suddenly gave way in her head. It was like a big black ball of flies that had lifted up off the corpse of a dog once on a hot summer day when she had accidently kicked it in the long grass of the vacant lot next door.

The black, buzzing swarm lifted in her head, but it didn't escape. It lighted on the rafters there, somewhere, and almost every time she moved, Randa could hear the furious buzzing, the scratching of thousands of legs against mandibles, the shrilling of the wings.

She heard a streetcar gong on the next street. Back of her fence (broken and with many broad slats out, like a half-decaying mouth) was the alley and in the back of that was Mistuh Rogers's house. Mistuh Rogers had his radio going in the window, playing music, and he was pacing around in the long grass of his back yard with his overcoat on. A crazy man. His hands clasped behind him, stopping at every flower or weed to ask it some question (mouth around a stogie), skin as black and wrinkled as a prune, eyes like chipped yellow glass. Most likely a hundred years old. Maybe borned in slavery, his granddaughter liked to brag.

Now, Mistuh Rogers stood there with his overcoat hanging to his knees studying a little goldfinch on a twig. Only Randa, seeing his head up and stationary, faced toward her, behind the little cherry tree, felt a twitch of terror, thinking maybe he was looking at her right through her back window. Crazy people's got the power and the vision, she reminded herself.

Then the swarm of black flies left where they were eating in her head and rose and stung all about them, while Randa moaned and lifted her chin with her eyes closed.

You one sloppy goddam woman.

Claude's voice scattered her sensations like birds and she almost hiccoughed. She turned around, and there he was standing in his bare feet in the doorway, holding the salt pork in his hand.

I wake up and smell somethin' strong and I look under the bed and what do I see?

Randa shook her head.

I see this here piece of meat! That's what I see. Just how the hell do you suppose it get there?

He walked across the kitchen and threw it into the sink. Did he watch her as he walked? The flies were in a fury, striking the walls of her head like tiny pebbles kicked up by a speeding car.

Claude was silent. He picked up a newspaper and walked out onto the back steps, slamming the screen. She could hear his breathing, even after he sat down. She heard him rustle the newspaper, cracking it finally into the position he wanted. Then he called out to Mistuh Rogers, who was standing near the back fence, rubbing his wrinkled old hand over the boards.

It was evening and Claude had gone down the street to Verity Williams's house. He'd be drinkin' and whorin' and gamblin' (she shuffled them all together in her suspicious mind, not caring which came up first when she needed something to brood on). He'd be mean and muttering when she woke him up at three in the morning to go down to work in Angelo Durando's produce house.

Full of bootleg whiskey and greasy chicken from the Williams's back room, where Williams himself kept his three hundred pounds of lard stuck in a rocker and charged the hard-working men a nickel a hand for poker.

And he'd be four hours nearer crazy. Four hours sleep, four hours going crazy. Eight hours sleep, eight hours going crazy.

Randa went over the equations in her mind, licking her lips and wiping her hands on her skirt. Her new plan would mean a sacrifice. She wouldn't be able to sleep until they dragged him out the front door, screaming and kicking.

At dark, Randa got the same piece of salt pork Claude had thrown into the sink and went outside. The locusts and katydids sang and screeched and old Mistuh Rogers's radio was still on. She could see it, a small dark shape in a lighted window, and she wondered with a tremor of anxiety if the old man was still out wandering around in his overcoat, talking to the sleepy flowers.

She went around to the side of the house and got down on her hands and knees by the bedroom window. The grass and briars were thick about the edge of the house, but she forced herself through and into the crawl space under the house. She shifted her eyes warily, as if looking for rats, but she couldn't see a thing. Still, she turned her head back and forth, like a tomcat, as if she could sense the moment when a rat might come near.

Her palms and knees sank into the dust beneath the house. She hadn't imagined how silken and soft the ground could be. Suddenly, she drew back the hand with the salt pork in it. A deep pain curled around the palm to the back and she could feel blood going down into the creases of the flesh on her palm and the fingers. At first she almost moaned, for she thought that it had been a rat. But then she realized by the sharpness and length of the cut that it must have been the jagged edge of a broken jar she had put her hand on. Probably something Ransom or Paul or Jacob had thrown carelessly under the house.

She turned and tried to gauge exactly where she was by the dim light at the edge of the crawl space. Judging that their bed must be somewhere above, she dropped the pork after spitting on it and recited:

> Salt pork, rot and stink
> and make his brains so they cain't think.
> Salt pork, stink and rot
> Turn them brains into snot.

For a moment she stayed there, waiting to be sure everything was all right, and then she crawled out again.

Straightening up, she smelled the sweetness of the night air and listened with pleasure to old Mistuh Rogers's radio. It was like coming back from the land of the dead. Then she thought of her hand, still throbbing mightily, and she went into the kitchen and wrapped it up in the rags from one of Ransom's old shirts.

She had liked the music she heard on Mistuh Rogers's radio so she turned on her own radio and sought out the station. She turned it up loud and wiped the sweat from her forehead with the back of her bandaged hand. Through the screen door she could see moths circling the naked yellow bulb hanging from the small roof over the back porch. The flies in her head were quiet. They were feasting upon something dead . . . breeding sleepily. Maybe it was the salt pork that still lay in her mind, a valuable token of all the sunny, lazy days ahead, with no pregnancies, no miscarriages, no Claude to come lurching through the front door, blind drunk and muttering.

For perhaps an hour she sat at the kitchen table, her elbows planted firmly on the oil cloth cover, gently massaging pomade into her hair with her good hand. Six straight miscarriages. Something in me don't LIKE babies no more, she said aloud, time and again.

Then she looked in her kitchen mirror and ran her fingers through the tight, kinky hair above her ears, mumbling: White women WANT curls for their hair, and me, I wish I didn't have NONE.

Oh, how sickable life is, she said, seating herself again. How can a man like that Mistuh Rogers stay alive so long what with nothin' but the sun comin' up and goin' down? Him and his flowers he goes around talkin' to. Him and that overcoat in the middle of July. He say it keep him WARM! Everybody crazy.

She stared at the clock on the window sill above the sink and it said nine-thirty.

Ain't goin' be able to sleep NO time, she reminded herself.

In fact, thinking about it, she was afraid even to go into the bedroom. What would she say when Claude noticed she wasn't coming to bed? She was surprised he had noticed the salt pork that morning, and that was a fact.

She went into the front room and lay down on the rug. If Claude came in and saw her there, she'd say that it was the coolest place she could find. But maybe, with luck, she could get a couple of hours sleep and then wake up before Claude returned.

For the next two days, Claude was silent and morose. He ate his food with his head down and left the table immediately. When he went to bed in the afternoon, Randa would wait until she was sure he was asleep and then she would go and stand in the darkened doorway and watch him.

She hadn't felt well. Her hand had gotten big and heavy with blood and the throbbing was worse than ever. On the second day she had put mutton tallow over the cut, dabbing it in with her fingernail, but it hadn't helped anything. The flies in her head were restless. They tickled the insides of her brain and she wished that somehow she could get her good hand inside her head to scratch and scratch until everything stopped itching.

Claude had not even mentioned the bandage on her hand. He had not even noticed that Randa was not sleeping with him. He hadn't tried to touch her and Randa was suspicious about that. It had been six days in the summer when he knew she wasn't sick. Six days. Was there another miscarriage building up inside her? She moaned and sucked on her good fingers at the thought.

Outside, Mistuh Rogers was walking around what he called his "garden." Everything was dead and brown and dying there just as it was everywhere else. Still, the old man walked and smiled pleasantly at nothing at all. He was a happy old man. Maybe the slave days weren't so bad, compared to a life with six miscarriages in a row.

On the third morning, Randa stood in the kitchen and held her hand to her burning brow. The flies were bad, swaying from side to side in the slow move of their swarm. Her hand was hot and swollen, shiny as a knob with blood. Her legs were unsteady. Something surely was wrong.

Claude was at work. About noon he would come walking up on the front porch, smoking a cigarette or maybe a cigar, loose-jointed and cocky, his eyes half-open and a slight grin on his face. That's what she had liked in him when they first met—his devilish good looks and his don't-give-a-damn ways.

And why had he left her alone for seven days now? Seven days straight and he knew she wasn't sick.

When Claude went to bed that afternoon, Randa decided that she would have to do something else. The salt pork wasn't enough. She would have to cut off some of his hair and flush it down the toilet.

When the hair reached the river, Claude would go blind, staggering crazy. He would throw his hands up in the air, dance when there wasn't any music, vomit his soul up through his nostrils.

Randa grinned and held onto the kitchen table as the flies left their roost and flew away, expanding and contracting, like an accordian dangling from one end. She couldn't find any scissors so she picked up a paring knife and went up to the bedroom.

Claude was sleeping on his stomach with his legs outstretched and his hands thrown up near his head. Randa could hear him breathing fast, as if the heat were pressing on him.

She walked up to the bed and reached out to one of the wiry clusters of hair above his ear. Gently, she started sawing it off with the paring knife.

Suddenly, Claude stopped breathing and she could feel his eyes open and roll around to the side of his head. Then, he slowly reached his hand up and closed his fingers around the wrist of the hand which held the paring knife. Claude looked at the knife so closely that his eyes were almost crossed. Then his eyes loosened and he was staring at her.

You think I don't know what this means? Claude asked in a flat voice.

She was unclear about things after that. Actually, nothing happened, but she was unclear about just how she got out of the room. Claude was sitting there holding the knife, not saying any more. And there was a kind of sleepy scowl on his face. She said something about not getting pregnant again.

Then she was downstairs and great pulses of nausea were coming up into her stomach and head and she was wondering if she might not be pregnant after all, but then she realized that this was something different.

And then Auntie Kye was on the other side of the screen door . . . a woman as small and hunched as a monkey, who had been dead for twenty years. Mistuh Rogers was walking around in the front room, smelling a dandelion and saying something about people not enjoying the little things in life. And while she was lying on her back on the floor of the kitchen, her three boys came running in and each one of them stepped on her, pinching the flesh of her thighs, her stomach, her breasts with their heavy shoes and scuffing on into the front room.

Oh, why didn't that salt pork WORK? she groaned.

Then, in a quiet moment, still lying on her back, she understood that it HAD worked. She wouldn't have realized it, except for the fact that her hand started hurting and burning as if she had suddenly plunged it into the chicken scalding water.

That salt pork had worked and it had her blood on it!

All that time it had been lying there, rotting in the soft dust under the house, it had been working on her blood, not on that happy, mean, uncaring head that slept above it!

And here she had been pacing the house without sleep, with a bad cut that seemed to be filling her with poison, while Claude had been miles away in his head, thinking of other things . . . other WOMEN more than likely.

Randa picked herself slowly up off the floor and crawled through the screen door and sat for awhile on the backsteps, in the sunlight . . . letting the heat boil away her sickness and the crazy feeling in her mind, while the flies buzzed and buzzed and looked out of the dirty windows of her head at the glassy yellow and green of the world, where Mistuh Rogers spoke to flowers and wore his overcoat on the hottest days.

She stood up and managed two drunken steps before she fell in the dirt at the side of the house, shoving the heels of her hands into the ground and feeling the jolt in her shoulders and breasts as if a man had beaten her all over with his fists.

But her hand hadn't hurt one bit when she fell. It was numb before her, as comfortable as if it had been a hammer she was holding . . . only, of course, this was the whole arm that jutted out before her like the dusty cherry leg of an expensive piece of furniture.

Finally, she crawled to the bedroom window and, separating the grass and briars at the edge of the house, she peered into the crawl space.

A strange dim land lay before her: a land of small animal tracks in the dust, tin cans and shattered bottles, filmed with a powdery dust, and an old hip boot that lay over a cement block as if the broken leg of a man might still be inside.

She shoved her body forward and miscalculated to the extent that she banged her head on the house. A white light streaked in front of her and a high ringing noise blotted out the faint sound of birds and Mistuh Rogers's radio, which had been playing far off in the fuzzy distance.

Crawling forward slowly, Randa's forearms gave way and she slid chin first into the dust. She tottered to her hands and knees and looked around her for the salt pork, muttering:

> I'll get that pork sometime today
> and from the insane asylum I'll stay AWAY!

Then she saw it, curled on the ground and part of it stained brown from her blood. She saw brown spots all around it from her bleeding hand.

Suddenly, she seemed to be seeing things through thick glasses and she couldn't find the pork. Panic came up inside her. This time, it was not flies, but sparrows that beat at the rafters in her head, wanting to escape.

Somethin' inside me just don't WANT no more babies, she heard her voice say. She thought she might be in the waiting room of the hospital, her stomach mountainous and white nurses and doctors leaning over her, their faces looking like lard . . . cold, unfeeling, inhuman.

I want a colored doctor, she moaned. I want Dr. Jones!

Then rats were running across her belly and flies were once more in her mind, and she felt almost cozy with their familiarity.

Certainly, the salt pork was there, among broken glass, and it had to be lurched for. Randa lurched and her arms gave way and once more she felt her skin split open on glass. She felt the air enter into her arteries and it felt cool . . . even on so hot a day, in such a place.

The blood spurted before her eyes in a fountain a foot high and she wondered which arm it was that had been cut.

But before she could leave, she must find the salt pork and burn it up. Otherwise, they would drag her over her own rug, across the floor in that white canvas coat without sleeves, her screaming and biting her tongue and cursing at how strange things were in a world that was just naturally upside down.

THE LAST ABANDONMENT

"I'm going to fatten you up," she'd cried. "I'm going to put some meat on those bones!" At odd moments, her words came back to him, riding edgily on a voice that any man would have to admit was not attractive, not calculated to contribute to that essential restfulness that is what a man after all (he understood this now)—beyond all the turmoils and confusions of sex—wants from a woman.

Her voice wasn't something that swam to the murky surface of his mind when he was idle or at peace in the hammock on the back porch of the cabin. At such times, he might hear the voice of Tillie, his dead wife, saying something like, "Hal, don't forget your diet," or "Hal, don't strain yourself lifting that; you be careful!" (Of course, it had been a long time since he'd tried to lift anything heavier than a pair of shoes or a half-gallon carton of skimmed milk.)

No, it wasn't at such quiet times that he heard *her* voice, but in sudden tangles of crisis or tension: hearing a car horn blare from behind when he was caught napping at the wheel under a traffic light, or turning the corner on the gravel walk as he walked down the steep path to the lake, and hearing the pounding of footsteps behind him as the Larimer boys raced toward the canoe and passed him in a hot flush of air.

Then he would hear: *"I'm going to fatten you up!"* And momentarily Sylvia Kate Dunham's face would float like a balloon in the air, past his mind's eye, and one of Sylvia Kate's eyes would wink at him, as if it—though only imaginary—saw more, and knew more, than he saw or knew.

"Aren't you the *funniest* little old thing," Sylvia Kate had said the first time they'd met. But no, that was later. Maybe the third or fourth time. Sylvia Kate had been dressed in her spotted bikini (Hardly big enough to have spots *on* it, old Mrs. Cosgrove had murmured between scarcely-parted lips), and she'd been sitting in the big bucket chair on the big sun porch of the lounge when she'd said it.

His foot had slipped in the shower stall, and this is when it had all come back to him. (This memory, this time.) Most reality was made up of memories, now, even things that had just happened—Good God, they might as well have all happened forty years ago!

By the time his heart had stopped lurching (he might have fallen and broken his hip or elbow), Sylvia Kate's ghostly, remembered head had joined him, and her voice was cranking out that somehow-obscene utterance; and he was trying to remember when and where she had said it.

Then it was that he remembered: it had been on the sun porch of the lounge, and Sylvia Kate had been sitting in that bucket chair with her pretty knees sticking up higher than her heavy, plump, rounded hips, and her bleached hair white as a wedding cake, and her deep gray eyes as perfect as the inside of seashells, smooth and (like them) echoing of inhuman depths.

If it had been only the voice, it wouldn't have mattered. He could have coped with that, easily; a man doesn't collect all those years without learning *something*, he'd said. (But inside his mind, at this very moment, Sylvia Kate's head had been turned, talking to Mrs. Stillwell.)

No, that wasn't it. That voice would have sunk just about any woman's chances, but the first glance at Sylvia Kate was enough to tell you that she could have croaked like a frog or grunted like a pig and it wouldn't have made any difference. Because she was *just plain damned too much;* she was just so plain damned beautiful, it sort of hit you in the pit of the stomach, so that you were a little bit sick and thought of turning your head away so you could throw up.

And she wasn't just beautiful, she was overwhelming. She was tall, rawboned, with a stride that made you want to harness her to a sulkey. Broad-shouldered, heavy-breasted, and with a rounded bottom that a man could hug with both arms and close his eyes and whisper, "Thank you, God, for making this!" Yes, looking at Sylvia Kate, you would forgive her any kind of voice; she might have cawed like a crow or whooped like a baboon with pink sideburns . . . and you could forgive that voice saying anything . . . or (he told himself, plunking his teeth in the plastic water glass and staring at them) *almost* anything.

Why had she fastened on him? Did she guess he was lonely? Did she sense he had money? (Of course, you damned old fool, he told himself—and then forgot.) Could she perceive in his poor blasted old features the lineaments of a once-commanding and quite handsome profile? (Go back to the money, the voice inside his mind said—and he forgot again.)

And what was he doing here at the Pine Bluff Lodge (seventy dollars a day and smiling attentive help) when he knew that any time he stuck his old hawk-nose outside he'd be risking trouble. Better stay away from the world (he said, and listened), because it is out to get you sooner or later. But it was a little hard to think of Pine Bluff Lodge as the world . . .

or at least it had been, until Sylvia Kate Dunham appeared. Which somehow turned it into *more* than the world . . into Heaven or Hell, either
one (he didn't know which) . . . but, he knew with a certainty that came
from someplace deeper than her heartbeat, *one or the other*.

"What are you doing here, Mr. Sibley?" one of them asked. "Just
taking a vacation? Taking it easy?"

He wasn't sure which one it was. One was named Treskell and the other
was named Chambers. (Last names; he didn't know their first, and didn't
care. Whichever one it was, this was the fat one.)

"I'm recovering from an illness," Howard Sibley answered. He started
to say more, but then stopped. Instead, he looked out upon the lake,
forgetting Treskell or Chambers, whichever one it was, and thinking: my
granddaddy farmed land that is now somewhere at the bottom of that
lake; if we could bring granddaddy back, he wouldn't know his land any
more than if it was an alley on the moon.

"I hope you're feeling better," Treskell or Chambers said, touching the
tips of his fingers together and sounding like he might be going to lead
somebody in a prayer.

God, it had changed! Not just the land turned into water, but all the
old ways, the people, the air blowing through the pines. He thought of
the old song:

> In the pines, in the pines
> Where the sun never shines,
> In the pines where the cold wind blows.

But to save his life, he couldn't think of the melody. His dead wife,
Tillie, would have remembered it. If he'd mentioned it, Tillie would have
sung the music, as sure as spit hits the ground.

"You're all from this part of the country, aren't you?" Mr. Treskell
said politely. (Yes, it was Treskell; Chambers was the little bald skinny
one who wore fancy shirts open all the way down to his belt buckle.)

"I was born and raised near here," Howard Sibley told him, nodding at
the lake. He almost said, "Sixty feet under water about two miles north
of here," but that would have made Treskell start asking questions all
over, like a barrel springing leaks. Sibley sneaked a glance at him, and saw
the fat young man leaning far back in his chair, rubbing his hands idly.
He was staring at the water, too, not realizing that he was practically
looking at the old Sibley place right then.

"It all goes down the drain," Sibley said, and when Treskell said,
"What? What?" he could have kicked himself for a damned fool, because
now there'd be no stopping him. Treskell's eyes were too close together
and he had a big mustache underneath a snub nose and had sort of bangs
over his forehead. As if that wasn't enough, he had huge soft, fat, hairy

arms and a sort of sissy voice. Briefly, he wondered if Chambers and Treskell were, you know, but then he dismissed the question from his mind as being deficient in interest.

And yet, he'd known Treskell's type way back before he'd gone North to make his fortune, turning his back on the land and people of his heritage. (He'd never felt guilty about it, but sometimes a little uneasy.) There was a type of sissy produced by the fierce old culture-maddened women and the Bible schools that Northerners had trouble understanding, especially when these sissies could upon rare occasions surprise you—cope with a lot more than you'd expect, and maybe even prove stalwart or vicious (depending, of course) when all the cards were on the table.

Then, too, there was that type of aggressive Southern woman, volted with charm and cunning, whose thoughts in a one-day period could provide a battalion of psychologists with enough enigmas for a year of study.

Tillie certainly had not been one of these. Tillie had been a pretty, bright, lovable, strong-spirited woman from Milwaukee, whom Hal (he'd become "Hal" six months after leaving the old plantation) Sibley had met when he was just starting to do pretty damned well by trading in commodities, which an acquaintance had once said is a little bit like trying to land Hereford steers with a fly rod. But that faintly offbeat simile notwithstanding, Howard ("Hal") Sibley had, by God, made good at it, and when his wife had died seven years ago, he'd been worth something like $800,000 . . . even after a few spectacular losses in which the steers had smashed line, rod, and tackle.

When you get old, what happens is you make a lot of connections you didn't make as a younger person. Some people think that old people don't *make* connections, but this is wrong. They make too many; they are embarrassed by a richness of connections; connections, with the elderly, are too common to be respected, therefore they are treated with contempt, and sometimes (as is natural) forgotten or ignored. The connections you had made when you were younger no longer have quite the same authority they had then. The arbitrary character of most human meanings has finally sunken in, and you are not as gullible (i.e., *interested*) as you once were. At least, this is one way of looking at it.

Also, the connections that do remain are changed; the relations they form are altered. The lofty perspectives of time afforded by a long life see to this, so that recent events often rub shoulders presumptuously with those of long ago, and an old man may gaze upon a young girl who reminds him of a high school sweetheart, causing her image to merge (however briefly and inconsequentially) with that of a woman long dead, some of whose children, even, may be resting in the grave. What a resurrection is this; and what a connection!

Actually, however, Hal Sibley was not all this ancient. He had been ill, as he'd informed Treskell. He was certainly *getting* to be an old man, but he was not yet as old as a hickory tree or a carp can get. And the fact that he had never in all his life encountered a woman like Sylvia Kate Dunham was sufficient to relegate him to the helplessness and innocence of youth, if not to youth itself.

For he *had* never seen a woman like her. No one had. Discovering Sylvia Kate and hearing her speak for the first time (including what she said) was a significant moment for most men. As for most women, they preferred to ignore the whole business as best they could. Take Hal Sibley's poor dead wife, Tillie: if she had come upon Sylvia Kate in Hal's presence, she would have had a seizure. She would have smiled and carried on an intelligent conversation, but deep down underneath she would have been having a seizure. Tillie was a pretty woman—everybody said so—but Sylvia Kate was an act of God, like a tempest or a mud slide.

Not only that, she was politely tactless. Or perhaps she was merely tactfully impolite. Whatever it was, she probed, she manipulated, she *found out;* she was something of a bully. Hal could hear all the familiar accents, identify all the ploys and tactics (and, yes, real affection) he had known in the women who'd surrounded him as a little boy and youth . . . but none of them had put it all together the way Sylvia Kate did. And once Sibley found himself speculating that if he'd met a woman like this in those early days in Chicago, he would not have made a fortune in the commodities market; he probably would have become an idiot, or perhaps the sort of hebephrenic who giggles and dribbles and eats things like socks and matchboxes.

Out on the long deck of the lodge, Hal Sibley sat and waited. The day had been peaceful, and he was gratified that Sylvia Kate's words had not once obtruded upon his mind, startling even the nerves in his arms and legs. That morning, in his room, he had gazed upon himself in the mirror, and had recognized his thinness. (He had always faced up to facts, he frequently told himself.) Then he had said, "Thin, yes; emaciated, no."

But of course, Sylvia Kate had never said he was emaciated; she had said only that she was going to fatten him up. She had said only (also) that she was going to put some meat on his bones. She had said this at odd moments (but shrilly, unabashedly—as if Sylvia Kate could act in any other way); and yet, the context was unclear. Hal Sibley could not remember what had framed those memorable utterances, just as he could not fathom her glaring tactics. ("There are men just as rich as I," he said to himself, "who are younger and more vital by far!")

What he guessed he really wanted to do was just die in peace. No fuss; no theatrics. With as little static from others as possible. Especially Treskell and Chambers, and *especially* especially Sylvia Kate Dunham . . . who was somehow beginning to give the impression of *stalking* him.

"What does she want?" Sibley had cried deep in his spirit. This was also on that very morning, as he'd crawled out of bed and approached his grinning dentures in the water glass. And then, like a sigh of regret: "I have nothing to give her but money, and money is impersonal . . . worse, it is nothing; and it is everywhere." (Like many wealthy people, Hal Sibley thought wealth was available to all, practically for the asking; he had forgotten the poverty of his own youth.)

Before dinner, the guests usually gathered on the long porch and gazed out upon the vastness of the lake, discussing such topics as sunburns and fishing and the weather. Sibley liked such conversations, for they made no demands upon him, and yet they gave him a sense of community. But this afternoon, as he was sitting there (Treskell and Chambers had not appeared yet), he felt his head suddenly jarred forward, and Sylvia Kate's face leaned over in front, upside down, smiling brightly.

"Do you know, I've just always wanted to do that to a man!" she said to nobody in particular. Several older women were sitting nearby, however, and Sibley saw them lift the corners of their mouths in automatic smiles, as if they had been raked by the brief salvo of Sylvia Kate's words.

"Do what?" Sibley asked.

"Why put a flower in a man's hair!"

"Do you mean . . ." Sibley started to ask, groping at his head. One of the smiling women nodded busily at him, and sure enough, he found a flower there.

"You looked just like a Polynesian Prince or somebody," Sylvia Kate cried, pouting and picking up the little white flower he'd dropped by his chair. "And now you've gone and thrown it aside."

Then she came at him again and grabbed him like a blacksmith about to shoe a horse, and stuck the damned flower in his hair. And it was at that instant he heard a sharp intake of breath and—startled more than he could ever have described—he turned ninety degrees to the side and saw Tillie sitting there . . . his dead wife, Tillie, dressed in baggy shorts and with her poor pointed nose red (the only unattractive feature in her face) and her dark-brown eyes sizzling like sausages as she watched the damned old fool fumbling at his hair, trying to extirpate the flower that Sylvia Kate had planted there just a second before.

He couldn't help noticing how pear-shaped Tillie had gotten since her death. Or he had forgotten how plump she'd gotten toward the end. Either one. Or perhaps both. Perhaps she had put on a lot of weight since she'd died, which wasn't at all fair, when you stopped to think about it.

That night it came to him: Sylvia Kate was crazy. All that utterly indescribable beauty marred (rendered human) by a whangy voice and a cracked brain. Nature is full of such compensations; Sibley knew this well. And he was not about to fool himself; he may have been old and in delicate health (he pored over his printed diet the way men once pored over homilies and sermons), but he had common sense and dignity.

He vowed that if the occasion arose, he would tell Sylvia Kate that. Come right out with it. Let her know the score, which was . . . well, that *he* knew the score. But that wouldn't really solve anything, and he knew it, because, damn it, Sylvia Kate Dunham *wanted* something. What was it?

Sibley shook his head and looked at the television set. This was evening. The TV set was moaning over there in the corner, flashing feebly in the darkness, so he walked over to it. The channel selector was set on an impossible channel. How had it gotten there?

He switched to channel 9, where there was a western playing . . . in fact, there was a gunfight, and when Sibley turned up the volume, the pop, pop of the guns filled him with a sort of muted horror at the thought of these grown men (now mostly dead, which increased the obscenity of it all) playing at death. The horror was sufficient to prod that old mechanism, and Sylvia Kate's voice floated by saying, "I'm going to fatten you up if it's the last thing I *do!*"

He turned the set off and wandered out to the kitchenette. Through the window he could see the lake glowing dimly, framed by the pines beside the path. Where was Sylvia Kate now? Was she romping in the sack with some appropriate stud, her happy feet waving at the ceiling?

Sibley shook his head and made a face. "Crazy," he murmured to the growling refrigerator. "Crazy, crazy, crazy!" Only that wasn't really an answer to anything, and he knew it; for even if she was crazy, there was still a motive behind the crazy things she said and did (and said she was going to do) and it was *that* which perplexed him.

He went to the front door of his cabin and opened it. A fresh breeze washed over him, smelling of the lake. The dust of his granddaddy's farm, like that of his body, had long since been settled, quieted forever and ever. Sibley thought about this for a while, and then he wondered why, indeed, he had come back here to a changed place. How would he have answered Treskell if he had been forced to say something sensible?

Well, that was a mystery, too.

And then a little later, still standing in his lighted doorway, Sibley whispered to himself, "But God, how beautiful she is!"

Poor Tillie hadn't really been there. Nor had her ghost. Sibley knew this, and felt a brief spasm of comfort pass through him from the knowledge.

But if you live with a woman over forty years and love her (far more than a man could ever love that damned Sylvia Kate) and learn to fit comfortably into her ways (as she has learned to fit into yours) and learn to expect her voice, saying particular things upon particular occasions . . . why, there is little wonder that parts of her last on, sometimes even as visibly and tangibly as those more conventional presences we call living people. After all, a human being is not an electronic component; he is not wired so that when a particular circuit is cut, the sound and image fade swiftly, leaving a surface as cold and dead as a pearl. Most of our realities are internal, after all; and it is not really so strange that since Tillie's death, Hal Sibley had spoken more words to her than to any other human being.

This did not prevent his being mightily irritated with her, of course. It would be a long time before he could forgive her for that business on the porch, when Sylvia Kate had stuck the white flower (hell, he didn't even know what kind it was) in his hair. Tillie had acted as if it was all *his* doing! And all he had really been doing was sitting there looking at the lake. If it was true that he wasn't at that very moment thinking of Tillie (*remembering* her), it was equally true that he hadn't been thinking of Sylvia Kate, either.

What had he been thinking of? He groped and tried to remember. He was dawdling over his dessert in the Lodge Dining Room as he did so. His waitress was a little redhead named Brendalee, one word, and Sibley had commented on it one day, making him realize that Brendalee appeared never once to have given a single thought to her name.

Anyway, what he had been thinking of at that very moment was Treskell and Chambers. He didn't know what he had been thinking, but they were the subject of his thoughts. Very definitely. He was probably wondering where in the hell they were, since they spent so much time on the porch (the big fat one, Treskell, especially) and were such a damned nuisance, asking him questions and all.

Only this evening, they didn't ask questions. And as a matter of fact, they didn't show up until after Sylvia Kate had walked off, shouting in an old woman's ear as she held her two arms above her head in a sort of parentheses (God knows what she'd been talking about); and then Treskell and Chambers had crawled out on the porch, like creatures too afraid to risk the heat radiated by Sylvia Kate, and yet needful of the lake breeze on a hot evening.

When the subject had arisen, Sibley didn't know. He'd been sitting there half-listening to Treskell and Chambers talk, and then Treskell had said something directly to him, Sibley, and Sibley had said, "What?"

"I said," Treskell told him, popping each syllable distinctly in his mouth, "that you'd better be careful. That's all I said, isn't it?" He asked this of Chambers, who didn't answer but merely stared at Sibley appraisingly, and then let his gaze wander off as if he was suddenly tired of focusing his eyes.

"Be careful of what?" Sibley asked.

"He says be careful of what!" Treskell said, chuckling in the direction of his friend, who was now gazing at the sky above the trees.

"Why am I in danger?" Sibley asked, and was about to ask another question, when something strange happened: the image of Sylvia Kate was in his mind; she had just received a cue to speak, but then she stopped and waited.

"I think she pronounces her name Sylvia Kate Dunham," Treskell said; then he closed his eyes and bobbed his head up and down. Apparently, he was laughing.

"She has you in her sights," Chambers said with the corners of his mouth tucked up in a grin. "That's what he means."

"Nonsense," Sibley said in a scarcely audible voice.

"Not at all, not at all," Treskell said. "You'd better watch out! She shows all the signs."

"Signs of what?"

"Of having *plans* for you."

"She has you in her sights," Chambers repeated, looking up at the sky once again.

"What makes you think that?" Sibley asked, trembling a little.

"It's perfectly obvious," Treskell said, nodding and tapping the tips of his fingers together.

At precisely that instant, they heard Sylvia Kate's whooping laugh from somewhere deep inside the lodge. It was startling, as always . . . but also because Sibley had seen her go off in the direction of the lake. She'd circled. What was she doing inside the Lodge?

"If she doesn't sound like a siren," Treskell said, "I don't know what does."

"She looks like one, too," Chambers said, savoring the twist in meaning.

"And *acts* like one," Treskell added. "I'm afraid for Mr. Sibley here. Afraid he might crash upon the rocks and never be heard of again."

"Nonsense," Sibley muttered, gripping the arms of his chair.

A sudden breeze from the lake had come up, agitating the flowers in the flower pots upon the railing. Sibley stared at them and realized that their petals were white. It had been one of these that Sylvia Kate had stuck in his hair.

"You'd better watch your step," Treskell went on. "She looks like dynamite, if you ask me. Too much for one man to handle."

"Oh, I don't know," Chambers said, gazing steadily at Sibley as he spoke. "I think Mr. Sibley has learned how to take care of himself by now!"

At that instant, there was a shout of laughter behind him. Sibley turned and saw two rockers nodding back and forth. They were empty, but they had the appearance of rockers that have just been abandoned by two people in a great hurry.

Could it have been the sudden wind rocking them?

Not at all.

Then who had been sitting there?

Treskell and Chambers suddenly drifted off, and Sibley was left alone, thinking of who might have been sitting in the rockers.

But of course, there was no question. None at all.

Tillie and Sylvia Kate had been sitting there together, and they had heard everything.

Later, Sibley remembered this conversation on the porch and took comfort in it. Treskell's and Chamber's awareness that Sylvia Kate was after him was reassuring—he had not been imagining it; it was really happening, all of it.

But the mystery of what she wanted from him still remained. Her attacks were so sudden and violent, and her departures so unexpected, that Sibley didn't know what to think. Sylvia Kate gave the impression of being visited by seizures of inscrutable responsibility that took her suddenly elsewhere; she gave the impression that as soon as she took care of various kinds of pressing business, she would turn her full attention upon Sibley and fulfill all those dire threats and prophecies of fattening him up that had been echoing in his head for over a week.

At times, Sibley thought she was talking about marriage. What else could she be talking about? How else would she fatten him up? How else could she put meat on his bones?

Sibley was walking down the path toward the lake as he contemplated these questions, and while stepping over a wrist-thick root in a particularly steep section of the path to the lake, he misjudged the height and tripped. The fall would have been spectacular, if anyone had been there to witness it: Sibley dived forward over the path, part of him taking a rather remote interest in this brief sensation of flight.

But such ecstasies are not to be trusted, and when Howard Sibley came down, it was with brutal force, jamming his shoulder so hard the pain reached clear inside his ear, like a long-buried fishhook being suddenly yanked, and then a forlorn scalding ache spread like a seepage of hot mustard throughout his shoulder muscles; and his arm and hand were trembling; and he knew with clinical certainty that something had broken inside, for he was already remembering the heavy, dull cracking sound, like a pool cue being broken under water.

How long he lay there, and what dreams struggled like torpid fish through his mind, no one knows. Old Mr. Cosgrove was the next person to come down the path, and of course he saw Sibley lying there with his arm all crumpled and mashed beneath him. He cried out, and Vernon Peters, the lodge handyman, heard him, and sobered by Mr. Cosgrove's admonition not to touch the body he hurried up to the lodge and phoned for the emergency squad.

Sibley was taken to the hospital, where it was determined that he had broken his collarbone and dislocated his shoulder. The pain had been extreme, and it was no wonder he had passed out. The resident physician was a man named Gifford, and Sibley eventually decided that he was probably the grandson of a man he had known forty years before; but he did not ask Gifford about this, nor did he let on that he was anything but a random guest at Pine Bluff Lodge.

The day after next, Vernon Peters brought him back in the Lodge station wagon, talking volubly upon various topics, including the fish not biting. Sibley, on the other hand, wanted to ask about Sylvia Kate Dunham; but he did not. And yet, he thought about her; he thought about her mightily, with a sort of yearning that was not unlike suffering a dislocated shoulder and broken collarbone; and once he even found himself wondering if Treskell and Chambers were still there at the lodge, or whether they had picked up and departed for parts unknown.

No one was waiting for him, and he took note of the fact, calling himself a damned fool for expecting anything else. His shoulder ached so badly he took one of the painkillers the doctor had given him, and then lay down on the bed, flat on his back.

He did not fall into sleep, but was, rather, sucked under . . . with a rapidity and force that would have proved a little bewildering, had he been more fully aware of it. The rush of darknesses, representing different layers of sleep, drifted upwards past the descending wafer of his mind . . . a wafer that normally disintegrated precisely as it sank, but in this instance (possibly because of the sting of the painkiller) resolutely retained its shape.

But then, just as suddenly, it popped into nothingness, and Howard Sibley was reduced to an equal Nothing. At least he would not remember anything afterwords, which is tantamount to a dream's not having existed at all (and which small enclaves of dark rhapsodists often cite as sufficient cause for our concluding that life itself is less than a dream, since eventually nothing is remembered).

Independently of this, Howard Sibley slept—whether the sleep of the wicked or the innocent, there is no way of knowing—and rose and fell on dim powerful waves of breathing, cross-currented by the systole and diastole of another rhythm deep down inside his after-all-sturdy body.

Sometime late in that dimness, he awoke and was startled to see dear Tillie sitting cross-legged in the velveteen-covered chair that came with the room. (How she would have despised that expensive but meretricious and vulgar chair when she was alive!) Seeing his dead wife, Sibley's heart went out to her. More than his heart, for he actually cried out, even as he told himself that this could not be as it seemed. Tillie evidently understood and sympathized, for she smiled tiredly and nodded at him, lifting her hand and waving it as if to dispel the very illusion of herself.

But of course she did not disappear. She did not even ripple, so hearty was she at this moment. And seeing this, Sibley could not help but notice once again that poor Tillie had put on considerable weight since her death, and her long pale gray shorts and blouse were mussed and wrinkled, as if they had been packed in a suitcase during her voyage from the dead, and she had not (poor woman!) had a chance to iron them out.

"Tillie!" Sibley groaned. "For God's sake, help me!"

But all Tillie said was, "Hal, you got yourself into this, so don't be surprised."

What she meant by that, only God could know; Sibley was so astonished that he could not even ask for a clarification. He lifted his arm and saw that it was in a sling, but suddenly nothing hurt. It was almost as if he had been faking it, for there was not even an echo of pain, not even the merest trickle left from that storm of agony that had inundated him the day before yesterday.

"I want to get out, Tillie," he said. He had had enough; he was too perplexed, too confused by the storms and turmoils within, too bewildered by the terrible galloping of existential cowboys across the neat lawns in his mind, firing their six-shooters and killing everything in sight . . . all of which managed somehow to come alive again, in time for the next reel being fitted on the spindle by inhuman hands.

But what Tillie said was the greatest surprise of all: what she said was, "Well, if you want to, go ahead."

And even then, even at that deepest moment in the mire, Sibley realized that she was not talking about the same thing at all; she was not talking about calling it quits.

The next day he felt a little better. In fact, there were times when he felt well enough to think of Sylvia Kate and her mysterious utterances. What would he say if Sylvia Kate proposed to him? (*Ridiculous Old Fool,* he cried in anguish, and then turned his head so he wouldn't hear.)

Long and grandiose scenarios of qualification unwound in his mind. Many had to do with his calm and dignified acknowledgment of the fundamentally mercenary character of her infatuation, along with his acceptance of this. "I am myself the power I have generated," he said in one of these scenarios, only to scratch it out in a spasm of disgust and self-loathing.

Later, however, he faced up to Sylvia Kate (inside his mind, of course, where all these adventures were happening), and said, "I do not intend to relinquish my diet."

"But I'm going to fatten you up!" she cried in that now familiar war call.

"Absolutely not!" Sibley thundered. "Don't you know that the doctors say that fatty foods and sugar will *kill* me?"

"But don't you know that those doctors don't know *anything?*" Sylvia Kate cried, shaking her head in an ecstasy of negation.

This dialogue ended inconsequentially, for it was not tied to reality . . . and Sibley very well knew it. And was content, for by dinner time he was feeling well enough to go to the Lodge and face them all: Treskell, Chambers and above all, Sylvia Kate.

He lifted his arm and probed it carefully through his shirt sleeve. The route it took was a delicate one, bordered on all sides by fiery pain, and his fist was weighted with lead. At four minutes till six, he was ready—his arm in the sling and the jacket thrown over it all, like Louis Hayward in an old movie from the time of his youth, ready to march forth (though wounded) to claim the heroine.

He walked—most carefully and yet with as nearly a lighthearted spirit as he had felt in years—toward the Lodge, and entered in a fanfare of muted light glancing off the lake and vibrating subtly upon every niche and corner through the high windows.

After he ordered, he looked around and saw . . . no one he could remember from before. Treskell and Chambers, that obnoxious duo, were nowhere in sight. When he asked the waitress (not Brendalee, not redheaded, not familiar at all), she said that she thought they had both checked out. Eating quietly, he occasionally lifted his eyes to glance about the dining area. Mrs. Cosgrove was not there; Mr. Cosgrove was not there. Perhaps even Vernon Peters had gone, and was retired—living with a fat daughter and raising coonhounds somewhere under the water.

"Where?" he asked, but no one turned around.

Later, in the lobby, when he found out that Sylvia Kate had also left, he smiled at the clerk and nodded. That nod said that Sibley had known all along. He almost winked: he knew all the tricks. He could take care of himself, as Chambers had said. Indeed. He was almost frolicsome with the knowledge.

Even later, after sitting alone for over an hour on the porch, crowded with sudden strangers, Sibley returned to his cabin—stepping carefully— and went inside. He took another painkiller, and retired early. Softly, he drifted down through the layers of darkness; and later on that night when he awoke, he saw that Tillie was not sitting there in the velveteen-covered chair . . . and he was almost relieved, knowing that she was slender and pretty, as he remembered her, and free . . . knowing that some things, at least, last on even as they change.

After that, he felt the silence closing in; the stillness was absolute, like the darkness in a photograph. He knew that on the big porch of the Lodge, all the rockers were still. He knew all of this and found it breathtaking, for in spite of its terrible beauty, he had to acknowledge that it was more awful and more true than anything he had ever known.

Jack Matthews is Distinguished Professor of English and twice director of the creative writing program at Ohio University. He is the author of five novels, *Hanger Stout, Awake!; Beyond the Bridge; The Tale of Asa Bean; The Charisma Campaigns;* and *Pictures of the Journey Back,* along with two previous volumes of short stories, *Bitter Knowledge* and *Tales of the Ohio Land.* His *Collecting Rare Books for Pleasure and Profit* is now into its second edition. Several anthologies, including *The Best American Short Stories* and *Prize Stories: The O. Henry Awards,* have featured his work, as have such publications as the *New York Times, New Republic, Nation,* and *Mademoiselle.*

THE JOHNS HOPKINS UNIVERSITY PRESS

This book was composed in Baskerville text and Venus Light display type by Horne Associates, Inc., from a design by Susan P. Fillion. It was printed on 50-lb. Publishers Eggshell Offset Cream paper and bound by The Maple Press Co.